YEARS ARE SO LONG

YEARS ARE SO LONG

A Novel

By JOSEPHINE LAWRENCE

FREDERICK A. STOKES COMPANY

NEW YORK   MCMXXXIV

YEARS ARE SO LONG

YEARS ARE SO LONG

CHAPTER ONE

Gᴇᴏʀɢᴇ ᴄᴏᴏᴘᴇʀ paused somberly in the doorway of
the old parlor to survey the group waiting for
him. The narrow, chilly room with its deeply recessed
windows, its slate-gray carpet and walls provided a
depressing background. His father and mother sat
side by side upon a small, hard, red velvet sofa, and his
two sisters occupied the matching chairs. Richard, his
handsome, dark brother, nodded unsmilingly from one
of the window-seats let into the side wall. The steadily
falling January snow had banked the outside sills and
made the old-fashioned recesses snug.

"Glad you went ahead without me." George settled
himself in another window-seat and felt in his pocket
for his tobacco-pouch. "I started late, and the roads
are drifted a bit."

His mother hastened to reassure him. "Oh, we knew
you'd come, George. Your father wouldn't say a word
till you were here. We've just been visiting." She
leaned back contentedly. "You can begin now, Bark."

"There isn't much to talk over, but your mother
thought you all ought to come down." The father's

I

bright, darting hazel eyes scanned each face. Barkley Cooper prided himself that he didn't look his seventy-three years. The gray hair that swirled to a peak above his forehead still contained a good deal of its original reddish brown. He was a small man, but erect and trim. "I've reached the end of my rope." He could be dramatic in his quiet way. "From now on it's up to you children."

George, the oldest of the four children, foresaw accurately that in this Sunday afternoon conference he must force the issues. Though he appeared absorbed in filling his pipe, secretly his vulnerability in the face of the impending crisis nettled him. At fifty, he thought, a man ought to have acquired suppleness, if not ease, in dealing with difficulties. "Just what do you mean that it's up to us?" he said.

"Your mother and I have no money. My job's gone for good. That's simple enough, isn't it?" The father spoke with some acerbity.

"Well?"

"Well, we do happen to have five children." He missed something in the attentive faces of the children present, but was unable to define the lack.

The mother, reflecting that George and his father had never got on together, automatically murmured pacifist phrases. She was a rather massive old woman whose high blood pressure, at the slightest hint of agitation, flushed her full, sagging face to the roots of her beautiful white hair. Loyalty to her husband struggled with maternal pride in the look she flashed her favorite son. "Don't be impatient, George, your father only wants to get things settled."

Nellie, the most affectionate of the Cooper children and the least nimble-minded, said, "Oh, but Papa darling, you can't count on five of us. You know since Addie moved to California she practically forgets she belongs to this family."

Her father frowned. "I hope no daughter of mine will ever completely forget her parents. However, that's immaterial at present. As I wrote George—and I presume you've all read my letter?" He paused to collect a nod from each as they stared at him wide-eyed. "As I wrote George, my earning days are over. The factory's closed for good. No one wants a bookkeeper my age. Without a salary I can't keep up this house. It's too much for your mother, anyway. We must make a change." His nervous, combative nature expressed itself in the brevity of his jerky sentences.

He had not been seriously disturbed by the death of the factory owner and the subsequent decision of the heirs to close the old building where he had been employed forty-seven years. At frequent intervals during his life he had contemplated his old age as a period when he should no longer post books. He did not altogether dislike the idea. His children, he confidently assumed, waited eagerly to have their father and mother as permanent guests; there would undoubtedly be some competition among the five homes as to which should offer the most lavish hospitality. He might have to make as able decisions as Solomon, in order to escape the accusation of partiality. Biblical images visited his mind when he pictured his old age. The rôle of patriarch, honored by his children and his grandchildren, appealed to him. He imagined himself consulted, deferred to, his gray hairs venerated in each household. For the last week, pending this conference, these fancies had taken clearer shape in his thoughts; and since no doubts had ever assailed his calculations, he resented the hesitation of his children in fitting into the plans he had drawn.

George, silent, continued to smoke. Richard reached out a long arm to crush his cigarette in a fluted shell that ornamented a small marble-topped table beside him. Cora's thin, kite-shaped face tightened as if screws turned in her temples. She raised scimitar-shaped eyebrows at Nellie, who manifestly had the fidgets, the term she herself supplied to describe the twisting and turning of her body as she vainly tried to adjust herself to the rigid chair.

"Just what," George exchanged a glance with Richard, "do you expect us to do, Father?"

The old man put a hand on each knee. Failure to respond to his mood had always annoyed him, and he seemed to remember now that this oldest son had de-

lighted to oppose him. "I expect you to do no more
and no less than any other sons and daughters would
do under similar circumstances; make some return for
the care we've given you, the sacrifices we've made in
your behalf. Isn't that it, Lucy?"

His wife smiled in agreement. Her soft, uncorseted
figure, constrained only at the waistline, quivered in
its envelope of black-and-white voile. Her desire for
comfort had long ago triumphed over her pride. Years
before the fashionable abandoned corsets she had ceased
to wear one. "I thought we could take a smaller house
somewhere," she said in her unhurried voice. "Either
that, or we can come live with you."

The duet of Cora and Nellie rose strident: "I may
have to close the house and go away for my health.
The doctor says . . ." "You know, Mama, I haven't
an extra room. With four children . . ."

Richard added another to the pile of stubs in the
shell. "That's out of the question for us. John and
Dariel live with us, of course, and we have only the
two bedrooms."

Nellie, brown-eyed, plump, untidily put together,
fumbled with the half-dozen metal bracelets on her
arm. "You have no children, George."

He regarded her thoughtfully for a long moment.
His habit of deliberating before replying, together with
a certain objectiveness that led the family to describe
him as hard, rather awed Nellie, who was secretly afraid

of him. Still, she reminded herself obstinately, George *didn't* have children and the rest of them did. George and Anita were well able to take care of Papa and Mama.

"Do you all feel that way about it?" George in his window-seat patiently relooped a rebellious fold of lace curtain that dangled across his face.

Cora, quick, assertive like her father, answered first. "You see, you and Anita have no real responsibilities, George. In a way, you've both had an easy life."

"It will be quieter for Papa and Mama with you, George." Nellie's bracelets rattled. "They're not used to children and their noise."

George turned his attentive face from her to interrogate his brother mutely.

"We're still paying on the house. And Grace—" Richard faltered. He leaned forward and began absently to finger a little white-and-gold china dog that stood on the table top. Whatever gift for expression Richard had lay in his beautiful, sensitive hands. He hated talk.

Perplexity, a hint of anger, clouded the old man's narrowed hazel eyes. He vaguely feared the trend of the discussion, which not only excluded him, but which, he fancied, pointed to mutiny. The parental authority he believed still invested in him demanded a measure of respect; his children, he insisted, must look up to him. He bristled. "We'll not live with any of you, if this is the way you feel about it."

"I guess a smaller house *would* be the best plan. Then we could keep our things." His wife's glance lingered on the two black iron urns ornamenting the marble mantelpiece. They had been a wedding gift. She thought complacently that they would lend tone in a new setting. Her mind roved contentedly through the modern, compact house she hoped to acquire. For fifty years she had kept twelve large rooms in order, but she had often rebelled at the necessary routine. They had continued to live on in the old house after the children had married, partly because of its proximity to the tobacco factory where her husband had been employed since their marriage and partly because both instinctively opposed alteration or change except that forced upon them.

"Well—" George did not follow up the monosyllable, but, dropping his pipe into his pocket, crossed to the marble-topped table. It occurred to him, as he fingered the litter of knick-knacks, that his mother had a positive genius for collecting useless things.

"For heaven's sake, why don't you act halfway sensible?" Cora impatiently tapped her long, narrow foot. She imagined that everything had a direct effect on her health, and now she told herself that she had simply wasted money on her last osteopathic treatment; a scene like this inevitably tied her suffering nerves into fresh

knots. "We've got to decide on something this afternoon," she rasped.

George surveyed her as he might a stranger. He set
down a paper-weight in which a cloud of snowflakes
whirled with something of the mysterious, absorbing
fascination of the storm outside, and noiselessly returned
to his window. Hands in his pockets, bracing himself
against the sill, he said in his even, pleasant voice,
"We'd better settle a few issues first. I don't get Father's idea at all, and the rest of you seem to be merrily
passing the buck. Forget my childless state for a moment, and perhaps we can talk intelligently."

His father, roused to watchfulness, challenged him.
"I warn you, I'm not going to listen to nonsense from
any of you."

"I'm afraid," observed George patiently, "that you'll
have to listen to our nonsense."

He saw his mother touch the old man's arm, noted
that her lips formed the words, "No, Bark!" How in
God's name, thought George, letting his shoulders sag
as if the actual weight of the task confronting him
crushed his strength, was he to induce these two to face
the facts? The twisted reasoning of some seventy-odd
years reared a protecting wall of tradition behind them.
They had dwelt securely, his father and mother, in the
belief that the chief duty of grown children was to care
for their parents. One had children to the end that
one might be provided for in old age. This duty, like

a chain, shackled one generation to another, and hell-fire waited the ingrate who dared dispute it. Ask my father why he didn't look ahead and plan for the years when he'd be laid aside, mused George, and he'd be honestly amazed. I don't suppose he's ever discussed the topic with my mother. They *were* insured against old age, they'd tell you. They had five children. And the worst of it is, the son admitted, the accumulated false sentiment of centuries of lame thinking is on their side. They can find confirmation for their views in every preacher's sermon and in a million magazines and books. This is going to be a terrific blow to them. Aloud he said, "Suppose we decide just what our adult obligations to our parents are."

Nellie, who would rather meet snakes than an array of hard facts, bounced up impulsively to kiss her mother. George interpreted this as a gesture of reassurance, intended to soften whatever might sound harsh. His sister's excessive flutterings reminded George of a clucking hen. Come to think of it, Nellie with her reddish brown hair and comfortable dowdiness did resemble a Rhode Island Red.

"Your father and mother are always your father and mother. You can't change that." The old man drew his spare figure erect.

"But the relationship doesn't remain unchanged, does it? For instance, you're no longer responsible for us."

His mother, anxious only to relieve the tension,

smiled placatingly at her oldest son. "We still feel responsible for what you do, dear. You'll always be our children."

George said mildly, "What about us? How should we feel toward you?"

His father shouted, a purple vein suddenly marking a triangle above his left eye. "You ought to feel respect for us. Respect, at least, if you have no love."

"Why?"

The old man sputtered. "Why? Why? Well, for one thing, you owe your existence to us. We gave you life itself."

Richard's cigarette stubs had overflowed into a second shell. He spoke unexpectedly, striking a match as if he slashed something with a knife. "Bunk. Not many of us are grateful for the privilege of living."

I wouldn't have said that, George reflected, studying his brother's familiar, stolid profile. Poor old Rick keeps mum about his troubles, though. I wonder if all parents assume their offspring are pleased to be born?

"It wouldn't have mattered much to me, if I'd never been born." A pulse throbbed in Cora's stringy throat.

"Well, my goodness, you needn't say such perfectly dreadful things!" Nellie looked frightened. "Mama always said it was wicked to wish you'd never been born, didn't you, Mama?"

A growing hostility edged the father's tone. "What about gratitude? Don't you owe us gratitude for our love and care? For the sacrifices we made to educate you, the things we went without to give you more?" His knees trembled, and the nervous tremor secretly alarmed him.

This is, of course, absolutely indecent, thought George. The gratitude his father demanded couldn't be compelled, yet the childish image of one's parents, ranked by their own rating one step lower than God, died hard. Perhaps one never quite lost the youthful awe, George acknowledged. He noted that his mother ceaselessly rubbed hand over hand as they rested on her ample stomach. It sickened him to guess what emotions might lie behind this, her habitual signal of distress. But it isn't as shocking to hurt her with the truth, he assured himself, as it would be to encourage her to wallow in emotional lies. "No, Father, I can't see that we should be grateful. You apparently assume that we wished to be born, in order to be the subjects of this love and care you talk about. No child has ever asked to be born."

His mother, honest terror in her gray eyes, cried out, "George! Haven't you any natural affection at all?" Perspiration, even on this winter day, glistened in her heavy black eyebrows like glass beads. Her fingers shook as she settled her steel-bowed spectacles more firmly in place.

Nellie, her mouth half-open, continually shifted her gaze from her father to her brother without turning her head. She managed to extract a vicarious pleasure from any controversy in which she was allowed to maintain a spectator's rôle. Now she centered her attention on trying to remember the words George used, so that she could repeat them to Harvey, her husband, that night. She would tell Harvey that George was as hard as nails and had scared Mama half to death.

Her father, frowning, apparently stared through Cora without seeing her, though he started when she coughed her affected, hacking little cough, which she considered safer than words. The old man remembered that he had left his box of slippery elm lozenges in his other coat, but the confusion in his brain switched his thoughts quickly so that he forgot what had suggested the lozenges to him.

All of 'em lie low and let me get in deep, George meditated cynically. Well, just this once, I'm damned if I side-step the mud. There'll be solid ground under my feet at least. He saw that Richard, his face shadowed by the absurd scrolled pattern of the parted curtains, held himself rigid, his hands locked around his knees like a vise. No man could sit as motionless as that without intense, directed will. It relieved George to hear the tap-tap of his father's foot on the floor.

"Why don't you answer your mother?" The old man rubbed fretfully at his close-cropped chin beard.

George, impassive of face and manner, began quietly to speak. "How do I know what 'natural' affection is?

Take a child from its mother at birth, bring it up away from her, it will have no natural affection for her. Let the mother bring up the child, and a bond between them develops. That's animal instinct, not a reasoning force. What's admirable in such an example of 'natural' affection?"

"Then the struggles of your parents to support you, to educate you, the years of actual self-denial by your mother, mean nothing to you? I don't expect you to give *me* any credit, but if you can look at your mother and not remember what she's done for you, you're more heartless than a—than a Gila monster." In the long ago this father had taken for granted, too, the maternal devotion that in retrospect impressed him as sacrificial, fine. He forgot that his wife's solicitude for their children had sometimes irritated him, that her tendency to sleeplessness and worry in any situation that involved them had often been a cause of marital discord.

"Sorry, but my theory is that we do the thing that gives us the greatest pleasure." George hesitated for a barely perceptible instant. "Mothers are no exception to the rule. They sacrifice for their children, they work over them, agonize over them, because they get a kick out of it. They'd rather do that than anything else in the world, or they wouldn't do it. You can't make the children out debtors on that score."

A tomb-shaped clock on the mantel-shelf ticked tinnily. The wheels of a wagon passing on the road

outside creaked, lumbering and shrill. In the chimney
the wind began to howl despondently, and a sudden
gust whipped a spatter of snow against the window-
panes.

"Lucy, it seems we've raised five children to mock
us in our old age. This is the thanks they give us."

Nellie, sliding her bracelets up and down her forearm, protested earnestly. "Papa darling, Addie didn't
even answer my last letter. She acts like she wasn't
even *related* to us anymore."

"My views are mine alone," said George as if he
flicked a whip. That gives you a chance, my dears, to
express your natural affection and back it up with tangible proof, he silently challenged his brother and sisters, not without malice.

Richard shuffled his feet, and Cora pretended to examine closely a frond of the Boston fern on a taboret
behind her.

The old man's darting glance traveled from face to
face, resting last on his wife, who breathed a little
heavily. Something in the stricken gesture of her large
hands as they helplessly rubbed over each other, roused
him to bitter rage. "Maybe you care nothing for us.
Maybe what happens to us doesn't worry you. But
you've got to support us. It's the law."

An invisible something passed from brother to sister,
from sister to brother, like a flexible wire that, the ends

fusing, banded them in an united circle for the first time that afternoon.

Now the real battle starts, thought George, taking out his pipe. "I think all of us admit our financial obligations," he said.

An hour later he still wearily reiterated, "Yes, Father, as long as we reside in this State, we have to support you. No one whose children are able to care for him can be a public charge. Only you can't dictate to us in this matter. The question of how you're to be supported rests wholly with us to decide."

"But you've got a crazy notion of separating your mother and me."

Cora's emaciated features reflected impatience. "Oh, Father, don't take everything so *hard*. None of us can afford to take two extra into our homes. For one thing, we haven't room."

Her father's expression changed and he laughed. A new set of wrinkles, kindly tolerant lines, printed his brown skin. "I guess you don't rightly understand. Your mother and I've been married fifty years and more. We can't live in separate places—we've grown together, you might say." The effort to imagine the upheaval their parting must cost him began to churn his thoughts, despite his determination to be calm. He had, infrequently, wondered what he might do if death took his wife from him; the possibility of losing her in life had naturally never entered his mind. The pressure of her heavy body against his comforted him. Her physical presence helped to ridicule the terrors that beset him, as her familiar hand on his quieted a nerve that throbbed the length of his arm.

"Oh, no, we must stay together, of course." Her placid, rather indistinct voice was as matter-of-fact as usual.

Her very casualness strengthened her husband and his apprehensions, thus confirmed, retreated. "I'd rather die than live away from your mother," he said, because he dared believe again that no such trial would be asked of him.

"It's out of the question for us to take you both. Can't you *see?*" George meant that his own generation, middle-aged now, had read the warning. "We've each got to lay aside something for our own later years."

Again his father laughed. Derisively this time, and he put up a hand to touch the throbbing purple vein. "It seems funny," he said slowly, his gaze on his carefully polished shoes; "it seems funny. We could take care of five of you, and all of you put together can't take care of two. Your mother and I managed to do for our parents. Her mother lived with us for fifteen years after we were married and my father for five—till he died."

Cora, slouching in her chair, jerked herself upright.

"That's all very well, Father. In those days everything was different. You lived in a big house which furnished enough work to keep a dozen hands busy, outside and in. Nothing's like that now. The entire scheme of housekeeping's changed. Most of us haven't even an extra bedroom. Why, I haven't the remotest intention of living with May, when I'm an old woman. Bill and I expect to be responsible for ourselves till the end."

Richard surprised them all with an unusual burst of loquacity. "My good Lord, Dad, you're a hundred years behind the times. Did you and Mother have five children for the sole purpose of providing yourselves with old age insurance? Is that why you've never saved a cent—because you relied on us? One generation's duty isn't to the past; it's to the future. We're in debt to our children, not to you."

"Rhoda talks that way, too, Mama." Nellie looked quite spent from her efforts to listen and comprehend. "She says we have no right to depend on our children to take care of us. She says parents should save for their own old age. It's the modern idea."

"Perhaps when Rhoda has borne five children—" The white head lifted proudly, because the old woman still believed her motherhood crowned her life with a spiritual halo.

"No one has five children these days," gabbled Nellie.

George observed mildly that they were getting no-where, but the bitterness of his father flowed in under his temperate words and swept them into discard. The blood pounded in the old man's body, roaring against his ears, shaking his limbs. "We might have saved plenty, if we had done less for you!" A poignant, unfathomed sense of betrayal increased his pain. The whole structure of his life had rested on his faith that he possessed obedient children, and if they failed him he was bereft indeed. The thought knifed him so keenly that he refused to entertain it. These men and women, his children, who defied him, must be forced to feed and shelter him; he must bring them to their senses before they abandoned him.

He suddenly stood up because a pressure like suffocation hampered his breathing. His hands clenched, he gasped, "I'll kill myself, before I let you go through with this!"

"Bark! Bark!" His wife's flushed, distressed face upturned, implored him. Her own head swam dizzily, but she continued to tug at his coat. "Bark, don't be so violent. We can fix up something, if you'll be reasonable."

He stepped back, and the edge of the sofa bent his knees for him. Seated he closed his eyes, panting.

"Just a minute, Father!" That was George, George deliberate, watchful, powerful, because of his self-control. "How long has it been since the last one of us left home?" George asked.

Nellie clamored, "Why, I was the last one married.

Don't you remember? And Harvey and I've been married twenty-one years next October."

"All right." George stared beyond her at the engraving of "The Stag at Bay" hung on the wall above his mother's head. "Do you realize, Father—Mother—that for twenty years you've had no responsibilities beyond your two selves? You married young—we were gone before you were old. You've had no expensive sickness. What was Father's salary with the factory? Fifty—sixty a week? You could have saved one hundred a month from that and paid it into an annuity for twenty years."

His mother indignantly protested. "Why, George, what nonsense! The rent of this house is sixty a month." To the suggestion that cheaper quarters might have answered, she responded vaguely, "We had all the furniture."

"Do you set yourself up as judge?" The old man dried his clammy hands on a handkerchief dazzling white against his shriveled brown skin. "What do you know about an annuity?"

"I'm trying to pay into one now. When it means future independence, it's worth the denial involved." To save myself being in your place, to avoid being brought face to face with a day like this, brooded George, I'd live on bread and water for twenty years. To have nothing, to be nothing—good God, what must that be like! He threw back his shoulders, drawing in a deep breath, as if the gray chill of the parlor stifled him.

His father mumbled, as if subdued, "You can't separate us."

"Yes, we can."

"I tell you, you can't!" His voice rose to a shout before hoarseness cracked it. "I'll never consent to any such damnable scheme—never!"

George shrugged. "All right. What will you do about it?"

The longing for a safe haven, a yearning for dreams realized, still drugged the father. He smoothed a fold of his wife's dress as he announced triumphantly that they would borrow the money to take them to their daughter in California. "Some one will lend to us, if you won't. And Addie will look after us, once we get there."

"Addie!" Nellie shrilled. "Why, we've *told* you, Papa, she won't even answer our letters. She telegraphed just once to say she didn't feel obligated in any degree for your support."

Richard inquired about the money—where did his father expect to borrow it?

He'd borrow it—they needn't worry about that. But the question scuttled back and forth in the old man's brain, a frenzied doubt. He'd always been able to borrow—small sums of money, yes. How could he ask, whom could he ask, for the price of two fares to the

Coast? He would have to confess himself a man without collateral, credit, or, most terrifying of all, a future.
Then, suppose Addie refused to receive them? He
glanced furtively at his wife. She had never been one
to worry. Their division of labor had always been
simple in the extreme—he earned the living, she managed the house. They had assumed contentment with
their even lot to be a virtue. The necessity for grap-
pling with the disintegration of their orderly lives dazed
the old husband as if new lines had been handed him
to speak after he had played one part for fifty years.
Humiliating panic chilled his stomach, while his mind
reached out vainly in search of some solution.

"Could we sell our things?" His wife turned hopefully to her daughters, who might be expected to appreciate the value of beds and tables and chairs. "We
could live on the money they'd bring." She thought of
what the accumulation of fifty years had cost her and
her confused reasoning convinced her that she had exchanged her vanished youth and some of her hopes
for the material possessions that surrounded her. This
idea enhanced the worth of very ordinary household
goods in her eyes.

Cora and Nellie, both talking at once, as was their
distressing and wasteful habit, declared that the furniture was "junk." Marble-topped tables, enormous beds,
they insisted, had no attraction for the modern house-

wife. "It gives me a backache, just to think of moving any of your pieces around, Mother," Cora said.

Her father muttered almost in a whisper, "Plenty of people will be glad to have us live with them." He stooped, with a stiff movement, to pick a pin from the floor. The under side of his coat lapel was thickly studded with pins. He practised all the small habits of thrift such as saving pins and paper and string. "I guess there's plenty of places we can fit in." He wished his wife would confirm his statement, but she remained silent. No one, his common sense told him, welcomed penniless visitors, nor had he ever befriended any one to the extent that he had earned the right to ask their aid. As for his brother or his few scattered cousins, they would be curious, nothing more. He cringed inwardly, picturing how they must talk among themselves, when they learned that Barkley Cooper had not a penny to his name. Well, he admitted, with a spurt of pride, perhaps he had always carried his head too high.

"If we can't live with you—" The mother hesitated. A pathetic timidity, new to her, tinged her fumbling for words. Hers was an imperious character; she had often been dictatorial, meddlesome, as mothers feel entitled to be. Yet she possessed intuition and could haggle with defeat.

"Yes, Mother?" George flinched in such shame from

pity himself that he dared not smile, lest he reveal how
deeply he pitied her.

"Well, if each of you gave me a little—say every
week—your father and I could maybe board somewhere." An external calm screened the sickening
churning that whirled inside her. To live with strangers, to have one room . . . Clean towels perhaps twice
a week . . . "Will you have ham and eggs, or bacon
and eggs, this morning?" We won't even feel free to
sit on the porch, if there is a porch, she worried. But
if they might be together, did anything matter? An
agonizing wonderment throbbed like a bruise across her
heart. How could their lives have crashed to this, after
fifty serene and peaceful years? What had they done,
or left undone, that the past could so completely fall
away, leaving them stripped, defenseless, besieged by
the present? She reminded herself heavily that she and
Bark had always looked forward to living in their
children's homes. They had confidently expected to
be tenderly sheltered, gratefully cared for, when the
burden of their years weighted them down. Reverence
for the aged had been bred into her generation, the old
woman reflected miserably. She had thought to instil
the same teaching in her own children and now she
knew that she had failed. It must be my fault, all my
fault, she fretted silently. I haven't trained them right.

George sighed. "Cora?" Whenever he looked at his
sister he speculated curiously concerning her secretive-

ness. She kept her own counsel, he told himself, as only a woman can who has something to hide.

"I can't make any definite promises." Cora moistened her lips. "You see, George, my doctor bills are perfectly huge. And May's teeth are being straightened. I might be able to pay five a week after a while, but not right now."

"Rick?"

"Oh, for God's sake!" The whole mess of his life printed itself in the lines of Richard's haggard face. "There isn't a cent I can call my own. Grace is a wonder, a genius," he inserted loyalty as an ingredient called for by the conventional recipe, "but we're paying for the house by the skin of our teeth. When that's off the books——"

"And Nellie, of course, barely makes ends meet——"

"Well, that's the truth, George. You may think it funny, but I tell you bringing up four children on a moderate income isn't any joke."

Her brother nodded to quiet her. Their replies had been less equivocal than he had expected. Was he, he wondered, inclined to believe himself the only one among them who practised honest speech? Not that any of us are absolutely honest, of course, he acknowledged. Rick is letting his house crush the life out of him because he is afraid of his wife and still more afraid of what he might be without her. God knows what Cora is keeping to herself, but it isn't what she tells her

everlasting file of doctors. I think Nellie, whose func-
tions run to the physical, wants to be free to be all wife
and mother. And I—well, I've set my goal. My end
won't be like my father's. "Mother, the easiest plan is
for you and Father to take turns living with us," George
said.

His father snarled. "You can't order *me* around as
if I were a child."

"Oh yes, we can," his son assured him, "if you're in
the position of a child."

The old man faltered. His chin drooped, the wrinkled eyelids, almost bare of lashes, shaded his eyes.
"What have I done, then, that makes me a child?"

"You are indigent. You have no money. You are
dependent, as a child is dependent. We must make
decisions for you as we would for a child."

Nellie asked indignantly if he had to be brutal.

"I'll be damned if I'll be maudlin. It's the facts that
are brutal, and we're up against facts. At least I am.
If you wish to step in and will be responsible, Nellie——"

She fluttered and clucked, agitatedly disclaiming any
intention of interfering.

"I suppose I could take boarders." The old woman
fancied that her thickened ankles throbbed. To be on
her feet for any length of time wearied her. "We could

take care of ourselves, then." But she trembled inwardly, for she had never even rented a room.

Cora said coldly, "Don't be childish, Mother. There's no one to board in this town, except factory Hunkies. You'd look nice, waiting on them."

Her mother could not dispute the truth, merely resent it. Foreign labor manned the small factories on the edge of the town and provided the only steady demand for cheap board. I never could stand a foreigner in my house, let alone at my table, thought the mother, and for a moment distaste became as pungent as an unclean odor to her. If she lived with George and Anita, or with any of her children, her days would be comfortable, orderly, clean. She would be spared the pity of her friends. Yes, at their time of life, it would be madness for an old couple to go into business for themselves, and every one said that keeping boarders didn't pay. "Perhaps I'm not strong enough to undertake it," she admitted.

George cleared his throat, but his father flung up his hand. "Wait a minute. I guess I can still take care of my wife." He had to force his eyelids open, for lately their tendency to droop annoyed him. "What's the matter with my getting a job. Eh, Lucy?"

They looked at him as if seeing him for the first time as an old man, tired, shrunken, through. He might prattle about finding a job, he might delude himself with plans for his rehabilitation, but they knew—and so did he—that he would never regain his lost grip. As he stared fiercely at them, the consciousness of his age mocked him. What could he find to do? He might earn a few dollars as night watchman, or neighborhood handy man. It would be insufficient to support two, and the humiliation must intolerably sear him.

He heard one of his sons, he thought it was Richard, say gently, "They want younger men than you, Dad."

A man with grown children, able to care for him, had no call to do menial work, he told himself. He had been a good father, he had performed his duty honestly, as he saw it, throughout his life. If for the present he must accept less than his rights, at least he saved himself the dreary round of the seeker for work. It won't always be like this, either, he stoutly assured himself, remembering his trunk of papers under the attic eaves. Strange things happened every day. Suppose the oil stock, or the copper stock, made out in the name of Barkley Cooper, or his shares in that Western fox farm suddenly paid dividends? The shoe would be on the other foot then.

He turned to his wife, and it seemed to him that fatigue, heavy and numbing, like a great blanket, muffled his movements, even his voice. "Well, I guess there's no help for it, Lucy. We'll have to do as the children say. Maybe I'll get on my feet again after a while." I'm glad it's settled, he thought and yawned. He recollected that he had had no afternoon nap.

CHAPTER TWO

Not even the gold-colored theatrical gauze curtains at the windows could create the illusion of sunshine in Anita's dining-room. The apartment, one of the cheapest in an expensive building, was of the studio type always in demand among the ambitious whose social aspirations exceed their incomes. Anita, forced by the impending arrival of her mother-in-law to find an apartment with an extra bedroom, had been thankful to discover five well-arranged and equipped rooms at a rental her budget permitted her to pay. She disliked living in the basement in proximity to the purring oil burners if not within actual sight of them, she loathed the network of pipes that disfigured her ceilings; but she refused to complain because she despised whining women as poor sports. To be a good sport constituted Anita's entire philosophy of life, and she had a far greater horror of letting any one down than of losing her immortal soul.

This morning she hoped her mother-in-law might forget to notice that no sunshine penetrated the concrete court. Lucy Cooper usually chose breakfast-time to comment on that fact. The thought of living in the cellar upset her theories of hygiene. Anita watched her

now as the old lady buttered a hot muffin, poured a
spoonful of hot coffee over it and began to eat it with
a fork. Her flabby cheeks quivered as she leaned over
her plate, and the mass of her white hair appeared to
weigh down her head. She looks a hundred years old
in this gray light, thought Anita, shrinking a little from
the sight of the gullies and hollows in the wrinkled
skin.

"Hark!" Lucy Cooper half rose from her chair, then
resettled herself.

"That isn't our bell, dear." Anita, in the effort to be
patient, clenched her hands in her lap.

Her mother-in-law sighed. "All your bells sound
just alike."

Anita, with seven telephone calls to make before half-
past eight o'clock, assured herself that she would be
stark insane, if she lived through three months of this.
The restraint she put upon her nerves began with her
preparation of breakfast. Mitzi, the maid, "slept out"
and seldom arrived before nine. Anita, mixing muffin
batter and frying bacon, had also to stand tactfully between her husband (who dreaded nothing so much as
being left alone with his mother) and her mother-in-
law, who followed him wistfully from room to room.

"If he'd just sit down and talk for five minutes with
her," Anita sometimes told herself. "It wouldn't hurt
him to be bored."

But when George, early and safely on his way to his

office, had left her to listen to his mother, then Anita
felt the muscles around her mouth tighten like wires.
The senior Mrs. Cooper ate well. She could sit placidly
munching toast and drinking three or four cups of
coffee as if she shared her leisure with the world. Her
teeth clicked when she ate and drank, and for Anita
that small but recurrent sound amounted to torture.
To be obliged to sit behind the percolator and supply
a fund of suitable comment, listening to the click of
false teeth and the inane reminiscences of a small-town
mind must eventually deprive any woman of her
reason, Anita had assured herself every morning for a
week. Her mother-in-law, less than ten days in the
apartment, had already thoroughly complicated its
routine.

This morning the older woman anticipated a cozy
chat. She hoped she and Anita might share as a topic
of common interest George's approaching birthday. It
was so difficult, Lucy Cooper had discovered, to adjust
herself to a new stream of talk. Her familiar conver-
sational bromides no longer served. At breakfast and
dinner she persistently contributed to every discussion,
eager to partake in lives which had no need of her.
Her pitiful little attempts to interest George and Anita
only bored them; the rushing, crowded present alone
enthralled them, and the past, as interpreted by the
elderly, seemed artificial, dull. Over her solitary lunch-
eons—Anita seldom came home at noon—the need for

some one with whom to exchange trivialities intensified the mother's loneliness. For half a century she had been listened to, and now she might as well talk to the deaf!

"Fried chicken, always, and a birthday cake." She helped herself to a strip of bacon. "That's what I had for George's birthdays when he was home."

The quantity of food her mother-in-law habitually consumed amazed Anita. She contrasted her own trim outlines with the uncorseted, billowing figure opposite her. At forty Anita could wear her fair hair in a mass of paper curls and still not look like a fool. It required time and money to preserve her blondness, but the work was skillfully done. She ate nothing except fruit for breakfast, but gave cigarettes the credit for keeping her thin. It added to her irritation that she could not smoke at table without distressing her husband's mother. However, she no longer lit a cigarette at breakfast-time. She would have refrained if tobacco irritated the throat of one of her guests, and her code dictated a similar concession to inflamed sensibilities.

"Finished, Mother? Mitzi has the ironing to do, you know," she said now in her carefully cultivated voice.

In the morning light she looked tired. She admitted frankly that she didn't begin to enjoy a day till noon. By night she could have walked ten miles. No matter how late an evening lasted, she rose at seven and had breakfast ready by quarter of eight. Possibly twice a

year exhaustion laid her flat in bed, unable to rise for
two or three days. Excepting these lapses, for which
she shamefacedly apologized, she drove herself without rest.

Lucy Cooper, who had never budgeted her time,
shook out her napkin, refolded it across her knees. "I'll
take another cup of coffee. And a muffin. Anita, I
thought I'd bake George a cake for Thursday. My
recipe never fails. If you'll speak to Mitzi, I'd like to
fry the chicken, too. George used to dote on chicken
fried my way." She smiled gently as she split a brown
muffin puff and critically examined the grain. Anita
made good hot breads. Her coffee had strength and
fragrance, too. One enjoyed watching the clear brown
liquid change to golden tan upon the addition of a
liberal allowance of cream. Like most old people, Lucy
Cooper thought a great deal about food. It had such
power to comfort her no longer lovely body that she
associated a sensuous pleasure with the act of eating.
Because she achieved a fleeting happiness as long as she
could enjoy food, she unconsciously tried to prolong
the meal hours. When she ate and drank, other de-
sires, unfulfilled or frustrated, beat less sharply for a
time.

Anita, eager to 'phone, rose. She was careful to hold
her abdomen flat as she stood erect. Diet, exercise,
posture, composed her discipline and drill. "Are you
talking of George's birthday, Mother? I'm giving him

a party that night." She sternly forbade herself to notice the clicking of the two rows of even, blue-white teeth. A pity if she couldn't control her nerves!

She knew far more accurately than her husband did how deeply this announcement of the party wounded her mother-in-law. "Why should I be the one who has to step all over her feelings?" Anita had argued with George. She had despaired of being able to put into words for him the delicate sensitiveness of intuitions that she herself had never defined. George further defeated her by demanding to know if his mother had ever said what his birthday meant to her. How could Anita know how his mother felt about it, if his mother had never *said* how she felt about it?

George's mother, buttering another muffin, hoped that she concealed the trembling of her hands. The pretense that she enjoyed a close, personal relationship with her son, that he preferred her as a confidante, might be shattered a dozen times a day; but she clung to the fiction as to a drug. She cloaked the hurts and slights the falsity of her premises made inevitable with a mantle of determined, gentle patience. She looked upon her daughter-in-law as the real interloper, the outsider, an unassimilated third, but she intended to be the last woman in the world to *hurt* Anita. The gray eyes smiled suddenly into the turquoise blue ones. "How many are you asking, dear? Shall I bake one cake or two?" Her tone strove to establish an atmosphere of companionable conspiracy. As George's mother she could afford to be generous to his wife.

"It won't be here." Anita, her mind racing ahead to dovetailing appointments—she taught classes in bridge —forced her voice to remain calm. She detested a woman who shrieked. The necessity for choosing her words hampered her, because she had little time to spare. Still, though one might theoretically refuse to pander to oversensitive natures, one could hardly tell a man's mother that her son was intent on escaping from her. It seemed to Anita that all spontaneous expression withered at the roots of her tongue in the presence of her mother-in-law. The younger woman accused herself of crawling around situations, temporizing with tears. "But I can't deliberately stab her!" The passion of Anita's protests often surprised her husband. "When I look at her I think living to be old is the most dreadful fate in the world!"

Now as she sketched in the party details, Anita softened her explanations, adapted her reasoning with pitying skill. Her own mother, she confided, had loaned her house for the bridge. A private home afforded more space. "Besides, after a couple of drinks, every one gets noisy. In an apartment building, some one is sure to complain." She expected to have ten tables, Anita continued, and no one had to think of food. A caterer, one her mother recommended, had been engaged. They could afford it once a year. All the good

players George knew had been asked. "Forty contract
fiends, all young married couples." Anita gave silent
thanks that her mother-in-law did not play bridge.
"You'd never forgive us, if we dragged you there,
Mother. You'll have a nice, quiet dinner by yourself
and enjoy a peaceful evening. Mitzi's ready to stay, if
you want her."

Half an hour later Anita, who drove a small, second-
hand car and dressed in imported tweeds four seasons
old, left to be gone till night. A desire to laugh assailed
her at unexpected intervals, the morning through. Her
mother-in-law, she had perceived, pitied her son because she believed his wife dominated him.

Lucy Cooper, after breakfast, liked to make her own
bed. She still felt homeless in the orchid-and-gray room
Anita had painstakingly arranged for her. The painted
furniture with its slim, tapering legs suffered in com-
parison with her cumbersome walnut pieces, the bu-
reaus topped with marble slabs as large as tombstones.
The old walnut had been the despair of the auctioneer
who had managed the sale. No modern housekeeper
could be persuaded to buy such clumsy designs and
most of the sets had been bought in for lumber by a
cabinet-maker who admired the grain. The memory
of her high, wide bed, the bed in which each of her five
children had been born, visited the old woman each
morning as she folded the orchid blanket and smoothed
the gray taffeta spread provided by her son's wife.

Noises in the court and basement alarmed her, the
penetrating, gritty quiver of the buzzers startled her
each time one sounded. She distrusted all these bells.
Her own home, as she recounted daily to Mitzi, had
been equipped with doorbell and telephone—no more.
One knew, when summoned, in which direction to go.
Here, in this bewildering arrangement of only five
rooms on one floor, the clamor of a bell had half a
dozen possible explanations. Easy for Anita to protest,
"You don't have to pay attention, Mother—just ignore
it." Every ring pulled the old woman instantly to her
feet. Unable to distinguish accurately between the
dumbwaiter and front door buzzers, the signal of super-
intendent, doorman, or the mail, she fluttered nervously
from post to post. Easy for Anita to remonstrate,
"Some one will go, Mother; it's not your worry." A
woman trained to listen to the machinery of a household cannot easily cultivate a deaf ear. Lucy Cooper
continued to heed the bells.

"Where's old Mrs. Cooper this evening?" Mrs. Waterbury whispered to her partner under cover of Anita's
explanation of a bid.

The partner, whose husband took bridge seriously,
looked flustered and said, "Sh!"

Anita's bridge class, six tables, crowded the living-
room, sweeping the unused furniture at awkward

angles against the wall. Sixteen women and eight men, in attitudes of intense concentration, watched Anita diagram a problem on her tiny blackboard. Her restless, haggard, yet strangely lovely face lighted as she explained her points with professional ease. She spoke the patter of the game, which was all many of the women desired to acquire. Presently she would give the signal to play. Then her slim figure in the dull blue velvet gown would glide from table to table, as she silently made notes. In the kitchen George mixed the first round of drinks.

Lois Waterbury's query had reached Anita's ears. The problem of what to do with her mother-in-law this evening had definitely troubled her. In the end she had conceded that nothing could be done. She might argue, she might explain, she might plead, Anita had reflected, but it was impossible to make a dent in the feather-bed disposition with which she must deal. Her mother-in-law's soft obduracy was proof against exasperation, anger, or the passing of time; restrained at one point, it gently functioned at another. The longing to be of help, a passionate desire to feel herself needed motivated the older woman's insistent and useless offers of her services and advice.

"Only tell me what you want me to do, dear. I'd love to help you with your party." A new anxiety to please shone in the gray eyes.

We know we're going to misunderstand each other
before we speak, despaired Anita, who said truthfully
enough, "There isn't anything for you *to* do."

"I guess there's plenty I could do, if you'd let me."
Wounded dignity was the second stage in these eternal
arguments. "You and George try to treat me like a
child." Her daughter-in-law's professional connection
with bridge bewildered the old woman. The spectacle
of her son's wife teaching "card playing," holding
classes in and outside her home, presented an aspect so
foreign as to seem almost illegal.

Anita, whose amusements paid a large share of the
household expenses, had begun to talk of renting a
studio for her games. "Don't let any one tell you old
people are just like children!" she flamed to Bess Post,
her closest friend. "Nor that they can be treated like
children. I'd rather manage six kids than one old person. Children are cooperative, open-minded, friendly
—most of them. Old people have none of these traits.
They live in the past and have only suspicion and distrust for the present. Besides, children fit into the
scheme of things. Old people demand that the scheme
be altered to fit them. They just won't interlock."

Mrs. Post, whose father had lived with her since her
marriage, shook her head. "I don't agree with you.
It's a theory of women that children adjust themselves
to the scheme of things. As a matter of fact, they fit
into homes only because women make them fit. It's

easy and natural to arrange the stage for a child. That is in line with the biological maternal urge. It's the devil of a job to arrange the stage for the old, because that reverses the biological drive." She added helplessly that there was nothing for old people to *do*. "The more civilized we get, the more of a social problem the aged become. We can't seem to teach them to adjust themselves to a changing world."

Ten minutes before the arrival of the first guest that evening George had asked, "What'll we do about Mother?"

His wife completed tying his dress tie before she answered, because she found she needed to count ten. "What do you suggest?"

"Well, but, Anita, I'm thinking of her. She'll be bored to death."

"She'll be heart-broken if we ask her to sit in her own room. In an apartment, a woman of such limited resources is sunk. She simply doesn't know how to amuse herself."

George suggested the movies. "I'll call for her after the second show."

"I thought of that. She asked me if I wanted to get rid of her. If we were ashamed of her. She's still sensitive, because we've left her out of your birthday party next week."

This conversation re-echoed in Anita's mind as she worked at her blackboard. From which direction would her mother-in-law appear? Of course, she told herself, old people ought to live by themselves. But George can't carry *that* burden alone. "Remember, if you're vulnerable, your opponents will push you to the limit," she recited. A door down the hall closed with a click. She continued to speak smoothly, forbidding herself to listen to the murmur of voices in the kitchen.

"You're not serving liquor?" The words were perfectly audible in the living-room.

Now, I can stand just so much, Anita informed herself grimly. But the relationship, not the provocation, would be remembered, she admitted, and registered a resolve not to supply a mother-in-law story for her guests.

George's response caused several of the men to grin. "Here's to you, Mother. One highball will make a new woman of you, and if you keel over, I'll put you to bed."

If she raises the Moral Issue I shall raise the roof, Anita promised her tingling nerves. At such times as this it seemed to her that the entire problem resolved itself into a matter of simple courtesy. Her mother-in-law happened to be living in another woman's house. Ordinary good manners demanded that she attempt to conform to her hostess' routine and plans, refrain from voicing personal disapproval. A little politeness, the exercise of common discretion, was all that was needed in the situation. Yet, Anita was gradually learning, the older woman not only overlooked the simplicity of such an adjustment, she remained ignorant of its necessity. To her the fact that she was her son's mother actually convinced her that she and her son were one. She believed she had as much right to his home, to his money, to the labor and patience of his wife as he had. Once she said, "I'll never be happy till Bark can come and live with me here." And had added to Anita, "If any more of your family come to live with you, you'll have to take a larger apartment." The startled Anita had murmured, "My family?" but her sense of humor had enabled her to laugh.

Bess Post raised her plucked eyebrows as George entered carrying a tray, his mother peering around him.

"I've never been used to liquor in the home," she informed her audience, "but I daresay I'm quite out of style."

Several men rose to fetch her a chair. She looked about her uncertainly, never quite steady on her feet. George shifted the tray to one hand and with the other guided her to a seat near the wall. Mrs. Waterbury, who in the course of her incessant chatter was often quite simply kind, leaned forward to say across her table that she admired white hair. "How do you keep yours looking so lovely?"

"Bluing, ordinary bluing." The old face kindled to animation. "I always use it in the rinse water. It prevents that yellow tinge." She waited brightly for an-

other question, but Lois Waterbury, a stout woman
with a green scarf knotted under her series of chins,
was already absorbed in dealing the cards.

A strange, new world into which she would never,
never fit, thought Lucy Cooper, who had told herself it
would look queer if she stayed in her own room. Naturally, she had deliberated, these friends of George and
his wife would expect to meet his mother at a party
given in his own home. She resolutely refused to consider these evening games a business proposition,
though she knew those who attended paid in cash.
The whole intricate pattern of tournaments and classes,
the elaborate fabric of a modern craze which Anita,
like so many others had capitalized, eluded the old
woman utterly unable to associate card games with
hard, exacting work.

The talk of these people confused her. They might
be speaking a foreign language, for all it meant to her.
On each occasion like the present she listened with
painful intentness, eager to be admitted to companionship, ready to exchange views, trying to pretend she had
found friends. The laughter swept past her. No group
ever turned to her, seeking her opinion. They would
have none of her experiences, her reminiscences, her
censure or her praise. Many of the women, she knew,
had children and were interested in their homes. Why
did they never talk about babies, or cooking, or their
curtains and rugs? In such discussion she would be

afforded an opportunity to display her authority; attention would be drawn to the dignity of her years. Instead, for the most part, when they were not harrowingly silent, intent on the game, the players chattered a jargon, disjointed, so casual as to bewilder the elderly listener, to whom bridge scores, mixed drinks and country club jokes were alike unintelligible. The radio orchestra that inevitably blared added to her distress; she usually jumped when the leader started to croon.

Tonight, sipping her ginger-ale, she narrowly missed dropping her glass when she heard Major Hackle's voice for the first time. A soldierly, white-haired man, meticulously barbered, he was really the attraction of Anita's evening. At dinner she had explained to her mother-in-law that the Major had invented a system of bidding that might make him famous. He was obviously a good deal older than most of the other guests, who admitted to awe of his skill. His table, set a few feet away from Lucy Cooper's chair, formed the center of a group.

"I never open with a two bid, forcing—" He spoke so like her husband that she almost cried out. The same staccato, clipped speech, the same way of folding his lips firmly at the end of each word. The hollow sham of her resignation, the pretense that she was getting used to living without Bark, collapsed in the feverish, tumultuous beating of her heart. How could George listen to this Major and not be constantly reminded of his father? She smiled faintly at her son, who took the tall glass from her trembling hand. No, she decided, George did not notice the resemblance at all. She wished the Major would speak again, then dreaded to be forced to listen to his compact tones. Perspiration dampened her face, her neck and arms felt wet. Loneliness, oppressive, heavy and dark as some wild beast, crouched on her chest. In the midst of this room of gay, chaffing people, friends who drank and smoked and laughed together, she was perishing, a solitary soul. O Bark! O Bark! she moaned silently, her big, stolid body placidly at rest while within her the pain twisted and pinched. Desperation drove her to make. another effort to establish human contact. Scarcely knowing what she did, she touched Lois Waterbury's bare arm with hot, seamed old fingers. "My husband used to be very fond of cribbage." Her gray eyes wandered hopefully from face to face, seeking a response from some one among the four.

Mrs. Waterbury nodded, keeping her gaze on her cards. "I'll be through this in just a moment," she murmured.

"Kibitzing, Mrs. Cooper?" A fat young man who clowned a good deal, leaned back to show her his hand. "Shall I cover?" he grinned.

The old lady smiled, dabbling her handkerchief against her upper lip. "I'm afraid I don't know." None of their phrases meant anything to her.

Major Hackle's voice no longer disturbed her. His appearance, so unlike her husband's, had helped dispel the earlier illusion. He must be, she decided, about her own age, but he would undoubtedly resent the label of "elderly." For a partner he had a young and charming woman, whose deference to his skill obviously pleased him. He had brought her with him, and Lucy Cooper had supposed her to be his daughter or perhaps a grand-daughter, until the clowning fat man had referred to her as "the Major's current girl friend." Well, Lucy Cooper mused, a man was as old as he felt. Bark, too, liked to pride himself that he was a "ladies' man." Attention from a pretty girl still went to his head. But he wouldn't like this sort of thing, Bark's old wife assured herself, trying not to choke in the smoky haze that clouded the room. If she coughed, some one would apologize and George and Anita wished their guests to feel free to smoke. No, Bark didn't approve of cigarettes for women, nor of drinking in mixed company. He would also, his wife indignantly brooded, criticize the freedom of contact between men and women she disdainfully characterized as "old enough to know better." In fifty years of life together, they had grown to think alike. She missed not only his physical presence, but the contact with his spirit, a wordless communication of which, until deprived, she had not been fully aware. This spiritual articulation had enabled them to sit together, in the kitchen, on the porch, for hours at a time, exchanging commonplaces in complete and perfect understanding. There's no one to talk to, she cried to herself, rising creakily as some one knocked over a glass. The dull ache of her loneliness sharpened again to a pain that stirred her to rub one hand over the other, her action of acute distress.

She skirted the flurried table where some one mopped at the rug with an inadequate napkin, and reseated herself behind the slightly pompous Major Hackle, huddled over a row of cards spread before him. The dummy, she had learned, might be spoken to without violating any mysterious rule. "It makes kind of a lull for you, doesn't it?" Her smile, half timid, half friendly, wholly conciliating, had in it such pathos that the Major, whose card sense provided almost his entire mental equipment, felt vaguely moved to respond.

"You're not playing, Mrs. Cooper?"

That brought upon him a rambling account of her total ignorance of cards, followed by a reminiscence of what had happened the one time she had been persuaded to play hearts at a cousin's home. "My husband used to play cribbage, though. Once a week, with a friend. I'd serve them supper on a table at their elbows. They were so fond of their game they wouldn't even stop to eat."

"I'm afraid we're interfering with the concentration of the other players." The Major indicated his partner and opponents, who murmured polite denial.

She whispered loudly, like a child. "You mean they can't play, if we talk?" Her foot struck the table, jarring it. "I'll just sit and watch you, then. Perhaps I can learn by watching. If I could fill in now and then, I might be able to help Anita and George." She had been so hungry to talk that it seemed impossible for her to stop. She kept adding to her sentences as if the words welled in her from a buried spring.

In the kitchen, Anita unburdened herself to Bess Post. George played in the latter's place, and the two women busied themselves with preparations for the buffet supper Anita served in the intermission between games. "You might know—" she counted napkins nervously— "that Mitzi's oldest would have appendicitis on an occasion like this. If it is appendicitis."

Bess, stacking plates, admitted that Mitzi had a variety of names for her gin parties. "But she's failed you before. Why the irritation tonight?"

"*Oh!*" Anita, remembering that voices in the kitchen carried, lowered hers. "The least George can do is to steer his mother away from Major Hackle. He wants to kill any one who speaks to him when he's following the play, and there she sits, 'entertaining' him."

The dark, chunkily-molded Mrs. Post said, "I didn't think she'd stick around tonight."

Anita, wearily measuring coffee, explained. When the movies had been rejected, it had been proposed that her mother-in-law pay Anita's mother a visit. "My mother's about ten years younger than Mother Cooper, but I don't think that's the reason they fail to hit it off. Mother's sister lives with her, and Aunt Jennie is exactly the same age as George's mother. Yet they never can find anything to talk about, either."

"I know." Bess Post removed the damp cloth from a plate of sandwiches. "I suppose old people lose the knack of making friends. Mostly, though, I think they want to live entirely in their children's lives. Old associations and memories are easier than deliberately to cultivate new ones." She lifted a triangle of bread. "Are these chicken?"

"Chicken and ham." Anita, harassed, brilliantly made-up, swooped to close the ice-box door like a darting dragon-fly. "Of course she's separated from all her old friends. I try to remember that. She misses her husband. I keep that in mind, too. But I am absolutely sure that if George and I—George especially—would devote our whole lives to her, she'd be content. She wants to be the center around which we revolve. As nearly as I can follow her reasoning, she visualizes herself as entitled to the homage of her son's house. After a lifetime of sacrifice for her children, she demands to reap her reward. She's beginning to suspect that we ignore her rather often, but God help her if she ever fathoms how we pity her!"

"What about George?"

Anita grimaced. "Few men allow any woman, even

their own mothers, to bore them. George has, I think,
a vague idea that I may be able to restrain his mother.
He certainly has no intention of experimenting in that
direction himself. And on one point he's like flint."
She explained that she referred to her husband's determination to force his brother and his sisters to share
equally in the support of their parents. "It's almost an
obsession with George. We couldn't, certainly, pay
their expenses in a home of their own for an indefinite
period. Neither could we afford to keep them both in
the apartment very long. We've got to consider our
own futures, and neither of us is a great money-maker.
George is rock-bound in his refusal to enter into any
such contracts even temporarily. I daresay he's right."

"You think the others would let him down?"

"Not deliberately. But they'd each have a hard-luck
story ready when their contributions were due. Illness
in the family, or unexpected expenses to be met—you
know how relatives are. They impose frightfully on
each other, and that breeds distrust. The birds manage
things better than we do; they sever all ties once and
forever, as soon as they learn to fly."

At ten-thirty the games stopped for an intermission
of half an hour. The card tables, deserted for the buffet
in the dining-room, conveyed an impression of untidy
desolation, littered with empty glasses and full ash-
trays.

"I met you one afternoon at Anita's mother's, didn't I, Mrs. Cooper?" A woman with a young, thin face and a curiously old mouth, lingered politely on her way to the dining-room. "I remember you didn't play contract. Take my advice and don't ever learn. It eats up your time." She smiled, lighting a cigarette. Her slightly theatrical costume, black velvet with white fur outlining the wrists and neck, displayed extensive sections of her bony frame. She wore a silver cap netted in pearls, and pearl drops in her large, flat ears.

These emaciated, casual women perplexed Lucy Cooper, but she was grateful for the smile. Hoping to detain the stranger, eager to retain her attention, she said, "I never had much time to play cards." Her eyes, smarting from the smoke, watered. "When you have five children to look after, you do the mending nights." She hesitated, glanced at the other's ringless left hand. "I'm afraid I don't recall your name, Miss——?"

"Mrs. Harbor, Caroline Harbor. I'm filling in to-night." Some one called to her and she glided away.

Left alone the old woman stared at the smoke curling from a half-burned stub. She laboriously tried to "place" Mrs. Harbor, mainly because the effort busied her mind. None of the people she had met through Anita's mother had impressed her. Nor had she and Anita's mother any common bond. The alert, consciously youthful Mrs. Gordon and her husband still kept up their own home. They still enjoyed a salaried

income, reveled in an independence as deceptively solid
as Lucy Cooper and her husband had once known.
She fancied they sometimes criticized her dependence
and always their complacent security mocked her.

A slight commotion in the doorway interrupted her
brooding—Lois Waterbury teetered toward her, followed by George.

"I want to sit down to eat." Mrs. Waterbury might
more truthfully have declared she wanted to sit down
to drink. She helped herself to a highball from the
tray in George's hand.

He arranged two salad plates. "Here you are,
Mother. I brought you ginger-ale, not coffee. Anita
thought the coffee might keep you awake."

"There's marble dust in ginger-ale." His mother
made it a point to mention this conviction each time
she drank the amber liquid.

"Are you tired, Mother? Want to go to bed?" He
decided it was her gallantry that wrung his heart. Her
attacks of self-pity tended to alienate his sympathy, but
he detected depths of pathos in her attempts to be
happy and at ease. He wondered, watching her
strained face as she turned worriedly from him to the
vivacious Mrs. Waterbury, whether she dreaded the
silence of her room.

She wouldn't go to bed just yet, she said, and he left
her. The expression in her eyes puzzled him till,
mulling it over, he concluded that she reminded him of

a person hard of hearing, who strives to intercept sound. She had the air of listening intently for something she failed to hear.

"I saw you talking to Caroline Harbor." Liquor loosened Mrs. Waterbury's tongue. She proceeded to sketch the life history of Mrs. Harbor in what she believed to be a discreet whisper, meant only for the old lady's ear. Caroline, a divorcee, had three children. She directed Little Art Theatres and made a living at it, at the expense of her health. "She hopes to get her children educated, but after that she doesn't know what will become of her when she's too old to work."

"Her children will take care of her." The white head lifted proudly. "They'll never forget what she has done for them, how much they owe her."

"Oh!" Mrs. Waterbury, seizing her glass, swallowed a hasty gulp. "Do you think so, really? My husband says children these days are getting away from the notion that they owe their parents anything."

Not good children, Lucy Cooper protested. Her voice trembled a little, because she did not really believe what she said. She had now constantly to defend her own children's conduct even to herself. Her love found it increasingly difficult to make excuses for them. The shock, comparable to losing her religious faith, so terrified her that she took every opportunity to reaffirm her beliefs, as if she recited prayers. "We get out of life what we put into it." The old voice uttered the old lie as smoothly as rosary beads slip through believing fingers.

"Well—you ought to know." Lois Waterbury had no child. "I've heard Caroline say she'll never be a burden on her kids. She talks of going into a Home. When she's decrepit, she says."

"A Home!" Horror widened the gray eyes behind the steel-bowed spectacles. "A burden on her children!" The phrases hissed like falling coals as she repeated them. "Why, a Home for the aged is the most dreadful place. Mitzi took me to visit one. Her sister's employed there." The vividness of her description was lost on Mrs. Waterbury, who had almost reached the glassy-eyed stage. She gazed fixedly at the old woman, and in her turn Lucy Cooper saw, not the disorder of this lighted, obviously lived-in room, but the spacious, dignified, empty parlors of the Ashby Memorial Home. The brisk, capable matron had shown her through. Not the spotless woodwork and waxed floor, the tiled baths, nor the infirmary "with a nurse in constant attendance," had impressed the visitor, whose silence had been disconcertingly profound: Lucy Cooper had carried away with her the memory of the faces of sixty-seven women, all old. The thought of being an inmate of such a place, subject to casual inspection by visitors in tow of the voluble matron, one of many without separate identity, appalled the old woman who witnessed it for the first time. The endless chain of the

generations in which she trusted had failed these
women solitary now. They had married, borne children, but no family circle closed them in.

"Take me away from here!" Lucy Cooper had ordered Mitzi. And to Anita she had said, "Promise me
you and George will never put me in a Home. I should
die."

"The old ladies have a very nice social life," Anita
had explained. "They like to talk to each other and
make rugs and knit."

"Well, Mother, you and Mrs. Waterbury talked
out?" George smiled down at her, held out his hand
to assist her to rise. "We're going to play again," he
told her.

Tables filled. The women, who had freshened their
make-up, looked rested, less tense. Mrs. Waterbury
pointedly concentrated her attention on the slight, bald-
headed man who had announced himself her partner.
George, not knowing what to do with his mother, saw
his uncertainty reflected in her manner.

She put her hand on his coat-sleeve. "You don't
want me to talk to people?"

His "No" sounded curt and he tried to soften it.
"They want to play cards. For heaven's sake, let
them."

His mother's mouth drooped. She stared forlornly
at the nearest groups, their interest centered on the

cards in their hands. No one spoke to her. She didn't wish to believe that if she left the room for a few moments, or forever, she would not be missed; yet she knew, and George knew, that this was the truth.

"I guess I'll go to bed," she surrendered.

CHAPTER THREE

O N THE date of George's birthday, his mother awoke
to the grayness of a rainy February morning. She
had had what she termed a bad night, and indeed her
changed environment had wrecked the sleeping habits
of a lifetime. Merely to accustom herself to sleeping
alone taxed her spirit; often she woke in the dark to put
out a groping arm that encountered only the smooth,
papered wall. She found it difficult to ignore the lights
and noises from other windows that faced the court as
hers did, and such distractions interrupted her rest at
all hours. Her bedroom was constantly too warm, for
she refused to open a window, and she as firmly insisted on closing the door. The very bedding contributed to her disquiet; the mattress she thought too hard,
the blankets too heavy, the sheets inferior to her own.

She dressed with habitual slowness, buttoning or tying each strong, white muslin undergarment securely
and smoothing it over her bulky hips. Occasionally
she talked to herself, a new habit, one of which she was
ashamed. She had always believed that it indicated a
failing mind. Now, in the strange loneliness that en-
folded her as she dressed or undressed in solitude, her
whispering voice formed brief sentences against her

will. At such times she glanced over her shoulder, half expecting to see a spare, erect figure before the mirror, brush in hand, pointing streaked gray hair to a jaunty peak. She had shared a bedroom with her husband for fifty years: did he, she wondered, miss her with the same piercing, aching hopelessness that lay in wait for her each morning and each night? The sense of seeking him never quite left her. In the other rooms she found herself listening for the sound of his voice, the alert quickness of his step. The futility of her expectations smote her with staggering force behind the closed door of her bedroom. Once, when the slow, painful tears had distorted her vision, she fancied that she sat in a cell. The windows let into the wall above her head and the glimpse of brick walls they framed, had heightened the impression.

This morning the sight of the ribbon-tied parcel in the lower drawer of her bureau mercifully directed her thoughts forward. This was George's birthday; she was the mother of sons. Lucy Cooper, arranging the heavy white hair of which she was innocently vain, gazed unseeing at her image in the glass. She was planning a ceremonial which should pay just tribute to her maternal rights. Her gift for George must not be ignored, nor presented in haste. No matter if he attended a hundred parties, his mother's observance of the day would hold a special significance for him. She had made it a gay and happy time for the little boy he used to be. Surely his sentiment had not all been lost. As she thrust the shell pins into the knot of her hair, she sighed for the birthday cakes she had baked and decorated with candles when her children were young.

When she opened her door to cross the tiny hall to the bathroom, the odor of broiling bacon teased her appetite. Breakfast was her best meal, she sometimes said, and she often wakened hungry at six o'clock. Then the time she must wait dismayed her.

As she washed, rubbing the knitted face-cloth up into the edges of her hair and holding it carefully away from the starched top of her corset-cover, she mapped her plans. If she called George into her room after breakfast, gave him his parcel there, they might both recapture something of that infantile joyousness, the one emotion, perhaps, she had ever honestly succeeded in sharing with her children. She constantly yearned to repeat these happy memories, as she liked to hear old and favorite tunes. Her vivid recollections not only of past situations, but of past responses shocked George, who was almost fanatically opposed to looking back. There was something positively superstitious in his efforts to ignore any reference to old times, and Anita declared he must dread the fate of Lot's wife.

Anita, in her tweed frock, but wearing a black satin hat as hard and round as a cheese box, greeted her mother-in-law from the telephone table in the passage-way. "Good-morning, Mother Cooper. I'm sorry, but we couldn't wait for you. I have an extra class this morning." She put up her wisp of a veil to squint at a list of numbers on a card. Anita needed glasses, but only, she explained, in a poor light.

"I'll have my breakfast with George." The tall figure in the long-sleeved, high-collared black-and-white percale, parted the portières that screened the dining-room.

Dialing, Anita called pleasantly, "Mitzi'll wait on you. George went early. I asked him to stop in and speak to you, but he was rushed. He has to— Hello, darling, I want to speak to you about tonight—" Her voice dropped to a confidential murmur.

The empty dining-room intensified the blankness of frustration that nagged at the old woman, whose lips trembled as she surveyed her grapefruit. They might have waited for her! Her thoughts had been centered on George's birthday, and he had not cared enough about her to say "Good-morning." Sometimes, Lucy Cooper told herself in the quick, exhausting anger of old age, she believed her son regarded her with no more interest than he did the piano or a chair. As a matter of truth, she had known in her heart for years that neither of her sons regularly remembered her except at the instigation of their wives. George's wife and Richard's wife at intervals said firmly, "Have you called your mother up yet?" Or, "You write your mother yourself—she'd like to get a letter from you."

In such ways do women preserve the shell of outward decency after sincerity or affection has died and among themselves they will try to shield even their enemies from the brutal indifference of men.

"The grapefruit sweet enough, Mother?" Anita, her 'phone call finished, hovered in the doorway. She would be gone all day, she added. "George and I are dressing at my mother's tonight. Mitzi is to get your dinner and stay as late as you want her."

Lucy Cooper said exactly as a child might, "George didn't see his present."

Anita, who had asked her husband to knock at his mother's door before he left that morning, remembered his refusal.

"I can't behave as she expects me to act." George, walking up and down as he dressed, had suddenly halted his circlings. "I suppose the ghastly fact is that I don't feel anything of what she feels, or thinks she feels."

"She has a present for you, she told me. You love her, don't you?"

He had picked a pin from the rug and stuck it carefully in the dresser scarf before replying. "How do I know? As a boy, I did. But the old relationships last only if one never examines them. We were an affectionate family, yet the girls and Rick and I are indifferent to each other now. My parents' attitude toward dependency has changed me, I think. I can't help wondering if their love for me was calculating from the start."

Old people merely *talked* as if they had children to care for them in their last years, Anita had protested. She didn't, she declared, altogether blame them. "Don't be bitter, George. Your father and mother were taught they were brought into the world to look after their parents. Naturally they feel the same way toward you. It's a terrible shock to old folks to be informed that sons and daughters no longer feel morally obligated to support their parents simply because they *are* parents."

"Now I won't see George on his birthday at all." Lucy Cooper, spooning grapefruit, waited hopefully for some suggestion from her daughter-in-law.

She's darn' lonely, and everything about it's all wrong, thought Anita, who resented being forced so frequently to admit the stark unloveliness of old age. Her husband can't protect her; her son fails her. She's had a richer life than I, but I'll be spared the pity of my son's wife. "You save that package for George and surprise him tomorrow, Mother," she said.

"Morning, Mis' Cooper. Your cereal." Mitzi, whose heavenly disposition was proof against wild nights out and dreary mornings in, smilingly set down a yellow bowl of perfectly cooked oatmeal.

"There's plenty of cream." Anita wished she had thought to remove the vacant chairs she and George had occupied. Yet the picture of a stout old woman

sugaring her cereal and evidently preparing to attack
her breakfast with a fine appetite shouldn't be pathetic,
worried Anita. She tried to regard the emotional effect
with scorn. If only, she informed herself severely, she
might learn not to be maudlin, she could hope to be
fair. God knew the Coopers had enough examples of
the havoc wrought by slipshod reasoning constantly before them. As she hurried to meet her first class of
nervous, intense women to whom she taught contract
bridge, Anita, not liking to be harrowed, shifted her
sense of guilt. It was all George's fault, because he
wouldn't spare the time to fuss over his mother. "I
can't make a fuss over her, can I?" demanded Anita
of the friend who helped her set out the card tables.
"It's getting so now that George actually tries to keep
out of her way."

"He always said no one could fry chicken the way I
did." Lucy Cooper, who had carried her dishes out
to the sink, lingered after Mitzi had washed and dried
each piece.

"Boys is like that." Mitzi added regretfully that she
had only girls herself. This strong, thick-set colored
girl, who should have been named something solid and
dependable, insisted on being Mitzi La Verne. She
often proudly mentioned a sister Bebe—pronounced
"Bee-bee"—who worked in an Old Ladies' Home. Mitzi and Bebe, with all the compassion of their race, pitied

the old. "You must-a been good to all your children,"
Mitzi said.

Lucy Cooper could talk only of George today, of his
little boy graces, of his childish prowess, of his then
fluently expressed love. She recalled the birthday parties she had arranged for him, described the gifts his
father had bought for him at her suggestion. "I have
a surprise for him today, too. He left so early, he didn't
receive it. I've a good mind to telephone him now.
Maybe he'll come up here to lunch."

Mitzi, with the bathroom to clean next, tolerantly encouraged her. Old ladies had to talk, and if they talked
into the telephone that relieved their immediate audience. "I'll dial Mr. Cooper's office for you." Mitzi
had no compunctions about interrupting another's work
when otherwise she must neglect her own. "I'll have
a good lunch ready, if he say yes, he come up."

"I only want to know if you're all right," said
George's mother into the 'phone. The mouth and ear
piece in one confused her and usually she held the in-
strument the wrong way. She had to repeat two or
three times that she had missed him at breakfast.
When she turned the receiver around, he heard her.
"You'll come up to lunch, George? Your mother won't
see you on your birthday, unless you do."

He had a meeting, he explained, a luncheon meeting,
at which he was honor guest. "I'm sorry, Mother, but

that's the way it is. Why don't you go to the movies early this afternoon?"

She replied with childish simplicity, "I have a present for you." She thought proudly of the six handkerchiefs, each marked with a "G," in the neat box. Nearly all her little stock of cash had been expended for the fine linen and she had strained her eyes over needlework she should not have attempted. She unreasonably enough expected her son to recognize how much of herself she had wrapped up with those linen squares. Like many women she demanded that those dear to her accept her own valuation of the gifts she made them.

At his end of the 'phone George sighed. The problems of a busy day nagged him. Each moment his mother claimed tied his routine in a deeper snarl, but if he pleaded the pressure of work, she would misunderstand. He knew that he and Anita hurt her in a thousand ways of which they must be unaware. So often he had seen his mother's eyes fill with tears in the few weeks she had lived with him, that he now tried to choose his every word to her. Yet in her presence he recoiled from her efforts to rebuild her broken life around him. Her constant attention irked him and drove him from her. Out of her sight he could and did successfully forget her existence. When he talked to her, an overwhelming pity gentled his manner and speech. He fancied he heard then something infinitely grieving, a murmuring undercurrent that saddened him, though his mother might not speak of pain. It was as if, unknown to her, her fussiness, her insistent clinging, parted at intervals, like draperies, to reveal her crying heart. Yet now she again oppressed him. An undercurrent of complaint in her tones hinted at dereliction on his part. Well, what more could he do for her than he had already done? She was well-fed, comfortably housed today, while he and his wife battled with rain and cold and the tedious drudgery of work. His mother had no responsibilities, no duties, no cares. She had no heavier call upon her time than to amuse herself. Only she still wants to be amusing herself by caring for her children, thought George in despair. When the child-bearing period is done for, Nature ought to choke off a woman's maternal passion for physical contact with her babies. Nature's all kinds of a fool! "Save that present for me, Mother," he said.

She let him go and wandered restlessly from room to room. Leisure appalled her, because physical activity had hitherto absorbed her hours. She found little comfort in papers or books, and she disliked the radio as so many poor listeners do. Nothing, she had once told Mitzi, could make up to her for the lack of *folks*. "I miss the people who used to run in and talk," she explained. "We had such good, chatty neighbors in my own town."

Mitzi, who must surround herself with people, too,

and who went home each night to renew her mysterious, smooth strength with laughter and love, paused
in her easy, rhythmic polishing of the porcelain tile.
"I'll toss you up a French omelet for lunch, Mis' Cooper." Food, Mitzi believed, could alleviate the troubles
of old and young. She had a theory that she could
drown most of the world's woe in cream.

Two hours till lunch! The restless, aimless figure
pacing the length of the apartment, halted in the bathroom doorway. "Mitzi, I believe I'll go down to my
son's office. I'll take his present to him."

The maid, vigorously scouring the basin, said doubtfully, "He mightn't like it." She sprinkled cleaning
powder on her cloth with a judicial air, as if she shook
out grains of wisdom. "Maybe he's busy."

Not too busy to see his mother, the old woman declared with confidence. She set about her preparations,
finding in a definite destination and purpose a tonic
more stimulating than wine. Nothing less than her
best gray silk dress would she wear. The box for
George must be retied. She spent twenty minutes com-
posing a message, which after many trials she copied
on one of the small blank cards she found in Anita's
desk. After she had adjusted her hat to her satisfaction, she decided that her shoes needed blacking. The
liquid dressing she used dried quickly, but she was conscious of its penetrating odor like the smell of dye. She
remembered her bottle of lavender toilet water and

painstakingly dampened the front of her gown with
the fragrant stuff. Her only cosmetic was face powder,
and she persisted in the use of a pearly white shade
much too light for her skin. George, she recalled, disliked a "floury" complexion, so she asked Mitzi if she
had too much on.

"No'm, you looks fine." Mitzi sincerely admired
something in the tall, wide-hipped figure that she
would have been at a loss to define. "You better take
a taxi, Mis' Cooper. The doorman'll get you a fifty-
cent cab."

The escort of the doorman, who had the outlines of
an imposing pine-tree in his green and silver uniform,
upset rather than sustained his elderly charge. In spite
of his caution she struck her head against the top of the
taxi and pitched forward, dropping heavily on the worn
leather seat. To the driver's request for an address, she
could only stare. "My son's office," she murmured
twice before she realized that she did not know the lo-
cation. "It must be down town," she amplified.

Mitzi, hovering in the lobby, gave the necessary information to the doorman, who relayed it to the driver,
and the cab rolled off smoothly, its solitary fare sitting
stiffly upright in a position best calculated to develop a
backache. To pay out money for taxi-fare, even on a
rainy day, seemed to Lucy Cooper the most wanton
extravagance in which a woman could indulge. Her
system of economy, never noticeably consistent, had

compelled her to forego cabs as a foolish luxury better left to the rich. She clutched her half-dollar tightly in her hand now, and to justify its expenditure assured herself that in this case time was money; she must see George before he left to attend his meeting.

"Shall I wait, lady?" The driver, who handed her to the pavement in front of the dingy granite building, glanced up hopefully at the windows from force of habit.

"Wait? For me? Oh, no." She paid him with evident relief. "No, don't wait. I don't know how long I'll be talking to my son."

She scarcely noticed the steadily falling rain, in the excitement of taking the second step in her adventure. The deference of the elevator-starter, who apparently summoned an elevator especially for her, pleased her. The operator, too, had a sympathetic manner. She told herself she was glad George had his office in a nice building, where every one was polite and kind. When she said to the pretty girl at the switchboard in the suite of the Henning Oil Burner Company—to which she had been carefully directed—"Is Mr. Cooper in? I'm his mother," she was prepared to like her, even if she did paint her lips.

"Mr. Cooper's out. Won't be back till after lunch. Any message?" The girl slanted a pencil above a pad.

She had missed him! Her whole existence darkened. As if disappointment, like a curtain, clouded her glasses,

she saw the office indifferent, preoccupied, unmindful
of her loss. The sound of voices and bells, the click of
typewriters, annoyed her. She tried to concentrate on
a message for George. "Say his mother was here. I'll
leave this package for him, and he's to call me up this
afternoon and let me know he's received it. Are you
writing it all down?" She distrusted the pencil that
flew so swiftly, for she contrasted the easy motion with
her own laborious, slow strokes.

The scarlet lips parted in a smile. "Mr. Cooper has
your 'phone number?"

"Why, I *live* with him." The words might have been
jerked from her. Didn't George ever speak of his
mother? Perhaps his friends didn't even know he had
a mother living. But, then, George was never one to
discuss his private affairs, she thought proudly as the
elevator plunged with her to the street floor. It isn't
likely that he says two words a day to a little painted
minx like that.

The traffic man at the corner, used, he assured her
with a beaming smile, to helping old ladies off and on
and out and in, put her on the right bus. The virtue
of her thrift sustained her the length of the smelly ride,
but she declared herself too exhausted to eat when she
thankfully reached home. "After all my trouble, he
wasn't there. He must have *hurried,* to get away as
quick as that."

Mitzi fed and comforted her as she would a fretful

child. "What you say you give Mr. Cooper for his birf-day? Handkerchiefs what you made yourself? My, my, ain't that grand! I bet he shows everybody the handkerchiefs what his mama made him."

After lunch Mitzi pushed a wing chair close to the doorway of the living-room. One could rest there and be within sight of the 'phone in the hall. Just what satisfaction it gave her to *see* the 'phone, George's moth-er could not have explained. She stared unwinkingly at the face of the dial till her eyes closed, but she ruth-lessly forbade herself to doze. To keep awake she tried to imagine how George looked and what he said at his luncheon meeting; she had never heard him speak in public. A dozen times she opened and closed the hunt-ing-case of her heavy, old-fashioned watch. Finally, she held it open in her hand. At half-past three she decided that the switchboard girl had probably neg-lected to deliver her message. It would be only busi-nesslike to get in touch with George. She asked Mitzi to dial for her, but almost snatched the receiver when she heard a voice reply.

"Oh, yes, Mrs. Cooper, I gave your message to your son." The high, clear tones matched the vivid creature the old lady as vividly remembered. "Yes, the pack-age, too. I doubt if he's opened it. He's been busy ever since he came back from lunch. Why, you couldn't speak to him just now; he's in the President's office."

The mother repeated the last sentence to Mitzi, because it reflected credit on George. He was busy, he was important; small wonder that he had no time to open a birthday present when his advice was needed by the head of his firm.

"I got to go to the store." Mitzi made her announcement as joyfully as if she contemplated a picnic trip. She would see folks in the cash grocery; the manager always had a word for each one who came to buy. "You're all right, ain't you, Mis' Cooper?" The colored woman had something of the dumb beast's sensitiveness to human moods.

"He works very hard," said the old woman aloud when she knew herself to be alone. "He works very hard, and he has very little time to himself." The words echoed hollowly in the silent room. They echoed as hollowly in her heart. She conceded that George had time for the party that night. Not, of course, she assured herself, that she wished him to forego recreation. A business man must relax. All work and no play, she quoted with satisfaction in her aptness, made Jack a dull boy.

She rose stiffly from her chair and drifted about the room, touching small ornaments that she did not see. When George spent an evening at home, how often did he speak to her? He played cards, or read, bringing to either occupation a concentration that rendered the most casual word from her an annoyance. The

tall figure halted before the copper smoking-stand at
right angles to a red leather chair. George's mother
identified his chair with his personality, and for that
reason she liked to sit in it during the day. Now, however, she merely rested her arm on the top and again
she spoke aloud. "He has no time for me." Her lips
quivered. "I'm in his way." She stared intently into
space. "He doesn't want me to live with him." Slow
painful tears dropped one by one on the leather, and she
rubbed her handkerchief on the spots.

Why remain in a household where one was not
loved? How, the old woman asked herself sternly, had
she remained so long? The obvious explanation was
that she had not realized that George no longer cared
for her. No mother could perceive a situation like that
until the knowledge had been forced upon her. Now
that she understood his hitherto inexplicable behavior,
she meant to leave his roof with the least possible delay.
The maid's absence cleared the way. Mitzi had a repu-
tation for prolonging her errands, so it was unlikely
she would return before a small black satchel could be
packed.

In her bedroom Lucy Cooper lumbered agitatedly
about, collecting her few toilet articles, folding a clean
muslin nightdress. Her hands trembled, perspiration
dewed her forehead, gathered in the hollows of her
neck. She started nervously every time a bell rang.
Once, thinking she heard Mitzi's step, she hurriedly

slung the bag under her bed. She had to fetch the broom to scoop it out, the awkward task cruelly twisting her back and knees.

When she had finished packing, she put on her hat and coat without looking at herself in the glass. She deliberated whether to write a note for George and decided that she dared not risk the time. Later she would notify him where to send her trunk. She closed the door of her room softly and tiptoed out of the apartment. Bag in hand, she stealthily skirted the magnificent oil-burners, determined to leave by way of the back basement door. The doorman must have nothing to tell.

She found the basement entrance more by good fortune than geographical skill and let herself out into an alleyway. Not until she emerged on the street behind the apartment house, did she admit to her uneasy consciousness that she had no place to go.

Her birthday present for George and the taxi to his office had so depleted her slender reserve that only a quarter remained in her purse. Any shadowy plan to join her husband that might have suggested itself, quickly faded. The bus fare to Locton, where Cora lived, must be as much as a dollar. Anyway, Cora wouldn't want me, she mused, trying to walk briskly, for the cold air numbed her. The rain had ceased, but the pavements were still wet. She knew she must sit as soon as possible and the small, gritty park two blocks away promised a bench. This cheerless, sodden haven appeared almost beautiful in her eyes before she had walked the short distance. Excitement, fatigue and grief had taken their toll of her. The tremor in her knees dismayed her, the weight of the small bag pulled at the socket of her arm. She spent two cents of her precious store for a newspaper to be spread over the damp seat.

Something that looked like a bundle of old dirty clothes huddled beside the stone posts of the park boundary, stirred at the sound of footsteps. Lucy Cooper perceived an old beggar woman holding a tin cup in terrible claw-like hands. Under the filthy shawl a shriveled face, the color of skim-milk, screwed into a mass of wrinkles, the toothless gums whined unintelligible words. If only I had more money, thought the other, but she dared not give away her few coins.

A bench, to some extent protected from the wind by a screen of shrubbery, tangled and bare, faced a boarded-up fountain. Lucy Cooper seated herself thankfully on her folded newspaper and for a moment the sensation of physical relief blotted out every other consideration; it was good to rest. Presently she found her mind functioning automatically, as it were, for a sentence fully formed beat against her consciousness as though it had been hammering several minutes for recognition. "I have nowhere to go," she heard herself saying silently, drearily; "I have nowhere to go."

She thought of Richard's wife, Grace, a strange, composed woman, almost a miser in her greed. Grace had indicated that she expected to do her share in the matter of supporting her husband's parents, but she had frankly declared that she didn't intend to be imposed on. To have her mother-in-law out of established turn would certainly be considered an imposition by Grace. Nellie, too, in her more gentle way, would resent the arrival of her mother before the time set. It was, of course, Harvey who must really be blamed. Nellie's husband disliked strangers in his house, and he persistently regarded his mother-in-law in that light. I never did get real acquainted with Harvey, Nellie's mother mused. Her feet hurt, and a drowsiness tugged at her eyelids. I can't go back to live with George, when I know he doesn't want me, she thought in despair.

Some one sat down at the other end of the bench. She turned to see a perfectly neat old man, plainly but comfortably dressed. He wore knitted wool gloves, and his nose was pink with cold. He said a little hesitantly, "You get tired, walking."

She agreed, glad to hear the sound of her own voice. "I was just getting rested myself." A gust of wind tore angrily at their backs, and they both shivered.

He lived, he revealed presently, in a Home for old men. They had to be in at five o'clock, in order to eat supper at half-past five. He found the place comfortable enough, but "the dang rules" kept anger at simmering heat in him. "Treat you like a parcel of kids, they do. I tell you if my children had lived, I wouldn't be there half a day. But a man without a family's got to do the best he can. I'm not complaining—I paid my way in, and there's worse places." He flexed his fingers to warm them, got carefully to his feet as if he expected his joints to crack. "You live with your folks? There's nothing like kin of your own."

The old woman watched him lurch stiffly down the path, trying to hurry toward his supper, for which he must be on time. It would be dreadful to live in a Home, she shuddered, wondering how people endured the terrible situations into which Fate pushed them. If my children refused to have me, I suppose I'd have to go in one of those places, she reflected, and Bark, too. The possibility menaced her with such horrors that she stood up as if to escape, and a sharp pain stabbed the small of her back. The park lights leaped into radiance, then settled to a steady glow. I must walk around, or I'll be too lame to move, the solitary watcher thought. She paced the length of one narrow walk, turned into a second cement strip. The idea of walking up and down, up and down, till George came in search of her, fastened on her mind. She pictured him entering the apartment, to discover that his mother was not there. The realization must smite him that he did love his mother, that her absence left a void. He will come to

look for me, the old woman confidently assured herself and smiled in the gloom of the winter dusk.

Then, like a crashing blow, the memory of the party
hurled itself against her dream and shattered it. George
wouldn't be home for dinner! He wouldn't be home
till all hours in the morning! Why, she might be out
in this wretched park all night and George never know
it till the next day. It would mean the death of her,
of course, to sit huddled on a park bench through a
freezing winter's night. Already she was chilled to the
marrow, and her rheumatism, she knew, was worse.
She stopped in the center of the walk to shift her bag
to the other hand and she wondered if women did ever
try to sleep on the benches as she had once or twice in
summer seen men do. A pang of hunger added to her
worries. She had so little with which to buy food.
Suppose a policeman, patrolling the park, discovered
her and bade her move on? Where did homeless
women go?

Lights twinkled in the apartments facing the park.
The clear sharp crescent of a new moon glowed through
the black branches of a tree. A boy on roller-skates
clattered past her, a parcel under his arm, and the smell
of freshly ground, cheap, strong coffee scented the air.
The apartment would be warm, fragrant with the
aroma of good cooking. Mitzi had corn pudding and
stuffed baked potatoes on Thursday nights. The comfort of a clean, soft bed, the convenience of a heated

bathroom, the security and shelter offered by her son's house, waited his mother now wandering in a deserted public park.

The old woman gazed fixedly at the cold, silver slice of moon for another long moment. Then she wheeled and began to trudge in the direction of the entrance. Beside the stone posts a bundle of what looked to be dirty clothes stirred, a feeble voice muttered pleading words. Lucy Cooper unfastened her little change purse with thick stiff fingers and dropped two dimes and three pennies into the tin cup.

When, at quarter of three the next morning, George and Anita walked into their living-room to discover two lamps burning, a slumped figure asleep in George's chair, a sock clasped in the relaxed hands, and the contents of the darning basket overturned on the floor, Anita lost her composure. "It's an act!" she cried. "There's no reason why she couldn't have gone to bed." Then she was suddenly sorry that she had spoken the truth.

Chapter Four

"Don't you find the house a little chilly, Cora?"
"Mercy, no! If you'd move around more, you
wouldn't feel cold." Cora Payne, who had recently
taken to wearing nose glasses, frowned so deeply that
they tumbled to her lap. The unexpected intricacies of
the Chinese costume on which she sewed baffled her,
and she wished her father would cease demanding her
attention.

"Do you want me to do anything about supper?"
He eyed her hopefully.

"Now, Father, we've just had dinner. Let me get
my mind off the kitchen for a minute, can't you? I
want to wear this to the club meeting tomorrow.
You'd better take a walk; you don't get nearly enough
exercise." She continued to pin her fabric experimentally, without once glancing toward him.

The old man stared wistfully at the kindling and
paper laid in the brick fireplace, ready to light. Bill,
his son-in-law, would touch a match to it, if he were
home; Bill liked comfort. Cora, on the other hand,
considered a fireplace untidy and discouraged its use.
Funny, Cora's father thought, tramping restlessly into

the front room, funny that he "hit it off" with Bill much better than he did with his daughter, his own flesh and blood. Perhaps it was because he and Cora were both shut up in the house so much that they constantly found themselves at odds. The anomaly of an idle man around the house distressed him quite as much as it did her, but a curt refusal met his offers to help. He had been accustomed to lending his wife a hand in the kitchen; he really enjoyed peeling potatoes, or preparing other vegetables, any work that he could perform comfortably seated. The discussion of food, the agreeable warmth and odors of a well-ordered kitchen, were associated in his mind with hours of placid companionship he and his wife had taken for granted on his days off. In the twenty years following the marriage of their youngest child his wife had grown more and more dependent upon him for actual assistance in her housework, as well as for fellowship. A certain clumsiness of movement had intensified itself with the passing years, and she mistrusted her hands. The care of her treasured bric-à-brac and china devolved on him.

As the old man pulled aside the curtains at Cora's front window, the cold dreariness of the first day of March, a grayness he fancied he felt in his very bones, rattled dully at the glass. The Paynes lived on the outskirts of town, and the street at this point was little more than a road. Few cars passed and almost no one walked by the house afoot. A tangle of trash and

paper, whirled by the wind into the mesh of the barbed-
wire fence on the opposite bank, fluttered and twisted
like something alive and trapped. The slight spare
figure, motionless, watched the aimless turmoil with
intent, unseeing gaze; on his empty horizon it served
as well as any other point of focus.

"Father!"

"Well, what is it?" He mustn't talk to her, he reflected, yet she couldn't let him alone.

"Are you wrinkling those curtains?"

He guiltily let the net drop back into place. Furtively he straightened the folds. Cora inspected the
front windows a dozen times a day. She knew if the
curtains were the fraction of an inch out of line, or if
the shades had been touched to be lowered or raised.

"Father!"

With a sigh he returned to the dining-room where
she sat, her sewing heaped on the table before her. She
was not a skillful seamstress, and handling a needle exhausted her nervous strength.

"For heaven's sake, can't you lift your feet?" Her
fretful voice jerked as she twitched at the dark blue
silk. "I declare I don't see how Mother ever managed!
Why don't you take a walk?"

He said, "Because I don't want to—that's why," as
an automatic assertion of self-respect. Invariably he
answered back, and he was as unable to avoid bickering or controversy as she. The habit of nagging, in-

grained in both, seemed unlovelier in her because she was a woman and the younger of the two.

Finally she had her way, as he had known she would. A walk to the post-office and back, she insisted, was exactly what he required. He felt cold, she told him, because his circulation was below par. No one who sat around the house all day could hope to be healthy.

"Walking's fine exercise for a man your age, Father. Not too violent, but splendid to tone up your muscles——"

"My good Godie!" He struggled into his overcoat, sputtering with inarticulate rage. "I know what's good for me as well as you do, Miss."

"Don't forget to ask for the mail."

He fumbled on the floor for his knitted gloves, which he had dropped, and she grumblingly left her work to help him search for them. "Here they are—under the chair. Don't lose them, will you? I can't ask Bill to buy one extra item this month." She ushered him out of the front door and closed it decisively against the wind.

The combativeness she aroused in him had ruffled his clothes as well as his spirit. He had to shake himself neat, adjust his collar, straighten his tie, before he felt sufficiently soothed to undertake his solitary walk.

He plodded morosely along the broken flagstone pavements of the main street, watching his feet lest he trip. In his mind he reviewed the few places where he might respectably loiter in town. He dismissed the hotel and the drugstore, because the stragglers there spent some money as a matter of course. The library, the railroad-station and the post-office offered the warmth of shelter, but the latter two were never clean. The old man, fanatically neat, distrusted the habitués who could kill time happily amid disorder and dirt. Yet he had to admit the restrictions of the immaculately arranged town library depressed him. Overheated, clean, severely classical as to decoration, the one-room building encouraged serious purpose. Self-improvement, not relaxation, was suggested by the smooth hard table and chairs. Each visitor became the object of the tense, eager librarian's solicitude, and Barkley Cooper, who liked placid women, dreaded Miss Gerry's fussy attempts to be kind. He stood looking at the library's plain exterior when he reached it this afternoon, debating whether to brave Miss Gerry for the sake of half an hour's rest. The buffeting of the wind tired him; it would be pleasant to sit down.

"Oh! Good afternoon—you're Mrs. Payne's father, aren't you?"

He jerked around to perceive a short, stout woman in a blindingly blue coat. Everything about her, he thought irritably, was too bright, from her immaculate yellow chamois gloves to her smile. But then he hated to be catalogued as "Mrs. Payne's father."

"I suppose you're going to spend the afternoon reading?" She spoke to him exactly as she might to a child of eight or nine. "I often say to Cora you're so fortunate to have your time free."

The old man thrust out his lower lip. His eyes watered, partly from the stinging force of the wind, partly from impotent rage. Damn these patronizing women who thought of him, Cora's father, as a puppet whom she controlled with strings. He lifted his hat and the twirling peak of his hair bobbed grotesquely. "If you'll excuse me, I'll be moving on . . . An appointment . . . Mustn't be late."

He scarcely minded the wind as he stepped briskly, his head held high. That Mrs. What's-Her-Name—he guessed he'd put her in her place. She had tricked him out of his rest in the warm library, but he had upset her notions of him as an idler. He hadn't lied, either. The stimulation of a legitimate errand completed the restoration of his self-respect. He eyed with disapproval the loafers congregated on store steps or lounging against sunny walls. The few loungers clustered in the vestibule of the grimy post-office nodded respectfully to him and moved to let him pass.

A capable, middle-aged postmistress, plump, curious as a rabbit, grimaced at him through the tiny barred slit. She had a puffy, white face and weak, pink-rimmed eyes. He never saw her that he didn't think of carrots. "And how do *you* do this afternoon, Mr. Cooper?" Expertly she sifted a cascade of mail. "Only

one this time, and it's for you. Guess your girl's remembered you."

He thanked her distantly for his letter, bent over the
dirty spotted radiator at the window, to scrutinize the
postmark. The warmth of the pipes burned his thin
old legs. He recognized his wife's transcription, small,
sharp, the lines evenly spaced as if ruled. In the weeks
he had lived with Cora, he had received two brief notes
from his wife. He had written her once. The labor
involved in transferring thoughts to paper daunted
both. They employed formal phrases, artificial, stiff.
"I am as well as can be expected," the old husband
wrote, instead of confessing that his wife's absence per-
vaded his very sleep. He often reared up in bed at
night when he discovered no one beside him and whispered drowsily to the empty space. Cora, hearing him
on one occasion, had accused him of talking in his
dreams.

The hot metal of the radiator insistently scorched his
shin-bones. Aware that the postmistress covertly inspected him through her wicket, he pulled his soft gray
felt hat more firmly over his eyes and prepared to brave
the cold. On the steps he hesitated, gasping for breath.
A raw film of grit, carried by the wind, flicked his face
like a dirty veil. Privacy in which to read his letter was
his immediate need. A recollection of the waiting-
room in the railroad-station, filthy but quiet, prodded

him. He retied his muffler and started off down the
street.

He and Cora had quarreled hotly over the removal
of the lock and bolt from the door of his room in her
house. Cora had justified her act on the grounds that
her father might be taken suddenly ill in the night.
"Old people often are. We'd have to batter down the
door to get to you." The standards of barren neatness
she superimposed on him afforded him no cover; he
had not even a bureau scarf under which to thrust a
letter, if she should push open his door to discover him
reading one.

The station waiting-room, divided by the circular
ticket-office into sections for women and men, offered
the privacy obtainable only in a public place. Two colored women dozed in a companionable huddle on the
women's side of the room. In the half reserved for men
a single lounger stared fixedly at his shoes. Somewhere out of sight the agent whistled dolefully off key.
Cuspidors, torn newspapers, and the butts and stubs of
half-burned cigars and cigarettes littered the floor. No
one noticed the old man any more than he observed
the cobwebs spanning the cracked windows, nor
minded the fetid air. The hissing radiator dripping
noisily on a dirty block of cement supplied enough heat
for a hotel. Barkley Cooper, selecting a corner seat,
glanced at the discolored clock-face on the wall. It had
only one hand. He methodically removed his gloves,

unbuttoned his overcoat, pulled out his own plain silver watch on a clumsy silver chain. Half-past four. He eased the timepiece into his vest pocket and drew out the letter, not knowing that he sighed. His strong fingers tipped with thick, long nails, tore a narrow strip from the envelope at one end.

A single sheet of paper, folded once, swirled to the floor. He stooped to retrieve it and perceived that it encased a bill. Five dollars, a green slip that, as he handled it, felt fragile, thin, and dry. He sniffed it critically, because he remembered that a postal employee had told him years ago that mail thieves could smell money through the envelopes. It seemed to him that the bill did have a faint odor, a musty, peculiar hint of decay. He glanced furtively about before he rolled the gift into a tiny green wad and stuffed it in an inside pocket. In all his life he had not carried a wallet. His wife had handled their actual cash. He wondered if she guessed that he now had not a cent.

The brief, unrevealing letter admonished him not to take cold, to wear his heavy underwear till late in the spring. She would be pleased to hear from him, his wife wrote. In a postscript she mentioned that she hoped he might be able to use five dollars which George had recently handed her.

He imagined her big, soft, shapeless figure squeezed into the seat beside him as he filled and lit his pipe. They had sat together in a station like this the first time they had visited George after he married. All the children had been eager to have their parents see them preside in their own new homes. Even Grace, Richard's wife, had been hospitable as a bride. The old man, recalling these visits and his wife's absorbed interest in the housekeeping arrangements of each of her children as they settled down, puzzled for the hundredth time over the present attitude of these same children and tried to trace the change in them.

George, the father reflected, had been, like the Coopers, indifferent to money, and Anita had shared his views at first. In the earlier periods of their marriage neither had practised thrift. No one knew what George earned, but he and Anita lived, not uncomfortably, in debt. Anita wanted children, yet suggestions that she adopt a baby angered her. "I want my own, or none. What is another woman's child to me? I want to see my husband's characteristics and mine repeated. Besides, I want the whole experience—all of it." She had asked her mother-in-law's advice, she had consulted physicians, attended clinics. She had even prayed.

Barkley Cooper sucked his pipe, dismissing the peculiarities of childless women. As always when he searched for an explanation of why his children had failed him, his reasoning stopped short at George and Anita, to him an inscrutable pair. Their obsession, the accumulation of an annuity, bewildered the old man. He approved vaguely of provision for old age, but he considered it foolish to dwell on a problematic future. Old people, with money and without, received care. His mind persistently reverted to his father, whom he had supported as a matter of course. Had his wife been modern like Anita, the old father might have been neglected, but thank God his wife had been taught the duty of a child. Her mother had lived with them for years, too.

An incoherent, furious resentment, gusty and sudden as a thunderstorm, scourged the old man's spirit. He muttered to himself, his hot, dry eyes staring fiercely at the dusty floor boards. Now that the first shock of the discovery that his children regarded him as a burden had begun to lessen, his anger against them mounted day by day. He called them in his soul ingrates, monsters of selfishness, liars. Bitterness seared him. His belief in the security of his future had been so absolute. . . .

The fury in him died. Fatigue confused his mind. He and his wife had not shirked *their* duty; they had cared for their dependents, and now surely they should reap their reward. The thought that to sow and not to reap might be his portion was as intolerable to the old man as the possibility that he might not live to see the ingratitude of his children punished. The lights flickered weakly in the dusty bulbs on the station walls. Barkley Cooper knocked the ashes from his pipe. He firmly believed that retribution occupied a large share

of God's attention, and he visioned a Deity who marked
the garments of those slated for punishment in this
world, not the next, with some kind of identification
mark, probably a faint white "X."

Time to be going home, he told himself, rising with
the slow dignity that ignores stiff joints. He felt of the
tiny wad he had stuffed in his pocket—it was safe. Its
possession gave him a measure of confidence, for with
money of his own, the way of escape need never quite
close. He resolved to tell no one. A train roared past
the small station, and through the windows he glimpsed
passengers eating in the dining-car. He buttoned his
overcoat, letting the anticipation of Cora's supper table
and her hot, fried food cheer him.

"My head feels as if it would split in two!" Cora,
spooning out hashed potatoes on her father's plate,
added salt and pepper as if she judged him incapable of
seasoning his food. "I've sewed so long it's a wonder
my eyes don't fall out of their sockets."

Bill Payne, who looked years younger than his wife
in spite of his frontal baldness, held out his hand for
his already sweetened cup of tea. Cora did the serving
with a zeal that discouraged self-service. Throughout
a meal her dark eyes roved the table, apparently mind-
ful of each bite of food consumed. She jumped up
twenty times in the course of a simple supper, to fetch
something forgotten or possibly needed. She fretted
incessantly, too, about the appetite of her only child,

May. Her father, who had forgotten the force of her nervous energy, longed to command her to sit still.

"May, you haven't touched your milk!" Cora pointed an accusing forefinger at the glass beside the little girl's plate. "You know what I've told you—well, for heaven's sake!" Her chair tipped. She lunged to grasp a tiny, grimy wad of paper before it struck the floor.

Her father, still tugging at the handkerchief which choked his pocket, swung round. He saw she had picked up his five-dollar bill. "That's mine!" He stretched his arm across the table. "Give it to me."

She examined the crumpled paper with minute care. Little May left her place and went around to her mother's chair to look over her shoulder. Stolid Bill Payne continued to eat serenely, crunching a stalk of celery in his big white teeth.

"You give that back to me!" The triangular vein bulged into view on the old man's forehead.

"It's money, isn't it, Mother? Does it belong to Grandpa?" May touched the bill gingerly, as if she expected it to tear.

Cora pinched her glasses more firmly on her nose. "So this is what goes on behind my back!" Her hostile glance included the two men who gaped at her in mutual surprise. "I work my fingers to the bone, trying to cut expenses, and you hand out five-dollar bills to Father! Well, let me tell you, if any one in this family needs cash, it's your wife!"

"Don't be a fool," her husband said calmly. "I never saw that money till now. Hand it back to your dad. And how about more bread? The plate's empty."

Of course he'd lie to cover her father, Cora retorted, ignoring the question of bread. Men always stood by each other. If Bill didn't give her father the money, where did he get it? She intended to keep it till she found out.

The old man hashed angrily at the potatoes on his plate. The money, he'd have her know, was his, a gift to him. "Your mother sent it, because she thought I might be short. Now are you satisfied?"

"George!" Cora's tone damned her brother. "I might have known! He and Anita can pass out five-dollar bills when the rest of us are wondering how to get the butcher paid. If George did his decent share, he'd look after you and Mother. He could and never feel it." She crumpled the money in her veined, transparent hand. "I'll apply this cash of Mr. George's on the next electric light bill. No one in this house, except me, ever thinks to turn out a light."

Her father let his spoon drop into his cup, spattering tan liquid on the cloth. "Bill!"

"I guess I'm still solvent, Cora," her husband said. "Let your father have his 'V'."

Cora clenched her teeth. "I'm entitled to it, after all I've done for him. Who's supporting him? Who has

all the extra work to do? Who cooks for him and does
his mending? He's living in my house, isn't he?"

"You stop right there!" Her father choked on a gulp
of scalding tea and put down the cup because it shook
in his hand. "That'll be enough from *you, Miss.* I'm
through living in your house. I want my five dollars,
and then I'll go away from here." He glared at her
through a haze of anger and pain. She had shamed
him before her husband and child. "I won't be a burden to you any longer," he said to Cora, hot sarcasm
swelling his voice. He said to himself that he would
shame her, in her turn. Common decency and truth
must compel her to assure him that her father could not
be a burden.

Cora, in her nervous rages, was incapable of putting
a brake on her tongue. She had gone further than she
intended; she had said more than she meant to say, but
it required greater self-control than she could summon
to keep still. "Where do you suppose you can go?" she
snapped, and because she enjoyed ruling, a faint thrill
of power quickened her pulse. This shabby old man
had no recourse but to do as she directed.

"I can go to Nellie's. That money will more than
pay my bus fare. Or maybe to George's place." Her
father looked hopefully from Bill to May and back to
Cora, seeking confirmation in vain. "I'll clear out the
first thing in the morning. It's too late to go anywhere tonight."

"Well, believe me, Nellie will have something to say about when you are to go to her house." Cora tucked the folded bill into the neck of her dress. "And Anita has her hands full with Mother now. You'd better behave yourself where you are, Father; you'd be jumping out of the frying-pan into the fire, if you left us before your time's up."

His head drooped on his chest. His figure appeared to shrink, so that his coat wrinkled across the white shirt he had carefully donned. The possession of a little money had lent him new self-respect, so that he had taken pains with his simple toilet before coming to the supper table. He scarcely heard Cora sharply order May to sit down and finish her meal. His son-in-law, uneasy, grateful for the cessation of bickering, plied him with offers of more food, which the old man automatically refused. He spoke no more but sat lost in a maze of painful, unrelated thoughts, until Bill Payne pushed back his chair and suggested that they all go to the movies.

"You take May, if you want to." Cora set her thin lips. "I have plenty of work to do."

As soon as they had gone, her father carried his own plate to the kitchen. "You better let me have that money, Cora. It's mine." He had decided to be patient, and he prided himself that he had regained his calm.

That greenback, Cora announced, scraping and stacking dishes as she talked, was going into the bank. She had seen enough waste, she declared significantly, to last her to the end of her days. "You and Mother apparently made no effort to save. A five-dollar bill to you was just something to be spent—I heard Mother say once that she never received more than two dollars' change, no matter what she bought."

"There's such a thing as being too small." The old man clattered a handful of flat silver.

"Maybe." Cora whirled unexpectedly to face him. "Maybe. But if I'm small, you'll never see me being supported by my child. May won't have me on her hands, when I'm old."

He resented only the criticism of his management and that of his wife. This strange, new abhorrence of dependence on one's children in old age merely puzzled him. He chose to regard it as a prejudice, an irritating modern idea introduced for the sake of controversy. But the implication that he and his wife had not handled their income wisely he could not let pass. From the bench in the breakfast nook, where he usually took refuge from Cora's frantic rushing to and fro, he said firmly, "Your mother and I did the best we could. If we didn't save money, it wasn't our fault. Remember we had five children to your one."

The enameled surfaces of the table and painted chairs reflected the gleam of the ceiling light. Cora rather pathetically expressed her desire for brightness in the drab monotony of her life by stenciling red poppies on apple-green chairs. The thin, dark woman brought an intense, hectic atmosphere to her simplest task. She rubbed the dish-mop over a plate as if her objective were to remove the flowered design. When she pulled the shade that screened the window above the sink, she almost jerked it from the roller by the violence in her lean fingers' grasp. The angles of her kite-shaped face sharpened as she frowned over her shoulder. "Don't forget you had twenty years with no children to make demands on you, Father. Twenty years free to save."

"Twenty years?" It sounded like a long time.

"After we left home, you know. You and Mother had only yourselves to care for then. Your salary was fairly good. Why you didn't put something by is beyond me." She scrubbed at a stain on the drain-board with an energy that knotted the veins on her scrawny arm.

Lost money, lost time—how could he account for either one? As vague, as baffling as fog, the disjointed memories that floated to the surface of his mind. Twenty years might have been twenty days, for all the imprint they had made on his life, he mused. No great joys, no numbing griefs, had marked the two decades. He and Lucy had lived then as they had always lived. He was unable to recall that the absence of their children had affected them deeply. Perhaps his wife had been lonely, but the change had been gradual enough to allow her to make an easy adjustment. Had it really been twenty years since Nellie, the last to go, had married and left them to themselves?

The old man put a hand to his back, which ached. The bench had no support. He was eager to justify himself in Cora's sight, because it seemed to him that that accomplished, she could no longer refuse to return his money. In the confusion of his reasoning, the charge of incompetency pricked him; did Cora think of him as a spendthrift in the past, or regard him as one now? He hastily computed his salary for twenty years and the total staggered him, as such fruitless mathematics invariably do. The recollection of his tranquil, small-town life, an existence surely devoid of extravagant luxury, comforted him. "We didn't live expensively," he testified. "Your mother will tell you that."

"You never even had life insurance." Cora shook out a wet dish-towel in a single flirt. "Bill carries a large policy. He thinks it's his duty."

This could be answered. "Your mother was opposed to life insurance. She wouldn't hear of it."

She knew, Cora admitted. Still, there were other ways to save. "I never let a month go by without putting something in the savings-bank. You could have done the same."

"Well—" His refutation faltered, and he watched her moodily as she put away the dishes in the cupboard over the sink. She had his five dollars; she was no bet-

ter than a damn thief. The intensity of his bitterness
rather shocked the old man. But it was tough, he told
himself, to be without money at his age. Pretty tough,
when he had never been without cash in his pockets
since he'd been old enough to earn his living—and he
had earned his first money at fifteen. He lost himself
in contemplation of the slim, eager lad who had carried
home his first week's wages with such pride. Cora's
voice, recalling him to the humiliating present, nettled
him.

". . . . Even five dollars a month in the building and
loan is better than nothing." She must have been talking steadily for a moment or two. "People like you
make the mistake of thinking it isn't worth while to
save small sums."

He dismissed her arguments as the vapid utterances
of an illogical female. Women knew nothing of the
terrific struggle men endured to support a family and
educate their children. A fortunate few, he reminded
himself, aided by luck, inherited wealth or exceptional
earning capacity, amassed fortunes, faced old age as
rich men and secure. The majority, he believed, were
no better off than he. The old platitudes, comforting
as old shoes to tired feet, relaxed his weary mind. A
man who had done his best, who had no regrets, he
must look to his children now. "Don't you be talking
about matters beyond you." His reproof halted Cora

midway between the ice-box and range. "I want my five dollars, too. Bill told you to hand it back."

"Yes, and I'll tell you what else Bill said!" She had bitten her tongue and she could have screamed with this pain added to the frenzy of her clamoring nerves. It would have been a relief to her to pounce on her father and shake him, but she could only clench her hands. "Bill said that you—you and Mother—are paying for your self-indulgence, extravagance and your ignorance of a changing world! Now!" She panted, conscious that the chords in her throat ached.

Her father shuffled his feet. "When did Bill say all that?"

"Last night."

He repeated the sentences to himself. His son-in-law he had supposed to be sympathetic toward him. He liked Bill, a good-natured man, patient, not unduly subservient to Cora, yet apparently able to live with her nerves in comparative peace. So Bill had said—what had Bill said? "I didn't exactly get that about a changing world." The old man's bright, suspicious eyes stared fixedly at Cora.

"He meant times have changed, Father." She propped one hip against the sink, letting the rest of her body sag. It always pleased her to explain; as a teacher before her marriage she had been patient and kind with submissive ignorance; opposition to her will then, as now, had been the unforgivable sin. "Bill was speaking of the way things are between parents and children these days. Fathers and mothers don't look forward to being cared for in their old age by their children, and the kids have no intention of supporting their parents. It's been coming for years, Bill says, only apparently you and Mother never sensed it. You're determined to cling to your worn-out theories that parents have divine rights."

Her father pulled himself out from the narrow space between the table and the bench. His back, as he straightened it, felt like a rusty hinge pinching his flesh. He grasped the table edge in case his knees wavered. "My good Godie, how much do I have to stand!" He heard the door open and felt a blast of cold air tunnel under the warm odor of cooking that still lingered, but he paid no heed. "You give me back my money this minute, so I can clear out of here. I'm going as soon as I can pack. I won't stand another night under your roof, after what you've said."

"Now, listen, you two pipe down." Bill, one arm around the little girl, closed the door with his other hand. "Run up to bed, May. You can tell Mother about the pictures in the morning." He added to his wife, "We didn't stay after the comedy; I didn't want to keep her out late."

May, a beautiful color in her usually pale cheeks, backed reluctantly out of the room, and they heard her stumbling up the dark front stairs.

"Bill, make her give me my money so I can leave here tonight."

"He's been going on like that ever since you left, Bill. If I don't have one of my bad spells in the night, it won't be his fault."

Cora's husband, hanging his overcoat in the narrow passageway between kitchen and dining-room, said bluntly, "I don't want to hear any more about it." He stalked into the living-room and snapped on a light. Presently the radio stuttered.

With a few agitated twitches, Cora arranged her dish-towels on the line near the stove and deliberately turned off the light. She flounced away, leaving her father in darkness.

He did not move. In the front room a golden contralto voice sang something in the German tongue. The alarm-clock, rapid, insistent, ticked companionably almost in his ear. Bill said a word to Cora, who dropped her shears on the floor, drowning her reply. The old man listened intently, as if he must tabulate the sounds. Under cover of these cheerful, inconsequential noises, one could steal out of the back door, tramp away to freedom, sloughing off humiliation and shame like soiled garments. He stepped forward, paused. Penniless, without shelter on a winter's night, where could he go? He had no money, he had no resources, his youth and strength were spent. There could be no adventure, nothing but failure waiting him in that cold darkness of the unknown. Better to be prudent, he counseled himself, groping his way to the door that led to the tiny hall. He could think more clearly in the morning, after a few hours' rest.

An hour later Bill knocked at the bedroom door to announce that he had dialed the "Western Warblers" on the radio. "They're your favorites, Dad. Come on down and be sociable."

"I don't feel like it tonight."

"But it's too cold for you to sit up there. I've got a grand fire in the living-room."

The old man muttered that he was in bed. He did not stir when, at the end of another hour, Cora bustled in without knocking, bringing an extra blanket. "You awake, Father? The wind's this way tonight, and I'm afraid you'll be chilly before morning. There—that'll keep you nice and warm." She spread the covering deftly, working by the hall light.

When the door closed behind her, the old man rose and turned on his own light. He folded the blanket she had brought him, bundled it into his arm chair. His thighs ached painfully in the icy chill that penetrated the bedroom after midnight, but his martyrdom had anticipated the self-inflicted torture of numb, stiff joints.

Cora, leaving Bill to lock up the house, retired early, too. Her day had exhausted her. Yet she couldn't sleep, and when she heard her husband creaking up the stairs, she opened her bedroom door to call to him. "Bill, I've decided to spend that five dollars on underwear for Father. He needs union suits." In every battle with her conscience, Cora won. Her clever solutions pleased her.

Bill waited, standing under the hall bulb till she closed her door. He heard her slide the bolt with neat finality. Then he went on past the bathroom to his own room.

CHAPTER FIVE

"BILL—" Cora's rapid, incisive voice reached her father in his room across the narrow hall—"is perfectly devoted to his home, his child, and to me. But of course his life can't be complete and hasn't been for years. Sometimes I think that when May is grown and settled in her own home, I'll give him a divorce. He really deserves it."

Cora's father, in the weeks he had lived in her house, had not accustomed himself to her garrulity with her women friends. That at forty-seven she could apparently enjoy long, confidential conversations by 'phone or tongue, with women whose lives like her own flowed evenly in the shallow channels of the middle class, amazed him. What did they talk about? What underlay the incessant, sly whispering? Cora, like a girl, sometimes stayed awake all night, talking to the dry, yellowed spinster whom she called her best friend. That Cora and Bill occupied separate bedrooms no longer provoked family comment, but the father revolted at the women who so frequently shared Cora's bed.

Downstairs his son-in-law, who made a serious business of reading the evening paper, smiled at him as he re-entered the living-room. "Find your clipping, Dad? Cora still confabbing with Miss Besmer?" Bill Payne's square white teeth flashed when he talked. He could be inscrutable when he chose, but his silences were friendly.

The old man pushed a chair to the center table, which held a white pottery lamp. Cora had half a dozen lamps in the room, but not one was a strong reading light. Her husband supplied his own bulb for his floor lamp and insisted on a plain parchment shade. Cora's father hated with equal fervor the ghastly blue-green silk in which she shrouded the rest of the lights and the incense she burned in the first floor rooms. A choking acrid odor now drifted languidly from the slanting eyes and grinning mouth of a fat brown pottery mandarin on the hanging wall-shelf.

"Well, I see steel's gone up three points." Bill patted the financial page spread on his knee.

His father-in-law asserted he had no use for stocks; that he considered people who traded in the market to be gamblers. "You buy and sell what you haven't got." He added uneasily, "What's Cora fussing around for so long up there with that woman?"

Bill, like most husbands, had trained himself to read and talk at the same time. He murmured that Cora planned to go in with Miss Besmer on the 10:40 bus the next day. "Cora wants to see a foot doctor. Mrs. Blake's to get dinner for you and May."

These trips to New York to consult specialists were
events in Cora's life. She had made the rounds. Her
egotism expanded in the sympathetic atmosphere of
medical suites, enabling her to dramatize herself in a
leading rôle. Anticipated importance rustled in her
manner like a starched frill as she swept into the living-
room and announced she must take a stitch in the dress
hung across her arm. "Fanny's having a bath. She
won't be down any more tonight." Cora accounted for
Miss Besmer as she threaded her needle.

"Old men have no business competing in the labor
market," stated Bill from behind the editorial page.

His father-in-law eyed him apprehensively, but did
not speak. The old man had learned, in less than three
months, that Bill and Cora's conversations generally
excluded him. They permitted him to listen to their
dialogue, but refused to reckon him as a third. He
would sit silently, evening after evening, his hazel eyes
glancing from one face to the other as if, like a deaf
man, he hoped to read their lips. Cora sometimes protested, "Don't stare so, Father!" Then he would announce that he meant to stay in his room after this.

"A man of sixty-five and over hasn't the right to com-
pete with younger men for the same job." Bill sounded
important. "He pulls wages down, because he can
afford to work for less. Younger men have families to
support. The old fellows ought to drop out and live
on pensions."

Cora inquired the source of pensions.

"We've got a state pension law, but it doesn't function till the applicant's seventy." Bill dialed the radio. "I'm in favor of lowering the limit to sixty-five."

"Could Father get a pension?" Cora, who had the full glow of the bridge lamp turned on her sewing, glanced speculatively at the old man. He sat forward in his chair, his shoulders drooping, hands clasped loosely between his knees. Cora characterized his look as "vacant."

Her husband explained, tuning out a crooner, that old people with children able to support them were ineligible for pensions. "There's a lot of red tape about it, too, but you don't have to worry, do you, Dad? You won't be grubbing along on a dole—that's what it amounts to—as long as your children live."

Mrs. Blake arrived at half-past eleven the next morning, serenely prepared to have the midday dinner ready by quarter past twelve. Competency stamped her every move. She liked men and children and they usually liked her. As she stirred briskly about the kitchen and dining-room, she inevitably reminded Cora's father of his wife. To be sure, Mrs. Blake's figure was tall and thin, her hair a marvelous yellow, but her wrinkled face betrayed her seventy-odd years. She lived alone and supported herself by sewing, nursing, and day's work. "I haven't seen you for 'most a month, Mr.

Cooper." She shredded carrots into damp, red-gold strips. "How do you like Locton now?"

He conceded that the town would do. The fragrance of the soup simmering on the range, the sight of the ordered table in the dining-room, blended with the presence of this comfortable woman to mollify his constant sense of loss. Physical and mental ease impossible to achieve in the same room with his daughter, relaxed his limbs. He stretched contentedly in a chair beside the kitchen table and plunged into talk.

When the little girl slipped into the kitchen soon after twelve, she too responded to the absence of tension or haste. May, with gray eyes like her father's, had inherited her mother's thin, kite-shaped face. The child, passionately adored by Cora, baffled her grandfather with a reserve which he felt screened her real judgments of them all. One couldn't get at her, he complained to Cora, who retorted positively that she understood her daughter as no one else ever could. May had accepted her grandfather's position in the household as she would have the addition of an end table or an extra chair. She never confided in him, but then she only confided in a certain fat little girl who was her friend.

Since May had only three quarters of an hour for lunch, they ate steadily, Mrs. Blake serving the steak with an accurate nicety that revealed her ability to carve. She had just brought in the salad plates, when

May asked if her mother had said anything about buying a screen.

"She promised to get the frame and cover it as soon as Grandpa goes," the clear, grave childish voice announced. "We saw a picture of one in a magazine."

"What do you mean?" The old man put down his fork. "I haven't said I was going anywhere, have I?" His close-cropped beard trembled as if further angry words tugged at the roots.

May continued to address Mrs. Blake. The child's interest centered on a picture she endeavored to translate into speech. "There are three panels, and you have to embroider them. Mother said she's too nervous to sew while Grandpa's here. When he goes to stay with Uncle Richard and Aunt Grace, then we'll make my screen. Mother says she is counting the days—" Instinct checked her.

Mrs. Blake said the necessary "Eat your dinner, or you'll be late for school."

The grandfather stared at the child, who obediently munched her carrot strips. His gaze traveled to the thin old woman, wholesomely intent on the contents of her plate. His dry, cracked fingers crumbled a bit of bread. "Maybe I'm not going to your Aunt Grace's," he muttered, but his defiance made no impression on the other two. They smiled and ate.

He repeated his assertion to Mrs. Blake in the

kitchen, after May had gone. People took a lot for
granted, he declared with the bravado of a boy whistling in the dark. They might be surprised, one of
these days, to learn he had a mind of his own. "Maybe
I'll go to my son Richard's, and maybe I won't." His
hand, thrust into his pocket, closed on a quarter and
two dimes, all he had.

Leisurely, Mrs. Blake scraped and stacked dishes and
put away food. She poured soap powder into her pan
of clean, hot water and stirred the mixture to a puffy
omelet of crackling foam. "I suppose it's hard to fit in
with other people's ways," she murmured, letting the
glasses slip one by one from her fingers into the suds.

"Hard!" The bitterness in his tone frightened them
both so that they stared at each other like people who
have uncovered something they dread to examine. "I
mind it more for my wife," he added in mumbling
haste.

Women, comforted Mrs. Blake, endured some phases
of life better than men did. They had more patience,
they resisted less. "When we get old, we don't expect
so much, and that in itself is a kind of lull. Men aren't
like that." She set three dripping glasses on the drain
board.

Her serenity irked him. She still had a routine to
follow; her life had not been ripped from its founda-
tions. His restlessness, his unhappiness, the dull pain
of an existence like his had not touched her. "A man's

got a right to expect gratitude and a little justice, hasn't he?" The twirling peak of his front hair nodded like a pert question-mark.

"My good land, there's no law against expecting." She rubbed a piece of silver gently with a snowy towel. "Getting what you expect is something else again." Her shrewd, light eyes peered thoughtfully into the dishwater depths. "Don't expect much from other folks," she advised.

He objected. Other people had expected a great deal from him, all his life. "I did what I had to do and didn't shirk. All I ask is a fair return, but it's different when the shoe is on the other foot. I've got five children, and not one of 'em remembers what I did for him."

She stood a plate in the draining rack, her hand swollen and puckered from the hot water. "Maybe children don't feel they owe their parents such a lot for bringing them into this world," she offered rather doubtfully, for she had never had a child.

This reasoning he dismissed as beside the point. Children owed their parents everything. No modern distortion of facts could alter the truth. The seething tirade that never quite died in him, rushed to his lips in a torrent of protesting words. A determination to compel his children's love and respect warred ceaselessly with the knowledge that he was foredoomed to fail. He might pit his strength in vain for years against their careless pity or indifferent selfishness. They would care for him, he knew that now, but grudgingly. Frustration, stirring the quick anger of old age, pumped the blood madly through his thickened artery walls. "I won't be put upon, or treated like a child. I've got some rights, haven't I?"

She nodded, "Yes," and began to scour a roasting pan. "Only—" she hesitated—"you'd be comfortable here, if you kind of did what they wanted you to do. I've been working since I was twenty, and I'm seventy-four now, and I've never really had my own way." She looked at his tense figure and fancied that his hazel eyes were bloodshot. "What won't bend, must break," fluttered in the storehouse of her mind. "The older we get, the easier it ought to be to give in, don't you think?" she encouraged him. "Nothing matters so much as it did when we were younger." Actually his position, as she had heard it outlined in the town gossip, horrified her independent, sturdy heart. She meant to work till her legs gave out. The thought of being totally dependent for her board and "keep" dismayed her. Not even children, she convinced herself, could persuade her to retire. She had no children, and she had nothing saved, but she regarded her future as bright because she had only to work till death overtook her.

The old man followed her to the front door when, the kitchen in order, she prepared to leave. He dis-

liked to be alone and would have lingered on the porch
to eye the few passers-by, if he had not recollected that
Cora pronounced the habit common. A newly formu-
lated decision to please her sent him indoors again, up
to his room. He removed his shoes and stretched himself on the bed. Once more the easy sleep of old age
provided merciful escape.

"When you go to Richard's," said Cora with increas-
ing frequency and an air of finality that shocked her
father.

She might have the decency to hide her impatience
to be rid of him, he whispered to himself. The habit
of talking aloud when alone had fastened on him. His
mutter embarrassed him, if he detected a listener, but,
undiscovered, he experienced relief in the dry rustle of
his own voice. Cora declared he was aging rapidly,
and certainly his alert, springy step changed. He began to shuffle, to scuff. His daughter maintained it
gave her the creeps to hear him drag his feet over her
floors. "For heaven's sake, Father, can't you *lift* your
feet?"

He had attempted to follow her suggestion that he
assume the duties of a handy man around the place.
Cora believed the neighbors could not misinterpret that
rôle. Her theory that her father would be happier if
he had something to do was honest enough, but his
efforts to help her with the housework upset them both,

since a similarity of temperament made them clash. Each resented the taking of orders, each insisted fiercely on mythical rights. The old man expected affection and filial respect, Cora demanded gratitude. They battled desperately over trifles, concealing their deeper, lasting wounds. Bill remained stolidly neutral, save when Cora acknowledged defeat by taking to bed. Then he said the bickering must stop.

So Cora's father wandered uncertainly between the house and garage, anxious to be of service, unable to cooperate or to subordinate his impulse to command. He resented Cora's directions and allowed his son-in-law's disregard for his expressed opinions to wound him. The old man's precision compelled him to take infinite pains, restricted his efforts to the methodical and slow. He was a neat workman, but he resented any demand for haste. He craved approbation, too, and to have his time and skill taken for granted, grieved him. As the weather grew milder, he spent more and more time away from the house. Cora secretly fretted, but made no open objection as long as he appeared promptly for meals. "I can stand anything till he goes to Richard's," she told her husband and May.

If she had known where her father spent hours of his time, her sufferance might have snapped. He and the caretaker of a summer home a quarter of a mile distant from the Payne house, had formed a friendship based on congenial tastes. The compact, handsome

estate, a small farm restored expensively and authen-
tically to its original Colonial charm, was the property
of a lawyer in New York. His caretaker, a man as
lean and dark as an iron picket, kept house neatly and
sufficiently in the kitchen. He had made the storeroom
into a downstairs' bedroom, and he boasted that Marcus
Evender coveted no man's place in the sun.

Cora's father, stopping to exchange comment, had
quickly appreciated the soothing philosophy of an individual who, without ambition, lived happily with
hours to spare. The old man sat with Marcus in his
immaculate kitchen on stormy or cold days, but when
the sun shone, the pair moved to the southern exposure
afforded by the back steps. Here they listened respectfully to each other's views, enjoyed their pipes and
found in their frequent silences a healing they wistfully
recognized as rare. In the recitals of their uneventful
histories, a mutual respect preserved them from the sin
of lying. Marcus had drifted from coast to coast, foot-
loose, untrained, always working desultorily at the
small, humble tasks open to the unskilled. In his middle age, he could boast of changing jobs twenty times.
Barkley Cooper, who had been bookkeeper for one firm
more than forty years, had never been one hundred
miles from his home town. Yet he had now no more
to show for his industry than Marcus, the rolling stone.
He had only more plausible excuses for his plight.

"A man with children—" he offered, and Marcus would nod assent.

Marcus had no roots. He did have a sublime confidence in the ability of the taxpayers of his country to support the relief institutions on which he sometimes called. The municipal lodging-houses in the large cities, the free wards of hospitals, received him when in distress. He accepted charitable ministrations as something to which he felt entitled. His old age, providing he attained it, he expected to pass in some county almshouse. The future for him held no terrors, no anxieties, no positive plans. He earned sufficient for his modest needs in good times; in bad he had always been helped. When he tired of one job, he moved on to the next. He cherished a theory that to have no special skill, only a smattering of many small trades, stood a man in better stead than an expert knowledge along one line. "You don't want a label tied to you; as long as you're unclassified, you can fit in anywhere," he preached to Barkley Cooper one sunny afternoon late in March.

"Suppose you're past the age limit?" A shower of ashes sprinkled the older man's vest. He nursed the bowl of his pipe in his hands.

"They can't set a limit." Marcus clasped his hands at the back of his head and stretched luxuriously in the sun like a cat. "I run into a man nigh eighty, operating an elevator, once. It wasn't much of a business, and they didn't need pep. Mostly he sat and read the newspaper. But he and his wife lived off the wages."

The older man said mechanically, "Guess he didn't have children to take care of him."

He hadn't, Marcus admitted. At that, he added, lots of folks preferred to be on their own. "If you live with your children, you get to be a wishy-washy yes-man, or the storm starts. If they pay rent for you somewhere, they feel entitled to run your life for you."

Barkley Cooper sucked at his pipe. That's the way it is, he sorrowed to himself, but it needn't be. "Honor thy father and mother." I took care of my father, glad of the chance. Lucy nursed her mother five years. Now folks pity us. He hastily called up face after face in his mind. The eyes in all the faces in Locton pitied him. Does Lucy shrink from pity, too? he wondered. He glanced furtively at Marcus, whose face was a mask. "You ain't one to adapt yourself, are you?" The old man believed he spoke lightly.

"Never had to." The caretaker showed his yellow back teeth in a yawn. "Now, next month I'm moving on. The owner wants a man *and* wife and I can't accommodate him."

He explained, dissembling his enjoyment in having an audience, that the owner of the place, a bachelor, wished to employ a couple for the summer months, a woman to do the housework, a man to tend the garden.

Wages and living perquisities he counted fair. He laughed. "But I don't aim to get me a ball and chain. I tell Mr. Hunter jobs and women is two things I got to change."

Before he left for supper, Barkley Cooper had in his pocket the name and address of the lawyer-owner written on a card. Not that he intended to make use of it. Americans didn't hire themselves out as servants. The idea itself would probably horrify his wife. She had never taken orders from any one. As for the children, the old man visioned them flushing crimson at the suggestion, bowing their heads in shame. When all the time, he mumbled to himself, when all the time they ought to bow their heads in shame for their own acts.

He wrote to G. Stanley Hunter that evening, while Bill and Cora and May attended the movies in town. The first letter of application he had ever attempted, he quite lost himself in the complicated sentences he wove. He stumbled over details. The thought that he demeaned himself looped his pen like a snake and twisted it in his hand. If I could only go where I'm not known, he faltered, hesitating midway in his painful task. It would be easy to hire out on a farm where we saw no one, and no one saw us. There must be jobs I could fill on a farm. He left the desk and squatted before the newspapers arranged in a neat pile on the under shelf of the fumed-oak table. Bill subscribed to the county weekly, and farmers advertised in that. The old man

squinted hopefully at the columns set in agate, till his
back and legs ached. No one appealed for a couple to
hire. He straightened up, catching at the table's edge
as his protesting joints grated in their sockets. "Got to
limber up," he muttered, cautiously swinging one leg
from the hip and ignoring the bones that creaked.
"Time to spade up gardens, first thing you know." He
limped to the desk and stood looking down at his letter.

The whole project daunted him. The thought of
working for a stranger, of subjecting himself and his
wife to the whims of an employer with whom contact
must inevitably be personal and close demoralized his
brain. As he balanced the extremity of his need against
the terrors of his imagination an inner coldness gripped
him with a nauseating clutch. Cora, he reflected, will
raise the devil and I can't stand much more. It will be
better to go to Richard's, after all. But at the surrender
there slipped noiselessly into the range of the old man's
vision a woman with cold, hard eyes and a voice that
repeated, "Money, money, money," like the Florida
Indians of whom he had read. I shall have to live under the same roof with Grace, he shuddered. Seizing
the pen, he sat down to complete the letter, deciding he
had finished when he reached the bottom of the page.

It would be quite dreadful if Cora intercepted the
reply. Her curiosity, which had so little on which to

feed, made the most of every mail. She prided herself
on never opening a letter not addressed to her, but she
inspected and shook and smelled and held up to the
light, every piece of mail matter that entered her house.
This dismayed no one. Her daughter had no corre-
spondents, and her husband received most of his mail
at his office. Her father, who had pilfered the necessary
stamps from Cora's desk, dreaded the comments his
self-addressed envelope must evoke. In his anxiety to
meet the rural carrier who delivered in the morning,
in his determination to let nothing interfere with his
afternoon trips to the post-office, he attracted Cora's
suspicious attention.

"I notice when it's mail time, you hop around like a
hen on a hot griddle," she shrewdly observed. "You're
expecting something special, I guess. Have you been
writing to any one?"

She was smart, he admitted to himself, smart as a
whip, but then women always jumped in the dark.
He reviewed his precautions, tried to feel safe. The
letter he had mailed himself. He could trust Marcus
not to blab. But the old man couldn't enjoy his food,
for picturing the scene Cora would make if she discovered his plan. Nervous indigestion plagued him, he
found it impossible to sit still. Cora complained that
he prowled about like a caged bear.

"Mother used to say he had something on his mind

when he tramped around the house like that," she confided to Mrs. Blake, who had come to help with the
ironing.

"He must have a lot on his mind." Mrs. Blake had
no desire to sound cryptic, so she added, "He can think
back over a long life."

Inevitably, in the period of suspense, Barkley Cooper
regretted the impulse that had urged him to write the
lawyer. Each day that went past without an answer
confirmed the old man's conviction that he had been a
fool. He reminded himself of his age and tried to believe that food and shelter summed up his remaining
needs. Each time Cora insisted on going out to the
mail-box herself, his spine prickled, his throat dried.
He refused to look at her when she returned, kept his
back toward her, holding himself rigid. The long moment he held his body braced for the blow sickened
him. If she remained silent, he assured himself that
she must be reading the superscription; if she coughed,
or indulged in any small mannerism as a preliminary
to speech, he clenched his hands. He yearned to
thunder at her, "For God's sake, has it come or not?"

His walk to the post-office in the afternoon afforded
him the relief of movement. He implored his God to
deliver the letter into his hands. All he asked, he carefully explained to Heaven, was an opportunity to read
the lawyer's reply, a chance to compose himself before

the reckoning with Cora. By the fifth day he began
to hope that the answer would be negative, in which
case he would have nothing to explain.

He was putting his razor away, after shaving at the
kitchen sink, early in the afternoon of the sixth day,
when he heard the front door slam. Cora had returned
from the cash grocery store. He had offered to go in
her stead, but she had irritably reminded him that the
manager sold him wilted lettuce. She did not come out
into the kitchen now, but turned on the radio, releas-
ing a soprano that echoed through the little house.

"Father!" The soprano gurgled, choked off. Cora,
seated on the divan, fluffed her hair as her father appeared silently in the doorway. "Come on in and read
your letter," she said.

He struggled to school his features to impassiveness,
tried to weight down the tumult that ricocheted in
him, pounding against his frail ribs. Suddenly it
seemed to him that his first sentence must be tremendously important, and in a panic of anxiety he shaped
two or three, without speaking, as if he could fit words
on his tongue like gloves on his hand. He discarded
speech, his desperate eyes tugging at the envelope Cora
perversely retained.

"Here—take it." Unexpectedly she thrust it at him.
"Wait a minute—where you going?" Her voice halted
him as he turned toward the stairs.

"Up to my room."

"Who's your letter from? I don't know any one named Hunter."

Her father hid the letter in the inside pocket of his coat, as if he feared she might wrest it from him. He mounted a step and halted. "This is *my* business. I don't ask about your affairs, do I?" He saw her round felt hat tumble to the floor and lie there unheeded. She had dropped her packages on the divan in a heap. A loaf of bread stuck out from a yawning paper bag. I don't suppose she got any better head lettuce than I did, he thought.

"As long as you're living in my house"—Cora rocked her head from side to side—"I've got a right to ask about your mail. You must have given my address. I'm responsible for you and any foolish mistakes you make. There's Bill to be considered, too; I can't let my relatives do anything that will reflect on him."

Her father pulled himself up another step without answering. Why, he raged silently, couldn't the lawyer have used the stamped, self-addressed letter sent him? No, the durn fool had to advertise his business, use his own letterhead. Vexation at the imbeciles who overcrowded an officious world nagged Barkley Cooper into ripping open the envelope with fingers that trembled. He read the few words. Could he come in to talk over his proposition tomorrow?

He straightened his drooping shoulders. The twirling peak of his front hair nodded buoyantly. "Well, I

guess I've got me a job." The unexpected easiness of
it intoxicated him. Any one who wanted work could
get it. He had only to offer his services in the open
market to receive a bid. Confidently, as if he had
signed a contract, he outlined his plans to Cora, who
for the moment seemed stunned. He reasoned that the
need for caution had been swept away.

"Have you no pride?" Cora flung out her arms, and
the sleeves fell back to show her elbows, sharp and red.
"If you've lost your own pride, you might think of us,
of your grandchild. Do you want to disgrace May before her friends?"

The old man folded the letter deliberately, taking
pains to preserve each original crease. He fitted it into
the envelope, which he placed in the inside pocket of
his coat. When he spoke, he appeared to be choosing
each word. "Nobody pays any attention to *my* pride.
You talk as if you couldn't get rid of me fast enough—
counting the days till I move on to Richard's house. I
can see I'm a burden, and I want to take myself out of
your way. You won't be disgraced, I guess, as long as
I keep out of jail."

Cora let her silence reproach him. She maintained
this attitude of the injured throughout supper to the
helplessness of the two men. May chattered uncon-
cernedly, but escaped to the house next door as soon
as she could decently be excused. Cora, declining offers

of assistance, gloomily washed the dishes and announced that she intended to go to bed.

Up in his own room, her father began confidently to pack. His preparations revolved around his immediate plans and his more distant but not less permanent future as he conceived it. For the next day he laid out his best clean shirt and a fresh collar on his bed, blacked his shoes, though they already shone, selected a pair of new socks saved for a special occasion. Then from the closet he brought his suitcase and transferred to it the contents of his bureau drawers. It was not a long task, for everything, thanks to Cora, was in good shape. He left the suitcase open on the chair because he liked to see it neatly arranged, ready to be closed. The can of tobacco Bill had given him, he placed in a corner of the bag, in a nest of clean handkerchiefs; he'd need the tobacco, likely, before he moved, but he could find it easy enough, if no one handled his things. His back ached a little from stooping, and he seated himself on the edge of the bed to rest. Eagerly he counted his loose change. Bill, who slipped him furtive quarters from time to time, would lend him enough to make up the bus fare into New York. Bill would have no outlandish notions about being disgraced. The old man, fingering his pennies and dimes, debated whether to empty his pockets into those of his other suit. He said aloud, as if an idea had surprised him, "Maybe I'd better press my good pants."

He enjoyed having the kitchen to himself. No one warned him not to slop water on the floor. No one cautioned him not to scorch the cover of the ironing board. He scuffled his carpet slippers without incurring rebuke. The cabinet drawer of clean dish-towels and cloths was his to rummage in until he found a strip of muslin that did not shed lint. As a cloud of steam ascended from his hissing iron, he hummed a jerky, aimless tune.

"Dad!"

What did Bill want? Let him come down, not shout from the upper hall.

"Dad! Will you come up to Cora's room for a moment?"

The iron thumped petulantly on the metal stand. Might as well go and have it over with, the old man grumbled, his brief contentment evaporating as quickly as the steam from his wet cloth. He toiled sulkily up the stairs and peered in at his daughter, propped up among the pillows of her bed.

"That you, Father? Come in here where I can talk to you." Cora's eyes without her glasses looked small and wounded. "You must understand you can't be a common servant, nor ask Mother to be one—Bill agrees with me this plan of yours is utterly insane."

Her husband, seated astride a ladder-backed chair, said uneasily, "Now, Cora."

"I'm going in on the nine o'clock bus." The old man malevolently eyed the smoking incense burner on the table beside Cora. The room reeked with the sickening stuff.

Cora sat up in bed and reached for a glass on the table, half-filled with amber liquid. She swallowed, choking slightly, her eyes closed. "Do you want to kill me?" she demanded of her father. Her flair for dramatics enabled her to visualize herself as a striking figure, her scrawny outlines softened by discreetly shaded lights; but her unhappiness was real enough.

"My good Godie, you've pretty well near killed me!" Her father, unable to control the tremor in his voice, made a pretense of straightening a rug near the door. He then pulled forward a small, fat cretonne chair and settled himself in it. The relief of physical action helped him to speak more calmly. "It'll be easier for me to earn my food and drink among strangers, than to go on living as I have been."

Cora began to weep. "Bill, you hear him? Are you going to stand by and let him go on with this crazy scheme? If you had any concern for me, you'd settle him."

Bill's slow, good-humored voice matched his smile. "I don't believe you and Mother could take orders at this late date, Dad."

"Tell you that better after I see this G. Stanley Hunter."

"Bill, he can't go in to New York! He isn't fit to make the trip. The worry's making me sick!"

Her father thought scornfully, you can scare your husband with your heart spells, Miss, but you can't scare me. Her ill health, the sword she habitually pointed at the breasts of her family, he discounted as a blind. He regarded contemptuously the solicitude of her husband whom he conceived to be the dupe of medical men. When he thought of the relationship between Cora and Bill, the old man despised the husband who lacked the guts to discipline his wife. Aloud the father said, watching Bill's ponderous nodding shadow on the greenish blue wall, "I'm of age."

"You'll have to let your father go in to see this man, Cora." Bill's few words usually conveyed authority, because he reserved his speech for conclusions. "Nothing may come of the interview, but your father naturally wants to talk over the plan."

"But it's so menial!" Cora dabbed angrily at her eyes. "Neither of you has a sense of fitness. What will people say, if Father, at his age, accepts the position of a servant and makes Mother one?"

Bill was silent.

"Well, let me tell you this—" Cora pointed a long forefinger at her father. "Let me tell you this: if you persist in going to see this man, and you don't get the job, you needn't come back here. Remember that.

Don't look to us to help you again, if your G. Stanley Hunter turns out to be an impossible fool."

A flush reddened the old man's face. He hoped it passed unnoticed in the poorly lighted room. "I guess I can get along." He felt a little sorry for the haggard woman on the bed.

"My nerves are in a terrible state; all the doctors say so," Cora whimpered, pulling her thin silk nightgown up over her bony shoulder-blades. "I should think you'd have a little pity for my condition. Scenes like this make me ill for days."

Her father murmured hardily that this might be the last of them. He clumped down the stairs to his unfinished pressing, but all his quiet enjoyment in the simple task had been destroyed. He heard Bill go out. That left Cora alone. The father wondered if a cup of tea might not soothe her. He had a vague idea that hot tea quelled all female complaints, mental and physical. With some clumsiness he brewed a pot of fresh tea and carried Cora a steaming cup.

"You've spilled half of it in the saucer!" She frowned at him as he seated himself on the side of the bed. "Oh, put it on the table! Maybe I'll drink it by and by."

"It's got the sugar in," he said hopefully.

Cora, ignoring the tea, laid a thin hand on his knee. "Father, I *wish* you'd look at this the way I do. Mother never worked for any one in her life. How you expect her to endure being ordered around?"

"We're ordered around now. Our own children say, 'You go here,' or, 'You stay there.' If I get this job, at least your mother will be where I am."

He didn't understand, Cora told him. He had never understood. In his youth, houses were rambling and large, two or three families could live together under one roof. There had been plenty of work then, Cora declared, for as many pairs of women's hands as could be brought to the unending round of domestic tasks. "Factories do most of that work now, Father. The washing, baking, sewing, all is done for us more cheaply than we can do it ourselves. It's the same way with outdoor work; your father used to help you by tending the garden, caring for the horse, milking the cow, chopping wood. I've heard you say so a hundred times. Well, none of us live like that now. Our homes are more compact; there's no need for extra help. Can't you see that?"

Yes, he could see.

"Well, then, under the circumstances, we're doing the best we can for Mother and you. You may not live together, but you know she is comfortable. She doesn't have to worry about you. I don't see how you can expect us to do any more than we're doing. You've no call to shame us."

He sighed wearily that he didn't intend to shame her.

"But you will! If you take this job—right here in
Locton where every one knows us—I'll die rather than
look anyone in the face!" When she cried she made
a desolate sound like something frightened and young,
and she held one hand clenched against her chest as if
it hurt her to breathe.

Her father patted the bedclothes in a vague desire
to calm her. He hated to make her unhappy, he mumbled, but she couldn't decide this matter for him.
"I've got your mother to think of." He stood up and
a curious feeling of being young and strong and tall
swept through him. "You've got your pride, Cora, and,
well—I've got mine. I'm going to take care of your
mother and myself after this." He heard Bill coming
up the stairs and was thankful, for the rising violence
of Cora's sobs secretly alarmed him. As he closed the
bedroom door he heard Bill take up the task of quiet-
ing her.

A half-dozen times during the night, the old man
woke to consult his watch. To do this he must rear
up, turn on the light. At four o'clock he tried to prop
his tired eyelids open long enough to allow him to close
the window. He wanted the room to be warm when
he dressed. He moved his legs as if to climb out of the
bed and instead slept.

Two hours later he woke again, shivering. His
blankets had slipped to the floor. He hauled them into

place and lay listening to a robin's song. His room was cold, as cold as the chill, wet air that rushed at him from the window open at the foot of the bed. No sense in rising yet; he had hours in which to make the bus. He tucked the blankets cozily under his chin and a sudden wild gust of wind and rain startled him. The fury of the storm, as unexpected as it was violent, lashed against the window-panes as he lowered the sash. He recollected that he had no overshoes. He pictured himself, bedraggled and cold, a forlorn figure in a handsomely furnished office. How, under the circumstances, could he hope to make a favorable impression? Exposure usually brought on his rheumatism, too, and who would nurse him? It would be only sensible to postpone his trip till another day. If, in the meantime, G. Stanley Hunter hired another caretaker, that couldn't be helped. When a man had worked steadily, year in and year out, with no periods of idleness, perhaps he was wise to rest when he could. Certainly, the old man reflected, yawning, there could be no disgrace in a man's ceasing from his labors when he had turned seventy years of age and had grown children to care for him. The spatter of the rain on the glass lulled him. He meant to lie still and think till breakfast-time, but his tired old body sagged inert and he slept.

Neither he nor Cora mentioned the New York appointment that day. Cora kept May home from school because of the storm, and the three of them worked at a four hundred-piece jigsaw puzzle with an intentness that completely absorbed them. They begrudged the time they needed for a cold lunch. The muscles of their necks and shoulders ached after a few hours, but they refused to rest during the afternoon. At five o'clock Cora fitted the last bit into place. They grinned amiably at each other like folk who had done a good day's work.

"I'm going to leave it on the table a little while, to show people." Cora, yawning, rubbed her shoulder-blades.

"I guess there's some good in the old man yet," her father boasted.

May suggested hopefully that, if it continued to rain, they might do another jigsaw the next day.

Chapter Six

PRECISELY three days before the three months of her
mother-in-law's stay with her expired, Anita Cooper invited Nellie Tuck to lunch with her. "We can
make arrangements for Mother to come to you," said
Anita smoothly into the telephone. Thus diplomati-
cally she reminded Nellie of her obligations and signi-
fied that the program would not be changed.

Nellie, breathless, untidy, affectionate, threw her
arms around her mother, hugging her all the way from
the hall into the living-room. "Why, Mama, Mama,
how *sweet* you look! City life must agree with you."

Her mother thought, it's been such a long time since
any one was glad to see me. Her eyes followed Nellie,
who tossed her hat on one chair and flung her coat over
another. She loves me, smiled the mother, her heart
warm as if her child's arms still pressed her with soft
strength. She remembered how Nellie had looked as
a little girl. Do you see my darling baby? she almost
said to Mitzi, who announced the serving of luncheon.

At the table, Anita controlled the conversation. Nellie, a little uncomfortable because the table appointments were on a more elaborate scale than her own,
wished to remember everything to tell the girls. Her

mother sat for the most part silent, brightening a little
if any one spoke directly to her. The old lady directed
her gaze at her plate and even between courses she seldom raised her head. Anita, more sensitive to impressions than Nellie, let the pathos of the inert, big body,
the humble searching patience in the still face when it
turned to them, hurt her. She was not a cruel woman;
she had never intended to browbeat her mother-in-law.
It was only that because she refused to adapt herself to
new patterns of living and insisted that other lives
accept her old design, she had been brushed aside.
Perhaps she isn't really to blame, mused Anita, ready to
be tolerant now that her ordeal drew to a close. You
can't mix two generations, that's the truth. She reflected that, if she could trust the others to pay their
share, the best solution would be to establish her father-
in-law and mother-in-law under some rented roof. She
dismissed the plan as automatically as she plucked the
parsley from the shad-roe. George's brother and sisters
couldn't be trusted; they'd leave her holding the bag.
"George will bring Mother to you day after tomorrow,
Nellie," she said.

It was difficult to get anywhere in a conversation with
Nellie, because that amiable person's mind was as incoherent as her sense of color. Anita maintained that Nellie was color-blind. Today she had buttoned her more
than plump figure into a bright wool green dress dotted
with emphatic buttons of brown wood. Nellie had

bought the frock especially for this occasion and she
had had her nails done. To her, as the mother of three
daughters, spring expressed itself in terms of clothes.
Dresses for her mother, she revealed, had been on her
mind.

"I know Mama must need new spring things, but I
don't see how I'm going to get her anything to wear,"
she fretted. "The girls' frocks cost a fortune; they
really do."

Her mother glanced at Anita, hesitated, then murmured, "Why, Nellie dear, I have all the dresses I need.
You don't have to buy me a thing."

"She ought to have a coat," Anita judicially observed.

Naturally it annoyed Anita, who had made her plans
in advance, when complications threatened to set her
studied arrangements at naught. She betrayed unac-
customed impatience on an April morning as she surveyed her husband's mother for whom new provision
must be made.

Anita, dressed for the street, tapped her foot sharply
on the floor. "You might know Grace would do something like this. Well, say something, George. I have
an appointment at nine." She stood stomach in, head
up, against the living-room wall. Her mother-in-law,
in the stiff attitude of the inexperienced traveler, occupied the small blue love-seat. She wore a dark dress, a
hat that was too small for her heavy knot of hair, and

new black silk gloves. Her suitcase rested on the rug
beside her. In the hall her trunk waited. George,
eager to reach his office, wondered why his domestic
affairs always developed crises on his busiest days.

"What happened?" His mother's eyes behind the
glasses, implored them to talk to her, to tell her.

George reassured her. "It's all right, Mother. But
I can't take you to Nellie's before I go downtown.
We'll go tonight." He hurriedly explained that Grace
had just 'phoned to say that Richard couldn't meet his
father till night. "You'll have to stay here another day,
Mother, and Father will have to stay where he is."

"You call Cora," Anita commanded. "Tell her not
to put your father on a bus till late this afternoon. He
certainly can't come here to wait—I have a bridge class
from two to seven." She kissed her mother-in-law hap-
hazardly, hurried to the door, then returned to say
rapidly, "Mother, why don't you spend the day with
my Aunt Jennie? Mother's away and you two could
have the house to yourselves. Aunt Jennie would love
to see you."

Lucy Cooper waited till the door slammed. "She
doesn't want me around." Her chin quivered.

"Sure she does." George, cheerfully positive, clicked
the dial. "Only with this bridge class on her hands—
that you, Cora?" He transmitted his wife's instructions
briefly and hung up, his mother suspected, before Cora
enjoyed her full say.

The old woman had not moved from the blue dam-ask-covered seat. She received his kiss silently, smiled when he reminded her it was not "good-by." He sur-veyed her rather anxiously, for he had feared a scene. "See you tonight, Mother. I've got to run."

She said, "Good-by, dear." After he had gone, she continued to sit quietly, her hands folded in her lap. Mitzi, curious, a little puzzled, left her for half an hour. Then the colored girl, tactfully announcing her ap-proach by clattering silver in the dining-room, ven-tured to intrude. "Mis' Cooper?"

The white head turned and the idle fingers began at once to stroke the fur collar of the coat folded over a chair. "I suppose you thought I'd gone, Mitzi."

"Not exactly. Is you here for lunch, Mis' Cooper? I can cook you anything you wants." Her dark eyes, gentle with the tragic patience of a race schooled to resignation, mirrored profound pity. To be old, to be shelved like a package left till called for, seemed to Mitzi a bitter load to be asked to bear. They might have stayed with her the last day, she thought indig-nantly.

Lucy Cooper convincingly lied. She explained that she intended to visit Miss Jennie Gear, aunt to her son's wife. "I wish I had my old hat; it fitted my head. Do you know whether it's thrown out, Mitzi?"

Mitzi salvaged the hat, a cloche that covered the white head decently. The colored woman also made fresh coffee and toast. "You wants to eat, when you has a heavy day." She did all the little things for a departing guest with a grave dignity and a rich tenderness that revealed the whiteness of her heart. When she had taken the old lady up to the first floor in the lift—Lucy Cooper had steadfastly balked at learning to operate the automatic elevator—Mitzi lingered for a moment to watch the bulky, pathetic figure, the wide hips accentuated by an ill-fitting coat, steer a weaving course to the intersecting street. "She ain't going to see no Miss Jennie," Mitzi informed the doorman. "I knew it when she wouldn't lemme call a taxi."

The bus Terminal, a subterranean modern cave constructed between the girders of a granite skyscraper, teemed with confusion and noise. Two runways, coiled, like greased black serpents, around the luxuriously furnished waiting-rooms. Departing and arriving buses jarred the brilliantly lighted windows and plate-glass doors. Blue-uniformed starters quieted excited passengers who dashed to the platform at each reverberation, determined to board any bus that came to a full stop. Somewhere a megaphone brayed mournfully, listing in unintelligible jargon the time and route schedules of the various lines. A crowd of transcontinental travelers mingled with throngs of local commuters, each finding the other supremely stupid and trying.

Lucy Cooper had to touch the starter's elbow to attract his attention. Her voice made no impression against the din. "The Locton bus," she screamed. "When does it get in? Where will I find it?"

Her scarlet face, the moist wisps of white hair that straggled from under her hat brim linked her in the starter's mind with a hundred old ladies who took their traveling "hard." He patted her on the shoulder, and jerked to the left with his thumb. "The Locton bus comes right *here,* Lady. You can't miss it. Just sit down in the waiting-room. I'll come get you, if you like."

She explained, shouting in his ear while a glittering coast-to-coast bus panted restively so close to her she could feel the heat from the engine. She didn't wish to go to Locton, only to meet some one from there. "My husband, but I'm not sure of the time."

"They roll in every half-hour. You just missed one." The starter felt his other sleeve jerked. "You sit down in the waiting-room, Lady, and at ten there'll be a bus. Yes, ma'am, what can I do for you?" He bent his head to hear another story.

In the waiting-room the minutes passed not too tediously. The old mother amused herself by watching a young mother with a baby. The child's grandmother, gowned in depressing, old-fashioned deep mourning, held the boxes and bundles while the younger woman fussed with the cocoon of pink and white flannel. I suppose the grandmother is a widow, mused Lucy Cooper, thinking how small and white the face appeared, banded by the folds of the crêpe veil. She probably lives with her daughter and helps around. A hope that she might be able to help Nellie with her children stirred the solitary watcher's heart. I want to be needed, she wept to herself, but the quick tears that stung her eyes goaded her to walk up and down the platform. I mustn't cry where folks can see me, she worried, staring at an electric light bulb till the wavering yellow blur cleared.

No familiar, slight figure with close-cropped chin beard and alert hazel eyes, descended from the ten o'clock bus. The starter's personal interest in her disappointment embarrassed her. She walked around to the other side of the station to wait. The arrival of a California bus held her attention for some time. The passengers and their dusty luggage disseminated a foreign air, impressive to a stay-at-home. A friendly, sunburned little woman smiled at the old lady, who was tempted to reveal that she had a daughter in California. No opportunity for speech presented itself. This was probably just as well. She never could remember exactly where in California Addie lived. Besides, one didn't know what it might lead to, talking to strangers.

A glimpse of the red-framed clock set in a stone arch urged her to hasten to the other platform where groups of people she had not seen before—where did they all come from, she wondered—jostled each other for foot-hold on the curb. The green-and-white Locton bus slid into place, directly beneath the correct painted sign.

"Bark!" She had not expected to cry out aloud. But then she had not expected to feel her heart turn in her breast, or her knees tremble so that she must rest one hand on an iron pillar for support. *He is thinner, he is older, he has changed,* a beating voice clamored within her. *Only three months, and already he is going down-hill.* She pushed aside the human obstructions that blocked her way and reached her husband. "Bark!"

He jerked around, startled. The hand he put out to her shook. He grasped her arm as if he doubted she were flesh and blood. They stared at each other for a moment without speaking. Slow, painful tears welled into their eyes. He kissed her then, a little awkwardly because he had never been demonstrative. The bus pulled out, a fresh crowd assembled, hemming them in. The old woman was the first to notice that impatient passengers buffeted her husband's clumsy bag sharply against his legs.

They found two seats in a corner, near the parcel-room. Even when seated their eyes clung, as if a great hunger had not been satisfied. "To think you knew I was coming," the old man repeated endlessly, closing his hand over hers. He added that if she had not met him, he would have spent the day alone. Cora, an-noyed by what she termed unnecessary delay, had taken him to the bus, instructing him to sit in the Terminal till Richard called for him that night. On no account, she warned him, was he to bother Anita. "Guess I ain't as popular as I used to be," he admitted.

His wife's terror mounted as she saw more clearly the changes in his physical appearance, but she automatically defended her children. "They're still mad at Addie, Bark. She's selfish, they say, though I tell Anita we don't know all the circumstances. It isn't that they don't want us—not exactly that—but each one's afraid the other won't do right. Don't let's talk about that. Tell me, have you been having that old pain in your back?"

He declared he was a two-year-old. He intimated that he had eaten Cora out of house and home. The right diet and intelligent exercise, he boasted, kept him fit. As he talked, the light streamed pitilessly across his sharpened cheek-bones, the stringy hollows of his throat. A look of pain endured shadowed the circles beneath his eyes. His wife estimated that he must have lost fifteen pounds.

A porter sprinkling wet saw dust approached them. The odor of cement dust, dampened, trailed him.

"Why don't we go to the little park near here?" Lucy Cooper bravely concealed the dismay that the thought of rising cost her. What if she should be bed-fast some day! She pointed to the parcel-room. "They'll check your bag there."

Outside, in the warmth of the April sunshine, they paused, a little helplessly smiled. They had no destination, no errand, no *home*. An old man, and an old woman, without hope, yet cruelly alive to the mocking promises of another spring. "I'd kind of like to see George," the father said.

Guiding him down the side street that terminated in a neglected little park, his wife murmured that she couldn't take him to George's house. "He's at his office all day. Anita has bridge classes. Now, see, isn't this nice?" She indicated the square of new, vivid grass, trampled bald at the edges, the half-dozen rusty iron seats flanking a mud-stained cement walk.

A woman, wheeling a stroller and leading two small children, abandoned one of the seats. They lowered themselves cautiously, for the bench rocked on its cement blocks. "When it's nice weather, all the seats are filled," Lucy Cooper remarked, glancing perfunctorily at the standard park population of mothers and babies, small children on velocipedes, inert, brooding men and women, who rested as if their feet hurt them.

The old couple, arm in arm, let the soft air, the sun and the misty green haze that silvered the hedge of willows soothe them. They spoke at long intervals and then in monosyllables. A great lassitude weighed their limbs. The joy of meeting had cost them something in shock. They shrank, too, from recounting to each other the humiliations, the disappointments, the wounds, of the past three months. The luxury, long denied them both, of sympathetic spiritual contact, still further reduced the necessity for speech. When they did talk, it was of their life together in the old house where their children had been born.

"You got a new dress, Lucy?" The old man remembered that it had pleased her to have him notice her clothes. He smoothed the fabric that covered her knees.

She disclaimed its newness. "I did have another hat, but I thought you wouldn't like it, so I took it off." The flabby softness of her withered double chin trembled. "Bark, I've been thinking—we were married fifty-three years ago, the sixteenth of this month."

"You said April was your favorite month," he reminded her. "Once you told me you wished you were born in it, so you'd get diamonds for birthday presents." They both laughed at the memory of a foolish girl.

He had removed his felt hat and the soft gusts of south wind lifted intermittently the twirling peak of his streaked gray hair. His shoulder pressed against hers, his left hand twined her right. If we could only die now, while we are here together, she thought peacefully, feeling the sun beat warmly on the back of her neck. A thrill of terror, because she remembered that death without pain or grieving never seemed to be the will of God, momentarily chilled her. A fat squirrel with a ratty tail leaped impudently across the walk.

The old man, watching the streak of gray dart fluidly

up a tree-trunk, said, "It's easy for him to keep a roof over his head. Human beings are the ones out of luck."

His wife pressed closer to him.

"Maybe we want too much." He squinted in the sunshine. "Now, if we made another start, in a small way . . ."

Her hand tightened convulsively. "In a little place, Bark. One room's enough. Plenty of people live in one room." The weight of misery that had lain like a chill stone on her heart for months, lifted, and she discovered that she could take a full, deep breath. "Maybe I can do plain sewing," she suggested.

"I'll get something." The old man began to jot figures on the back of an envelope with a businesslike air. "Have you any idea, Lucy, how much a room by the week costs?"

She couldn't help him, and suddenly statistics assumed compelling importance in his mind. He explained that he must have his facts. It would be necessary to borrow from one of the children to finance the simplest start. He tried to convince himself and her that the success of his appeal depended solely on his ability to present an incontrovertible argument in terms of dollars and cents. "If I can show them how little we need to live on, and after the first week we won't need any help," he insisted, the envelope quite covered with rows of sums.

His wife pointed a black silk-gloved finger across the

square. "There's a 'Rooms to Let' sign. Why don't we ask?"

The exterior of the house dismayed them both. Seen from across the park, it had appeared a rather attractive red brick, with windows and doorway outlined in green and white. A closer inspection emphasized the slatternly details of its gradual decay. Milk bottles and paper bags crowded the stone window-sills. The hall smelled dirty and sour. A tired, fat woman, whose soiled house dress Lucy Cooper suspected to be her only garment, answered their questions with a curious mixture of eagerness and listlessness in her asthmatic voice. Yes, she had a housekeeping room, a lovely room, with running water and a kitchenette, on the third floor. She couldn't climb stairs herself, but her little girl would take them up.

"How much do you ask for it?" The old man thought he sounded competent and brisk.

She got five dollars a week in winter, the woman explained, but for the spring and summer she might take four. "You could move right in today." She eyed him hopefully. "It's furnished complete."

They toiled up the narrow uncarpeted stairs, pausing frequently to rest. The little Minnie, summoned from her play on the sidewalk, dutifully led the way, but betrayed no interest in the prospective tenants. The halls were dark, for all the room doors were closed. Lucy Cooper, panting, stumbling, heard the common, cheerful sounds of living behind these doors: the rattle of dishes, the music of radios, chatter of human speech. She wondered if she would be expected to keep the door of her one room shut all day.

"There!" Minnie, ushering them into a third floor back room, darted from closet to dresser, from dresser to table, with bewildering speed. "Here's the stove. There's the sink. You keep your garbage-can under here." The child jerked at the grease-spotted shade drawn at the single window till it wound grudgingly on the roller halfway to the top. "You can look around," Minnie said.

The window faced a white-washed brick wall. A double bed filled more than two thirds of the room space. A table, the dresser, and one chair were the only other articles of furniture. The small lavatory, which must serve as a sink, was fitted into a narrow, black closet, one side of which was lined with zinc. A shallow shelf had been nailed to this wall. On this the two-burner gas stove stood and long strips of soiled pink crêpe paper concealed other shelves which held a few dishes, pots, and pans. Grease caked the stove. The odor of fried food, unaired bed linen and cheap cosmetics mingled with an older, musty smell of corners in which the dirt had been allowed to accumulate perhaps for years.

"Well—" Lucy Cooper seated herself apprehensively on the edge of the bed. She watched sharply, because she expected to see things that crawled. Perhaps, she told herself dubiously, young people could live like this. They might like to buy their food in delicatessen shops, and spend their evenings at the movies. The thought of sleeping in the same room in which she cooked three meals a day nauseated an old housekeeper. How could she market, then climb the long flights of stairs with her parcels? There was no refrigerator—what would they do for ice? How could they rest and read of an evening? One of them would have to sit on the bed. She compared her bedroom in Anita's apartment with this squalid space, and the memory of snowy sheets and orchid blankets, the cleanliness and comfort that had surrounded her assailed her revivingly, like a whiff of sweet, clean air. She glanced at her husband, who stood helplessly in the center of the narrow strip of floor. "We'll not decide right away, Bark." His evident relief did not escape her.

The other houses, the other rooms they visited, offered them little more. They assured each other they could endure shabbiness and inconvenience, but not dirt. Actually the thought of using furnishings that had been handled by a procession of strangers sickened them both. The old man regarded the beds and mattresses with suspicion, his wife found herself loathing the sight of grease-coated frying-pans and dishes with edges nicked.

"Maybe it would be just as cheap to rent a couple of

rooms unfurnished." Lucy Cooper, acutely conscious of her aching legs, stared hostilely at the fourth "Light Housekeeping" sign. "We could buy second-hand things."

Her husband brightened in quick agreement. It would be something like, he declared, to have their own furniture in their own place. He remembered they had passed a second-hand shop a block or two back. As they retraced their steps, he planned to paint and varnish the pieces they bought. No reason why even cheap furniture shouldn't be clean.

"You wouldn't want a better bed room set than that." The stooped old fellow who was the proprietor of the furniture shop, peered at them through a network of rampant table legs. He suggested a Brownie in the dim light.

Together he and Barkley Cooper had overhauled the jumbled furniture that stacked every inch of available space, till their faces were streaked with dust. Fatigue cracked their voices and they moved in jerks. The old woman, enthroned on a roll of carpet, drooped with weariness, too. The three shrunken figures appeared wraith-like, compared with the topheavy assortment of suites that towered above them in jutting crags. Head and footboards of massive, old-style beds, suspended by wires on the walls, threatened to crash upon them. The wild disorder of the single room that served as shop and storage space trapped them in an intricate labyrinth.

"We thought we'd furnish two or three rooms." Barkley Cooper seated himself experimentally in a chair tied about with heavy rope. "We had all our own things once, but we broke up." He looked suspiciously around the store as if he might find some of the familiar pieces with which he had lived for years. "The sale didn't bring much. People want new furniture now."

The proprietor muttered that people were fools. They wanted, he said, doll-house furniture, to fit their tiny rooms. "I got a dozen big bedsteads on my hands that'll probably be chopped up for firewood. Folks complain they ain't got space for 'em any more." He surveyed his customers with inoffensive curiosity. "Going to housekeeping again?"

They nodded. Their dreams flocked warmly around them, lighting an inner glow. They would start as the newly married did. The stark simplicity of the essentials encouraged them. Two or three rooms furnished for her; for him, a job. A nostalgia for his own home, his own fireside, shared with the wife for whom he was the center of the universe, gripped the old man with the intensity of physical pain. "There's nothing like your own place," he said.

The shop owner rolled his denim apron around his discolored hands. "Long as I can make out, I aim to

keep mine. Me and my old girl's getting older, but we
ain't asking no favors." He lived, he revealed, in four
rooms over the store. His wife at seventy-eight was a
partial invalid, but managed to do their housework.
Their living cost them little and a radio contented
them. The husband hoped to outlive his wife. "There's
no one except me to look after her. 'Course, if we had
children, it would be different."

Children, intimated Barkley Cooper striving to sound
impersonal, didn't always solve the problem. As a rule
children had their own lives filled; often they regarded
needy parents as an extra burden, an unjust one.

"Well, maybe you're right about that." The other,
calmly reflective, brought his foot down on a zigzag-
ging centipede. "I don't know that I'd want my children to support me. But they'd be somebody to call on,
if I got in a jam." He rubbed the frame of a mirror
with an oily cloth. "Think you'll take this little set?"

Reality confronted them. Where could they have
furniture sent, how could they pay for it? They had
been dreaming in this musty, pleasantly haphazard
shop. They struggled to their feet like sleepers reluctant to awake. "We may come back. We want to look
around a bit, first," Barkley Cooper lied.

Outside, in the sunshine, his wife anxiously questioned him. "Bark, did you have breakfast early? Are
you hungry?" The desire to minister to his needs
flooded her.

An odd embarrassment tinged his sallow cheeks dull red. "It's dinner-time. But I only got fifty cents left from the bus fare. It'll cost ten cents of that to get my bag."

She slipped her worn black leather change purse into his pocket. "It doesn't match my pocketbook—never did. There's something like two dollars in it. We'll look for a nice lunchroom that's cheap. Gracious, I never used to be as stiff as this!" Conscious of pain in all her joints, she watched her husband rub his knees as if to unlimber them.

The smoky lunchroom, crowded, cheerful, appall-ingly noisy with human voices pitched against the radio blast, served a special fifty-cent luncheon. The old woman discovered, too, that the place served beer. "You must have some; you always liked it," she urged her husband.

He demurred. "It costs extra."

She brushed that aside and persuaded him to order. When the waitress had brought his mug, he perceived that at other tables women also drank beer. "How about you, Lucy?" He nodded toward a group of girls being served. "It's all right."

"I think it looks common." She pursed her lips. When she had been a young woman, no respectable female drank liquor in a public place. Neither, she told herself, had paper napkins been permitted. The care-less service offended her. Inevitably she compared

Mitzi's fastidious neatness and consistently delicious meals with this cheap lunch. "I could cook for us better than this, and it wouldn't cost as much, either," she asserted, though she had never been praised as a notably economical cook.

They lingered at their table, aware that when they had finished they had no refuge except a park, or to walk. Both confessed to disappointment in the rice pudding dessert, but a cigar bought at the counter and a five-cent bag of mints restored them to good humor. They decided to walk, in order, they solemnly assured each other, to make plans. The old man asserted he thought more clearly on his feet.

The sun had faded, and a soft mist blotted their faces as gently as floating bits of down. Dampness seeped through the pavements; the gold of forsythia, cramped behind railings, appeared blindingly bright against the grayness of the mist. On such afternoons how she had loved to leave the routine housework and fuss in the strip of garden, the old woman recollected. She wondered how high the lily pips were now. "Perhaps we can visit each other in nice weather," she said.

He nodded and helped her over a curb. "Shouldn't wonder. But I'm not depending on visits. I got a scheme or two up my sleeve, if things only pan out." He sketched an escape, fantastic as a fairy tale, vague as a dream. They were to go away together, far away, to a Western farm where their hire included their living.

He had read advertisements. They could get a little house, their firewood, milk and eggs, perhaps a share of the planted crops. "The only place a man's independent is on a farm. His age ain't against him, either, since it's all done with machinery now. We could have a garden, too."

She didn't believe a word of it, but the woman's cue is always faith. Their fare, she agreed, provided the chief obstacle. They must manage in some way to provide the needed sum.

"Now here's one of those help-wanted places." The old man paused as they found themselves abreast of a sagging doorway about which stragglers gathered in a group.

Men and women with blank, indifferent faces stolidly read the fluttering rags of notices thumb-tacked to the door-casing, then shuffled their way out of the crowd. No one seemed inclined to obey the suggestion of a large painted tin hand that pointed hospitably in the direction of a dirty stairway. A woman, squeezing past the old couple, swore under her breath.

"Maybe I'd better see if there's anything." Barkley Cooper meant any employment for him. He instructed his wife to wait at the curb while he investigated.

A jovial, tobacco-chewing individual good-naturedly made room for the spare shrunken figure beside him. "Kinda ambitious, ain't you, Grand-pop? Most of the boys are warming park benches at your age." He directed a stream of brown juice at a blue paper slip. "That's a dish-washer wanted. In your line? But all they give is a dollar or two and your meals."

Somewhere behind them a hoarse voice growled. "They fire you, soon as you get your agency fee paid. You ain't got a cigarette, have you, Pop?"

I ought to go in and ask questions myself, thought Barkley Cooper, shrinking alike from the imagined contact as well as the real. The stale breaths of the men on all sides of him appalled him. The grimy set of stairs might as well have been a mountain leading to the fastness of an ogre. He shuddered inwardly at the prospect of facing the agency manager or his clerks. There must be better places than this, he reflected, places that cater to higher types of men. He detached himself from the milling figures and rejoined his wife. "It looks like the kind of place that would take your money and not care whether they got you a job or not," he reported.

"Oh, is there a fee?" She smiled, bewildered but relieved. "Well, we haven't the money for that."

Arm in arm they continued to walk till the backs of their legs ached with throbbing pain. The city offered so few places where one could rest without being expected to buy something. A stone seat, built in the pillared arcade of an office building promised them a moment's respite. The bench faced the handsome plate glass window of a large trust company, closed now for the day. This institution, recently delivered from criminal difficulties, had blandly resumed its rôle of advisor to the investing public. A handsome oil painting occupied two-thirds of the window space. The picture showed two figures, one a charming, hardy old lady seated. Jewels flashed in her laces and her white hair was trimly waved. Behind her, his hand resting on her shoulder, stood a ruddy-faced old gentleman, frock-coated, suave. He beamed directly upon the bank book open in his wife's black silk lap, a bank book that undoubtedly recorded a comfortable balance. Gold and black lettering, framed in gilt, explained: "They saved systematically in their youth."

After a long pause Barkley Cooper said, "I suppose I've been a plain damn fool. The children think so, anyway."

His wife glared at the complacent couple depicted on the wide canvas. "Maybe they had luck on their side. *You* never had a chance to save. Not with five children."

The old man wrestled with disturbing reminders. "Cora says we had twenty years after they were gone. If I'd saved money, and we had it now——"

His words echoed in their minds as hauntingly as noises of the outside world must sound to prisoners in their stone cells. If they had money now! They would have their own home, they would be together under one roof. No one would question their ability to direct their own lives. There would be no need to humble themselves before their children, no necessity to hold out their hands for crumbs.

The very depth of her passion of regret steeled the old woman against disclosure. If she confessed to mistakes, to blindness, to folly, they must both sink in the bitter waters of a common despair. She rubbed one hand over the other, as if chilled. Her lips quivered. "Oh, Bark, how could we look ahead? Time slipped away, and we thought we had the children to take care of us."

"Children!" He laughed derisively. "A fine lot of children we have. They as good as tell us we're no better than paupers."

Yes, his wife admitted, pain thickening her throat, the children had disappointed them. "But we'd do it all over again, Bark. And at least we have nothing to reproach ourselves for." The tears in her eyes dried. She honestly believed that.

He consulted his watch. "I've got to be at the terminal by six. We'd better start."

She made no movement to rise. "Suppose we didn't go back? Just walked on and on, till we found someone to take us in. People do drop out of sight." Her gray eyes searched his hazel ones.

"No." He rejected the idea, but gently as if regretting necessity. "No, we couldn't do that. One of us might get sick, or be run over. That would mean a hospital charity ward. And the one left would be in a bad fix. I guess, Lucy, we can't do any better for the present, than we're doing."

Stiffly she regained her feet, and very slowly they passed under the stone arch, out into the street. The tears she repressed swelled the agony that threatened to burst her heart. She forced her hand to lie lightly on her husband's arm, lest her grip convey to him a hint of the pain that choked her breath. This is killing me, killing me, she panted, moving silently with the passing throng. She glanced at her husband's profile, marked the twitching muscle beneath his eye. What if I never see him again? What if he is ill and dies away from me? She pressed closer to him, under pretense that someone jostled her. Men had such dread of witnessing for the truth! Her tears, her anguish, the awful uncertainty that crushed her breast must be concealed. Whatever her husband suffered he would hide from her. To his spirit any display of emotion savored of indecency, a kind of nakedness paraded.

Within a block of the apartment house she halted him. "Don't come any further with me, Bark. George and Anita might not like it. If they knew we'd been seeing each other, I mean."

"My good Godie, suppose they don't like it? You're not afraid of them, are you?"

She fingered his coat-sleeve. "It isn't that. But it's better if they don't get upset over things."

"I suppose it is." An unnatural composure, like a strange, new garment, lent him a sudden quiet.

His wife smiled, not knowing that her face worked. "See, I'm not crying. I'll ask Nellie to bring me to visit you." A sob betrayed her.

"Well—take care of yourself." His arms about her, he kissed her twice.

She waited, immovable as a statue, gazing after him. At the next corner he turned and lifted his hat. Then he receded into the distance, marching briskly, head up. She began to walk mechanically in the direction of an empty universe.

CHAPTER SEVEN

THE Tuck house, painted the color of a boiled sweet potato—Nellie Tuck, who had selected the tint from a chart, had been more surprised than any one else at the result—provided the typical setting for a suburban Saturday morning. A bicycle stood at the curb. In the center of the cement walk lay an over-turned express wagon. The muddy bird dog, Red, tem-porarily an outcast, sprawled untidily across the lower steps of the porch.

"Well, Red!" Grandma Cooper motioned to the dog not to get up. He acquiesced, but politely hunched his hindquarters to let her pass. She lifted a pair of roller-skates from the fiber door-mat in order to wipe her shoes.

Rhoda let her in. She was a tall girl with high cheek-bones, a large beautifully shaped mouth, and a mop of tightly curled dark hair tucked behind her ears. "Mail your letter, Grandma?" Rhoda's voice was like a firm hand held out to the tottering figure of age. "I told Mother I offered to go for you, but you spurned my aid. You oughtn't to get so hot and bothered over the news of a blessed event."

Grandma—within two weeks Lucy Cooper's other

identities had faded, save that Nellie still called her "Mama"—frowned. Perhaps she dreaded the stairs which taxed her strength. She pulled herself up by the banister railing, dragging one leg that constantly hampered her with a numbness she chose to ignore. At the top she stopped for a moment to draw a deep breath.

From her room Nellie Tuck recognized the step in the hall. "That you, Mama? You ought to let one of the children mail your letters for you." She followed her mother to the door of the guest-room, which had been turned over to her and watched the old lady as she seated herself on the side of the bed. "Don't you feel well, Mama?"

"It's Janet Ware." Grandma sighed for the grand-niece who had been married scarcely nine months. "You could have knocked me over with a feather. I never dreamed she expected a baby so soon. It must have happened right on the boat." She closed her eyes before the contemplation of intimacy on the high seas. "Right on the boat, during their honeymoon. And he's a clergyman, too."

Nellie, half-dressed, for she was preparing to go to market, appeared confused. She had never been able to argue with her mother. Rhoda, washing her hair in the bathroom, shut off the water fully to shout cheerily, "Janet's married. You can't exactly call her a fallen woman, Gram."

Hurriedly Nellie consulted her mother about brussels

sprouts. The doctor had ordered more vegetables in
her diet, but, like many elderly folk, Grandma cared
little for vegetables. Nellie, too fat, but gentle and
pretty still in her early forties, had not outgrown her
fear of her mother's decisive tongue. She cringed a
little under the old lady's arraignment of doctors in
general. Eventually Nellie retreated, murmuring pla-
cating little nothings, which infuriated Rhoda, who
would have preferred to respect her mother.

Twenty minutes later the knowledge that Nellie had
departed to market raised a little ladder toward the
shelf to which Grandma felt she was firmly being relegated. She climbed nimbly down, determined to take
charge of the rudderless household. For the moment
Grandma imagined that the busy hours stretched sun-
nily before her, that on her as the pivot of a home, the
happiness of a man and children rested. She peeped
in at Rhoda, who had dragged a chair to a sunny window. "You won't take cold, will you, darling?" She
bustled away, without waiting for Rhoda to answer.
Usually Rhoda did not reply.

The breakfast dishes, still unwashed, represented the
one domestic task that Grandma regularly performed.
She disdained the other housework, partly because she
thought her son-in-law, Harvey, should employ a maid.
Grandma had usually had a girl to help her in her own
home. Her husband had seen to that. Harvey con-
tended mildly that he might not be able to afford a

maid for his wife, just now, but at least he carried heavy life insurance. Barkley Cooper had never taken out a policy. Grandma didn't approve of life insurance; she declared that she would not be a female ghoul.

She scraped an eggy plate and put it to soak. Dishes she detested, and her stay with Anita had accustomed her to forego physical exertion; but she honestly wished to help Nellie, the dear. In spite of the patent fact that the noisy, busy household had no real need of Grandma, in spite of the evidence that, like Anita's and George's, their real lives touched hers at no point, the old woman had found it easier to adjust herself in this second home. This was largely due to the spontaneity of Nellie's affection and the natural manners of her simple nature, which had changed little since her childhood. She kissed her mother when she left her even for a trip down town; kissed her when they met on her return. Nellie brought her tiny presents, cooked special food to please her, tried to listen to her advice. To herself Grandma admitted that this daughter was a far better manager and housekeeper than her mother had ever been, but she made greater sacrifices, too. Grandma prided herself that she had been an excellent mother to her children, yet certainly she had never worn the same winter coat for five years, as Nellie did. It surely couldn't be necessary that all the new clothes go to Rhoda and Diane.

As if her thought connected with a signal, Diane,

little and fair and brittle, pushed open the swinging door that led from the dining-room. Her sharp, even features, her suspicious, curious eyes—blue eyes like her father's—her inexhaustible energy and eagerness, ought to have caught at Grandma's sympathy. But her only sister, many years dead, had been like Diane too long ago for Grandma to be able to perceive the repetition.

"Need any help, Granny?" Diane darted to the rack and seized a dish-towel. A hundred needs of her own, growing, spreading, demanding in her, called as insistently and silently as the advancing spring. She glanced hopefully at Grandma, for whom the clamor of unfolding life had grown distant and dim. "Where's Mother, Gram?"

A thrill, the power of authority in charge, straightened Grandma's drooping back. "Your mother's gone to market. Be careful of that plate, child."

Diane, drying a plate dreamily, announced that she had hoped her mother might visit the dentist. "She's afraid to run up another bill. She only got him paid for Patty and Colin last month. Rhoda thinks the reason Mother is so tired lately is that she needs to have her teeth fixed. I don't think it's that."

Grandma, who hoped her teeth looked natural, disliked dental conversations. "Your mother tries to do too much."

"At her age." Diane mopped the inside of a cup as

awkwardly as if domestic science had never been taught in the public schools. "I told Rhoda it's probably change of life. She's old enough for that to start, isn't she? And that would explain why she is so cross with Daddy some days."

To say, "Diane!" nearly strangled the grandmother. Her blood-pressure mounted another notch, and a roaring filled all the passages in her head.

"Well, she is! You don't always come down to breakfast, but I see. Once they didn't speak to each other. Mother never used to be like that. When they do talk, they argue. You know yourself, Gram, they are edgy, when they've always been wrapped up in each other before. Even Colin can tell there's a difference." Diane knew that Grandma adored the family's only boy.

The eager, searching voice continued. "That isn't all. Mother acts so silly, sometimes, at card parties. She giggles and flirts. She does, too! It's the closing door, *I* think."

"The closing door?" Grandma's stiff lips moved.

"When you get to the age where in a few more years you'll be really old—can't have any more babies, you know—you're apt to decide you want one more fling." Diane let one end of the dish-towel trail on the linoleum-covered floor. "I read about it. It isn't a woman's fault; it's Nature egging her on to have an affair before she is too old. Forever too old." The intense blue eyes stared, a little horrified, at the shrunken old woman body braced against the sink.

But Grandma had recovered in part. The real shock had been the realization that Nellie, in her mother's sight still a little girl, to her children was middle-aged. She scarcely heard Diane, computing birthdays, announce triumphantly that "forty-two must be the dangerous age you hear about."

"If you intend to dry those dishes, you'd better get on with them." In her day Grandma had put many a forward child in his place. "There are some things, Diane, that no lady will discuss."

"Well, of course, I wouldn't discuss this with Mother." Diane was unexpectedly lovely and gentle. "I wouldn't hurt her feelings for the world. But it's different with you, Grandma; you know all about it. I thought we could kind of talk it over. There isn't anything I can't talk about."

She said that with a thousand secrets behind her blue eyes, at the back of her little scarlet lying tongue. The things she couldn't talk about, the things no other human being would ever hear, she thought over at night, in bed.

And Grandma, whose heart ached with loneliness and lost hopes the greater part of her waking hours, who went back in her dreams at night to her lost, sweet girlhood, Grandma funked. She was tired, she was old, she wanted security herself. "I wish you'd clear out of this kitchen." The trembling in her knees angered her. "You've made me upset the box of soap flakes."

Every second Saturday Helen came to clean. She scrubbed her way through the house and out of the back door by four o'clock. This afternoon she remarked to Grandma Cooper that Colin worried her. "He hasn't moved since lunch. There he sits, up in his room, watching those white mice." Helen had two boys of her own. She was experienced enough to distrust their periods of quiet.

Grandma Cooper waited till Helen's red hat had disappeared through the side gate. Naturally Colin adored his white mice. He had bought them that morning, and any new possession engrossed him. Before another Saturday he'd be bribing Patty, his younger sister, to feed them. Colin's interests, intense, harassing, soon burned themselves out.

The third floor might be chilly, even on an April day. Grandma adjusted her white wool shoulderette as she slowly mounted the stairs. She seldom visited Colin's room, not so much that she disliked the climb, as that she dreaded the hordes of neighborhood children who constantly invaded the large, light place. Colin had it to himself, however, now. Not even Patty, his faithful shadow, shared his vigil. He scarcely stirred as his grandmother spoke to him.

"Colin! It's after four, dear. How much longer are you going to stay up here with those mice?"

The boy's tumbled dark hair accented the whiteness of his smooth forehead. He had a merry, impudent nose, a mouth like Rhoda's. "Nothing's happened yet." The disappointment in his voice alarmed his grandmother, who nightly served notice on God in her prayers that life must be kind to Colin.

She stopped a little, trying to peer into the slatted box. "What's the matter, dear? They look all right to me." Inwardly she shuddered, for all species of mice caused tumult at her stomach-pit.

"Not one's been born yet." Colin stamped his foot, which had gone to sleep. "I've been here since half-past twelve, and not a mouse has been born."

Grandma felt behind her and discovered a chair. She sat down. In heaven's name, she protested silently, what was the matter with every one in this house? She stared at the beautiful, open countenance of her grandson. Waiting for mice to be born— "You'd better come down and get ready for dinner." One ought to get ready for dinner surely, no matter what crisis loomed.

"I want to *see* them born." Colin thrust his nose between the thin wood slats and grimly eyed his mice. They cowered guiltily and squeaked. "The man said one of 'em would have a family any minute, when I bought them. I'm going to see them born. That's the only reason I bought the silly things."

"But you can't. You mustn't, Colin."

"Why mustn't I?"

"No one—no one watches such things."

"They do, too. Didn't people watch me get born? My mother was there and Doctor Cree and a nurse. Yes, and my father. He told me."

Overwhelmed by the situation, Grandma's temper rose. Not to know what to do made her so cross she could have flopped on the floor and kicked and screamed. "Babies are different," she snapped. "Mice don't have doctors and nurses, do they?"

Colin admitted the truth of this. He gazed at his grandmother with something like respect. "But they're born, aren't they?" he submitted humbly.

"Well, if they are, people don't watch them. Most likely they'll come in the night, when you're asleep. Puppies and kittens usually do."

"Ted Rogers saw their Boston bull, Bessie, have pups." Colin beamed as if this information must delight his listener. "She had seven. He said they don't all come at once——"

Grandma, who had no desire to widen her knowledge of animal obstetrics, struggled to her feet. "You come downstairs, and Grandma'll read to you," she bribed.

He'd listen if she brought the book up. Colin explained that he could watch the mice and be entertained, too. His grandmother flounced away indignantly, to shut the door of her own room with a crash. Where did her grandchildren—Rhoda, Diane, Colin, all of them—get their messy ideas? They got them, she decided promptly, at the movies. Even the films advertised as suitable for children were preceded or followed by stories worse than trash. Nellie did the best she could—of course she did. Still, one couldn't forbid the movies when every child in the neighborhood went more or less regularly, and educational films were run off in school. Not that you could drag a child to see an educational film outside of school hours. Grandma had learned that. It had never been quite clear in her mind how she and Colin, setting forth one evening to see the early run of a widely advertised travelogue, had wound up at the Bijou, where the chief attraction was a terrible nightmare labeled "My Sin." Colin had professed to be as surprised as she was. But he didn't like to ask for their money back, so they had sat through the thing.

Grandma, pacing her room restlessly, stooped to remove a thread of lint from the rug. She told herself she ought to do something about Colin. He was so handsome, so sweet and fine. It hurt her to think of his growing rough and coarse, like the other boys with whom he played. She wasn't sure how witnessing the birth of a litter of mice would coarsen Colin, but the

idea tortured her. The bit of thread held between her
forefinger and thumb, she stood motionless in the center of the room. For a brief instant she caught the
sound of life advancing, a torrent of sound. This roaring current that, unchecked, must bear her beautiful,
smiling grandson beyond her arms, menaced her love.
All she asked, she told herself passionately, was to protect him; to protect Colin from knowledge, a bitter
fruit.

"It's a wonder Nellie wouldn't stop gadding around
and pay a little attention to things!" The necessity for
blaming some one demanded relief. She closed the
window, hard. Some one was forever opening the
windows in her room. Thank the Lord, she had not
this modern fetish of fresh air. She'd slept with her
windows closed—except in summer—all her life, and
she was seventy-two.

Hunger—dinner would be late—increased her exasperation. Nellie must be planning to have that abomi-
nation, a cold meal. Grandma wondered if she could
coax her grandson down to the kitchen if she promised
to let him finish melting his lead. His mother refused
to allow him to use the gas range, unless some one
supervised him; in consequence the process of melting
his battered battalions of toy soldiers dragged.

A little pang of self-pity—and gas—stabbed Grandma's left side, as she once more toiled up the stairs.
Doctor Cree had explained that stair-climbing taxed

her heart. No one, except the doctor, ever urged her to be careful, or thought her frail. With a sigh, the old lady gained the top step and trudged into Colin's room.

"She just *won't* have babies!" Colin, pushing the hair back from his forehead, looked tired.

In the rocker beside him coiled a little girl, Patty, the youngest member of the family. She wasn't nearly as handsome as Colin, and she knew it. Her forehead bulged a trifle, her eyes were perfectly round. Colin's hair grew beautifully on his well-shaped head, but Patty had dark, stringy locks that straggled thinly over her prominent ears. She was a good child, as even her grandmother conceded, but distressingly plain. "We're waiting to see the mice born." Patty yawned. Like most of her sex, she had found it a tedious wait.

The lead-melting suggested, Colin only moved closer to the box. His fascinated gaze searched every inch of the cotton-lined space. "The man said she'd have 'em any minute."

"If you and Patty will come down to my room, you may take the things out of my box." Grandma yearned to stroke the round, intent face, but Colin jerked away from any caress. She adored him more, if possible, than his mother did. She and Nellie differed on many conclusions, but both agreed that Colin must be the finest boy in the world. Nellie, who quite simply loved her daughters after a more serene fashion, had once told her mother, "Girls are all right, but I don't think any woman feels she has done much till she has a son."

Patty answered, for Colin merely shrugged. "We've seen all the things in your box."

They had. The contents of the canvas telescope, which Anita had banished, but which Nellie allowed Grandma to store under her bed, no longer enthralled the children. Old photographs, Civil War letters, odds and ends of ornaments, scrapbooks, bits of ribbons and lace, each with its story, the youngsters had seen them all. However, Colin and Patty, who enjoyed repetition, had not exhausted the charm of the collection; it was only that for the moment, mice were new.

There remained the old-fashioned bribes. Grandma remembered a few pennies in her purse, peppermints in her china jar. Harvey had decided views, however, on offering children money and Nellie discouraged candy between meals. Stuff and nonsense, wearily scolded Grandma; she had used both methods with her children, and they had not turned out any more spoiled than other specimens she had seen. Still, she didn't believe in courting trouble. Besides, the six pennies would buy two postage stamps, and the candy she might need herself, if she woke hungry in the night.

"I haven't been around the block today, Colin," she said.

She took an unfair advantage of his kind heart. No one but what her son-in-law called "a female woman" would have done it. Colin had learned, from Grand-

ma herself, that Doctor Cree wished her to walk around
the block at least once a day. He thought it better if
she did not go alone. Sometimes Nellie accompanied
her mother, more often one of the girls or Colin. He
accepted the doctor's order with superstitious literal-
ness; if Grandma didn't walk around the block, misfortune might befall her. Now a momentary spasm
of rebellion churned inside him. She was so old! She
walked so slow! The mice would be born before they
got back. He grunted that Patty ought to go, once in
a while.

"Granny doesn't like the way I walk. She says I
fidget her. She loves you better than she does me."
Patty's statement held no rancor.

"Do you have to go today, Grandma? It's kind of
late." Be generous, pleaded Colin's anxious eyes.

Grandma could, she supposed, wait. "But I did think
I'd sleep better if I had a little breath of fresh air before
my dinner."

He capitulated without sullenness. His instructions
to Patty included specific directions for communicating to him en route any news that might develop in his
absence; she was to have his siren whistle and under
no circumstances must she mix her blasts. He went
into detail about what he wished noted, and Grandma
precipitately hurried him off. What did the child expect?

The leisurely stroll in which the old lady customarily

delighted proved to be a breathless, hurried tour. The lighted windows into which she liked to glance, even though she deplored the habit of undrawn shades, afforded her no clear pictures. The neighbors' lawns and yards she scarcely saw. His hand in hers, Colin towed her forward, her large white face, beneath the small, inadequate black hat, showing drawn and worn. The boy's energy and strength dismayed her, as if she had started an engine she couldn't stop. He had eyes and ears only for the event he had deserted. Her attempts at conversation went unnoted. Only when they rounded the last corner from which the house could be seen, did Colin relax, permitting himself a smile. "I guess they're not born yet," he beamed.

He shot into the hall ahead of her and tumbled up the stairs. A cheerful rattle from the kitchen indicated that Nellie had returned. In the living-room Harvey Tuck read his paper under a bridge light, a stout, cheerful man with ash-blond hair. Grandma privately considered him positively feeble-minded.

"Where you been, Grandma?" Harvey put practically all his sentences into interrogation form.

"Harvey Tuck, your son has spent his entire afternoon watching to see white mice born!" Indignation quavered in the old voice. "He's got Patty up there now. They put their faces against the bars and stare! Are you going to do anything about it?"

He dropped his paper. "Am I? Where are they? In Colin's room?"

Grandma heard him tackle the first flight of stairs at top speed, but she knew he couldn't keep that up. Harvey winded easily. She might as well follow him, for she didn't altogether trust his eager response.

In Colin's room three chairs were pulled up before the white mice box. Colin, Patty, and their father, sat in a solemn, silent row. They never turned their heads as Grandma crossed the sill.

Colin spoke. "Not one born yet. Can you beat it?"

"Want to watch, Grandma? Or have you seen white mice born?" The light struck Harvey's spectacles, screening the expression in his eyes.

Grandma loved the afternoon, when Nellie decided to sew. Diane and Patty had a store of wash frocks left from the last season, which might do another year. Nellie carried them down in boxes from the attic. She made it a practice to sort over the family's stock of clothing twice each year before purchasing new. Nellie inspected rapidly, deciding what each dress needed at a glance. Grandma did the ripping, cutting one thread at a time. She rocked companionably nearer to happiness than she had been in months.

"This is the way my mother and I worked." She smiled over her glasses. "We did everything together. Mornings, at eleven o'clock, we had a little lunch—just the two of us. Afternoons, we sat down to sew and talk." Some one to *talk* to her, was Grandma's constant cry. No one, she complained, talked nowadays. If they didn't play cards, when it was a crime to open one's mouth, they turned on the radio, which made it impossible for a body to think. Grandma's plea was the old, hopeless yearning for a sympathetic audience, for some one to listen patiently to the querulous, pathetic, foolish murmurs of old age. She constantly remembered the days of her active maternity, and brimmed with accounts of experiences she eagerly wished to impart. She had no doubt of the value of her advice to her daughter, whom she believed she perfectly fathomed. No adult children, she supposed, ever really comprehended old parents, a fact she had persuaded herself to be the most terrible tragedy old age had to face. The truth that no one human being ever thoroughly divines another quite escaped her.

"I don't think you should allow Rhoda to discuss Janet Ware's condition." Grandma frowned over the stitching in a green frock. She loved Nellie with a far deeper love than she gave any of her grandchildren. As a matter of fact, their vitality exhausted her. Returning in her old age to the sheltered existence of a baby, she had definitely begun to shrink from contacts with life.

Nellie emptied a bag of buttons on the bed and began an anxious search. "Why, Mama, you can't shut Rhoda

off on that. She talks babies to any one who will listen.
I've heard her say she intends to have a dozen of her
own. I don't believe I *have* a green button."

The way young girls talked! Grandma thought of
Rhoda, obviously and industriously engaged in the pur-
suit of a husband to support her family and her views.
The child's frankness shocked the old woman, but then
any bare truth did that. Harvey, her son-in-law, often
pondered why old people, to whom birth and death
and human desire should be as familiar as sunrise and
sunset, found descriptive phrases intolerable. He had
decided that a passing generation shied at words that
revealed thoughts. Grandma held frantically to her
secrets that would never be secret to Rhoda and her
kind.

"You'll be sorry when it's too late, Nellie." Grandma
ripped a stitch. "Nothing can replace the lack of early
training in a child's life."

Her daughter murmured. No one hedged children
about with too much supervision, any more. "We were
too repressed, when we were children, Mama." Every
adult in Nellie's circle said that.

"Why, Nellie Cooper! I'm sure no one had a happier childhood than you did. I never interfered with
anything you wanted to do, as long as it was *right*. It
was my duty, of course, to see that you were taught to
be good. I was responsible for bringing you up, wasn't
I ? But I don't see how you can say you were repressed,

when I spent my whole life trying to make you happy." Resentment shaped the old lips into a hard thin line.

Nellie agitatedly stirred the buttons into a mound. Why must Mama flare up at the most innocent word? She gets more and more sensitive, and that's why Harvey hates to talk to her, Nellie thought. Just the same, she did make a lot of mistakes with us. Nellie, fingering buttons, let her mind drift back to incidents that her adult knowledge invested with bitterness.

"Well, there's one thing I taught my children and taught them thoroughly." Grandma straightened in her chair. "Every one of you learned to respect gray hairs. If a child of mine had spoken to *my* mother as your children speak to me—I don't know what kind of treatment you expect yourself, Nellie, when you're old."

Her daughter pretended to match a button against a fold of piqué. Any kind of complication distressed Nellie, who had no diplomatic gifts. Currents beneath the surface, which should be smooth and fair, annoyed her. As she attempted to soothe her mother with the explanation that the children meant nothing by their careless speech, Nellie hoped fervently that the true situation might still be concealed. If the grandmother learned from Rhoda or Diane that her presence in the house was actually unwelcome to her son-in-law, then indeed, thought poor Nellie, the fat would be in the fire. "Do you suppose I'll have to buy all new buttons?" At that moment, fretted by a dozen cares, the failure of her search seemed to Nellie to be part of her general frustration.

It might be cheaper to buy new things, than to spend too much time and work on old materials, Grandma advised. A woman's time ought to be worth something, she observed. The recital of her favorite platitudes restored in a measure her good humor and enabled her to accept sympathetically Nellie's response—that with four growing children time was more plentiful with her than cash. Nellie carefully avoided the mention of doctor's bills recently incurred on her mother's behalf; Harvey had not paid them with good grace, but then his margin was always desperately small.

"Sometimes I feel that Harvey doesn't like me." Grandma said that without looking at her daughter. After an instant the shrunken, faded eyes met Nellie's glance, pleading tragically for reassurance.

"Why, Mama, how you talk! Isn't Harvey always nice to you? Of course, when a man's worried about business, he may be a little short now and then." Nellie wondered if her mother could possibly have overheard anything. Harvey sometimes raised his voice. He had lately argued that he was sure his mother-in-law wished to make her permanent home with them. His insistence that he wouldn't stand for it and his declaration that his position must be made clear had alarmed his wife. Nellie, anxious for her husband's peace, foresaw her mother's hurt. It would have been easier, she told herself weakly, if she didn't love them both.

Her mother said she could understand financial worry. She had had to count pennies herself when her children were small. "Your father's salary wasn't always enough, but I made it do. I had a girl in the kitchen, but I took care of my children myself. And, Nellie, it's the happiest time in a woman's life. I mean it. When your children are little and need you and you know where they are every minute of the day."

"Do you know, Mama,—" Nellie poured the buttons back into the bag. "All this talk about babies—" She slowly knotted the string. "I've been thinking. Mama, I'd love to have another baby, before I'm too old."

Her mother gaped. Nellie was forty-two; in the eyes of Diane, already old. Besides, the mention of a plan deliberately to bear a child again outraged the secretiveness the old lady believed should shroud procreation. She had accepted her own five children, but not all had been welcome. Rhoda had shrewdly referred to probable mistakes, an allusion her grandmother considered unspeakably coarse. "You wouldn't want to go through all that again, Nellie," the old voice warned.

"Well, of course Harvey thinks I am out of my mind." Nellie threaded her needle calmly. "We can't afford another child. Our income isn't likely to increase; indeed, as Harvey grows older, it will shrink."

The impulse to comfort a child prompted her mother's protest. "Why, dear, you may be well off some day. Harvey is very clever, I'm sure. His firm will promote him."

Nellie said, with her accustomed placidity, that Harvey was not the money-making type. "Rhoda is rather bitter sometimes about it."

"Rhoda!"

"Well, she's young. At her age money stands for happiness. Then, too, she has this modern idea that parents owe their children a college education and what she calls a fair start in life. If I had a baby now, I suppose Rhoda would leave home. She tells me we can't properly care for the ones we have."

Anger vibrated in the grandmother's voice. "You let her talk to you like that!"

"Oh, Mama, can't you see? Whether she talks or doesn't talk, she thinks like that. I'd rather have her be frank. Would you piece this belt?" Nellie valued her time and rarely neglected the task in hand.

Her mother agreed that it could be pieced underneath and not show. "It's utter nonsense—to say that parents owe their children anything!"

Nellie's red-brown eyes widened. She was not a quick-minded woman; her reasoning, hampered by her early training, remained consistently out of date, but even to her ears that speech had a hollow sound. "Why, Mama, you're always saying that children owe their parents a great deal. Is it all one-sided?"

"Your father and mother brought you into the world and cared for you till you could look after yourself." An emphatic nod of the white head punctuated each statement. Parents sacrificed their entire lives for their children, Grandma added. The children incurred a debt they could never repay. Not that fathers and mothers asked payment. "Any mother worthy the name does her best for each child. She asks nothing in return, except that they be happy and good."

Nellie silently basted a seam. She was unable to recall any specific sacrifices her parents had made for her, and she did remember, vividly, a number of thwarted wishes and ambitions which her father or mother had nipped in the bud. It seemed to her, too, that parents did ask something of their children in return; her own father and mother's dependency, for instance, had created a problem in four homes. Still, from her own maternal experience, she conceded that the rearing of children demanded a constant subjection of individual rights. In her own case, she would not have had it otherwise, and she suspected that her mother had also reveled in her maternal rôle. Not that she would admit it. She stressed only the responsibility, never the delight. Nellie wondered about her father, bit her lip.

Neither could her mother's thoughts be put into words. She dreaded pregnancy for Nellie at her age, or she supposed she did. Actually her fears and forebodings were for herself. The birth of another child

in this home menaced Grandma's security. Harvey
and Nellie, the intruder reasoned, would need whatever
surplus they had, nor would they desire an old woman's
help. Her methods of keeping house, of caring for a
baby, even if she had the strength for such tasks, differed too much from modern ways to win their approval. No family, she told herself heavily, ever needed
a grandmother less. "In my day, people didn't talk
beforehand about having a baby," she said aloud. Because she felt herself beaten, she must assert her su-
periority.

"I think it was perfectly silly of women in your day
to make a mystery of conception." Nellie, usually
gentle, found in harshness a refuge from a sense of
guilt. She *did* want another baby. Tiny babies were
sweet. At the same time she recognized the complexity
of her motives. If she had a child, she would be ab-
solved of her mother's care. The growing breach between her husband and herself would be healed. And
no one could criticize her, because maternity is beautiful to the sentimental in any guise.

The anger and pain in the old face were reflected in
the old voice. "Do you think that is the way to speak
to your mother, Nellie? I'm glad your father can't
hear you." Grandma rose, dropping her scissors on the
floor, tossing the dress on which she had been working
across the bed. "I never dreamed my own daughter
would treat me this way."

Heavily, wearily, she tottered to the retreat of her own room. She undressed more slowly than her wont, noting that her body felt clumsy and thick as she crept into the smooth coolness of her bed. Very old, very tired, she lay and sobbed to herself in the gathering dusk. Once she had to get up and find a handkerchief, because tears always made her sneeze and blow her nose. She wept for her little griefs of wounded vanity, of misplaced importance, defeated pride; but with her sobbing mingled too, the agony and heartbreak of greater sorrows, lasting, real. Loneliness, separation, uncertainty constantly mocked her; a future of despair forbade her to lift her eyes. She thought of the day in the park and wished that she and Bark might have died. After a time she quieted and turned on her side to watch the penciled crack of light under the door.

"Why, Honey! Didn't you hear the dinner gong? Are you ill?" Nellie followed so quickly upon her tap that Grandma blinked as her room light clicked on. Nellie's pretty, soft hands felt of the wrinkled forehead and wrists.

It pleased the old woman not to surrender too quickly. No one, no one cared a jot about her opinions, nor listened to her warnings. Her own daughter was disrespectful to her, her son-in-law and her grandchildren ignored her. "You go on and eat your dinner; they'll like it better, if I'm not there." A burden in the household, she continued, she would no longer impose. "I'll take my things and go 'way from here," said Grandma, who had no other place to go.

"Now, darling, now." Nellie, to whom endearments came easily, kissed and patted and soothed. Her eyes tender, she laid her soft face against her mother's withered cheek. Maternal, patient, she comforted her oldest and most fractious child.

When, later, she carried up a well-filled tray, Grandma graciously consented to be fed. To have Nellie wait on her, to be for however brief a time, the sole object of her thought and care, warmed the old body as no food could do. Her possessive love fed on each moment she had Nellie to herself like this. At such times she could almost persuade herself that she had never had to share her daughter's love.

"A mite more nutmeg wouldn't hurt your custard," said Grandma.

CHAPTER EIGHT

"THE boiled rice in the white bowl on the third shelf is for your lunch, Father." Grace, Richard Cooper's wife, decisively closed the refrigerator door. "There's a pint bottle of milk next to the ice—use that, too. I did think I'd keep it for gravy tonight, but you'll need it with the rice." She sighed, because this provision for her father-in-law's lunch added to her housekeeping costs.

He was the only one home at noon. Grace worked in the office of a laundry, Richard and his son, John, were skilled workmen with factory jobs. Dariel, John's young wife was a stenographer. The four of them usually left the house together each morning, in Richard's small car and did not return till after five. The honking of the horn now reminded Grace that the others waited. She glanced hastily around her immaculate kitchen, pulled a curtain straight and rushed out.

The old man scurried to the front of the house, to watch the car drive off. He dared not lift the ruffled curtains in the living-room, for Grace resented espionage, but he parted them in the center with his finger. He saw his daughter-in-law climb into the front seat, noted that Richard glanced toward the house, then

watched the car glide smoothly down the street. John
and Dariel always read a tabloid paper as they rode. If
she remembered, Dariel saved it to bring home to
Grandfather at night.

"Well, she's gone." Barkley Cooper fancied that he
didn't breathe right till his bustling daughter-in-law
had departed for the day. Certainly the early morning
program was always one of haste. To begin with, he
had to rise at six o'clock, and that fagged him. Grace,
who did a full day's work before she went to business,
demanded that every room in the house be in perfect
order before she left. The old man, who slept on the
davenport in the living-room, must rise promptly so
that his bedding might be aired. The family break-
fasted at seven, hurriedly, silently, in the kitchen breakfast nook. Grace had adopted the plan of telling her
father-in-law what to eat for lunch after she had discovered on one occasion that he had innocently consumed her dinner supplies.

The silence of the house, morning after morning
when he found himself alone, oppressed him. A cat
or a dog would have been company, but Grace disliked
animals, considered them an expense and a care. She
banned even a canary, because of the scattered bird-
seed. Her father-in-law tried to forget how fond Richard had always been of dogs.

Usually after every one had gone, the old man lay
down for a nap. In sleep the long, dull hours passed

quickly; he was neither cold, nor hungry, nor in pain. He carefully removed Grace's best pillows, spread his handkerchief under his feet, and drowsed on the mulberry-tapestried couch till noon. The heater fire, banked, gave little warmth, the sun penetrated few of the rooms. He used his overcoat for a coverlet, and if tobacco sifted from his pockets to the floor, he brushed it neatly into a paper, then ran the carpet sweeper vigorously over the spot.

His lunch—cold, cooked food that made it unnecessary to light the gas—he ate with an indifferent appetite. He liked to putter and would have enjoyed frying eggs or concocting one of his meat stews. Grace, however, discouraged any messing around. On the score of waste she refused to let him prepare vegetables for dinner, do her marketing, or do any of the housework. Even in the tiny back-yard garden, where green things had begun to thrust their tips through the red soil, she declined his aid. Two men were more than enough to have under foot, she declared, meaning her husband and her son. The garden reflected her fanatical neatness, methodical precision, and passion for economy, her father-in-law admitted, but he cherished no admiration for these qualities. Instead he preferred the front stoop.

He sought that familiar haven this afternoon when he had finished his rice and milk and washed his dishes, consisting of bottle and bowl. The long hours stretched before him; he had nothing to do. At three o'clock he could walk down a few blocks and get the paper. He liked to put that errand off because it afforded him a pretext of an appointment to be kept. He glanced at his watch as he settled himself on the cement steps and began to fill his pipe. After one experience, when he had locked himself out, he remembered to adjust the dead-latch on the front door. He had saved yesterday's paper to sit on, for the cement was damp and cold. "We don't have spring any more," he had complained to the friendly postman; "only winter and summer." But a young maple tree at the curb, leafing out, disputed him.

Up and down the short block other valiant young maples, girded in chicken wire, persistently testified to the arrival of spring. Scraps of lawns, fenced off with wire strands on which fluttered agitated bits of white rags, marked the boundaries of the narrow lots. In front of Richard's house white rags whipped in the wind, too. "You can tell every one owns his own home," Richard had said to his father. "A bunch of renters never take any pride in the way their places look."

The old man, smoking quietly, let himself be interested in the small activities of the neighbors, some of whom he already knew by sight. At the side of one house a man painted a rose trellis. Across the street a line crew worked on the installation of a 'phone. A woman carrying a spade jabbed fitfully at the roots of bushes planted the length of her porch. Just to see people moving about, to hear the sound of voices somehow comforted one. In the empty house behind him Barkley Cooper fancied his own voice hoarse and strange when, seeking to relieve the pall of silence, he sometimes spoke aloud. Strange ideas came to him then, suggestions that he was tempted to believe might be "signs." He smelled, or thought he smelled, the odor of funeral flowers, and he wondered if he had what his wife called "psychic power." She had always insisted he had, but he had condemned the claim as irreligious. Alone in the house he found the idea oddly fascinating, suitable to the chill gloom. Here in the sunshine the normal world, commonplace, indifferent, drew one back to the occupations of the sane. The lilt of the postman's whistle as he turned the corner was of the earth earthy, hopeful and gay.

"Well, Grandpop, how's the rheumatism?" The postman was perhaps twenty-two, a homely, beaming lad with a pug nose and a mouth filled with beautiful strong white teeth. He seldom had a letter or a card to leave at the Cooper house, but he never passed the old man without stopping to chaff.

"At least I haven't got flat feet." This hoary insult had its place in their every dialogue. The hazel eyes twinkled, the peak of gray and black hair bobbed in satisfied delight.

The postman rested his stuffed bag on his knee and thumbed a package of cards. "Wait till you walk as many miles as I do. Nobody but a fool would stick to this job."

He had a pension to look forward to, the old man reminded him. He'd be independent in his old age.

"At sixty-five?" Twenty-two tried to see down the years. "I hope I don't live that long."

After the postman had proceeded on his monotonous way, up steps and down, across the street and back again, Barkley Cooper tried to recall his own attitude toward old age at twenty-two. He suspected that then forty had been the first boundary of senile decay. Funny how we keep pushing the limits back, he mused, drawing circles on the stoop with a dead match. I'd feel young if I was sixty-five now. Don't want to die, as 'tis. That young fellow's got a lot to learn.

He consulted his watch and decided to pay his visit to the paper store. He walked slowly, prolonging the distance to enjoy the sensation of having something to do. At each newly-made lawn or flower-bed he paused to inspect the plantings, pleased if an amateur gardener volunteered a friendly word. Maple Avenue was a dead-end street, and each house precisely duplicated its next in row. There were ten streets in the development, each faced with a double row of small homes built from one set of architect's plans. Theoretically the home owners sought light and air in buying a detached house; in reality on the thirty-eight-foot lots, which included a driveway and a garage, the roofs almost touched.

The paper store, three blocks away, sold the usual miscellaneous assortment of supplies for readers, smokers and drinkers, adding, in season, tickets for the sweepstakes. Mornings and evenings the proprietors, two clever, raucous Jewish brothers, conducted the shop; the dull hours of the afternoon they intrusted the task to their bald-headed old father, a man who could neither read nor write. He had, however, a gift for friendliness, and he and Barkley Cooper enjoyed exchanging views. They were nearly of an age. Mr. Rabonwitz, dreadfully untidy, patient, endowed with compassion for all forms of defeat, listened more with his winking black beads of eyes than with his ears, partially curtained by a curly white beard. He wore a skull cap, which Barkley Cooper thought would have been the better for a thorough brushing. His criticism covered an envy of the old Jew, who had an occupation, one suited apparently to his failing strength.

"Still on the job, eh, Mr. Rabonwitz?"

"Going strong, Mr. Cooper. You want the home edition, eh?"

They grinned amiably, standing just inside the narrow entrance. The dim shop, heavy with the odor of sticky syrups, had no windows in its side walls. The Jew, kneeling stiffly to cut the cord tied around a package of papers, repeated defiantly, "Still going strong. My daughter Reba, she writes again for me to come and live with her. But till my boys are married—no."

His customer, who knew that the three cooked and ate and slept in two topsy-turvey rooms behind the store, listened with concern to the heavy breathing of the other. "Maybe this work's too much for you. Carrying in the bundles off the street, and all that."

"I can still work. If Ben gets married next fall, I go into the Sons of Israel Home for the Aged, a fine place where I have nothing to do."

Barkley Cooper took the paper extended to him and dropped two pennies into the counter cash tray. "I can't see this living in a Home. Not when a man's got children. You've got three, well able to support you."

The shopkeeper's little eyes disappeared in the wrinkled network of a smile. "For why should I be a burden on my kids? As long as a man can help, he has a right to be around. After that, no. Give the young a chance. Reba and her husband have four of their own. My boys have to get ahead, don't they?" He paused, then added simply, "I had bad luck with my first marriage. No children. So I am old before my sons are settled in life."

"I shouldn't think your children would let you go into a Home." Barkley Cooper drew himself up as if he, like his principles, were on parade. "My sons and daughters wouldn't hear of it for me."

The other explained mildly that he, not his children, had proposed the plan. A grand home for the aged, the Sons of Israel offered an old man the comfort of companions his own age. "If you move slow, you don't get in somebody's way. They cook soft things, if your teeth ain't so good. Where everybody's old, you ain't a special case. It stands to reason old folks and young folks want different things."

A little flurry of customers displaced the old Gentile, who assured himself that the idea of a Home was a Jew idea and dumb. Living on charity, that's what it amounts to, fumed Barkley Cooper, letting his feet drag a little as he walked. Nobody but a Jew could be happy in with a raft of strangers. 'Tain't natural to live separate from your kith and kin, the old man brooded. If I—or Lucy—ever get shunted into a Home, I hope the good Lord takes us quick. The pink glory of a magnolia tree fastened on the edges of his consciousness, and he told himself that the magnolias were late this year.

From the gutter a small brown dog watched him, tentatively wagging its tail each time it fancied itself observed. He could have sent it flying with a wave of his arm. Instead he whistled and the pathetically friendly creature trotted toward him. "What's your name, Boy? Nice little fellow—there! That's all. Sorry I haven't got a bone for you." He patted the wriggling body and motioned the dog back. Without looking round, he knew that the animal followed him. What a fool I am, talking to him, he chided himself. Now I've got him on my hands. If Grace wasn't so all-fired set in her ways, I could maybe keep him. He's a good breed. "Go back!" he ordered the dog, which stopped and stared at him attentively, as if anxious to understand and please. "I said, go back!" He pretended to hurl a stone. The dog crouched, but the pleading, shining eyes beamed with faith and good will. The old man sat down on the porch steps of a convenient house and took the dog's head between his hands. "You see, old fellow, it's like this—" he explained about Grace who didn't like dogs. He must just go on about his business and not follow his new friend home. "You don't want to get me into trouble, do you?" The dog thumped his tail, and as the old man rose, ran a little distance ahead. He waited, his ecstatic small body alive with yearning to serve his new master's pleasure, willing to obey every command except that to desert him.

"What's that dog doing on the front steps?" demanded Grace, who marketed on her way home and usually arrived with an armful of bursting paper bags.

Her father-in-law feigned surprise. "A dog? Oh, that must be the one that followed me. He's a spaniel, I think, Grace. That's a good breed."

Grace, shaking spinach into a pan, muttered that all breeds looked alike to her. She didn't intend to have a tramp dog tracking up her front stoop. "Go chase him off, won't you, Father? Likely as not he'll howl and keep us awake all night."

"Why don't we keep him in the cellar till morning?" The old man wished that Richard would come in; Richard had had a spaniel when he was a little boy. "He's probably some one's lost dog, and they may advertise for him. You can tell he's been a pet, Grace."

No one was interested in the dog. Richard, Dariel, and John, crowding into the kitchen a few moments later, had not even noticed the pleading little creature. Dariel, who looked twelve and was twenty, wanted to hurry through dinner, to sew on a new dress. The driving urge to finish one job in order to begin another motivated the entire family like a curse. Industry as relentless as any machine dominated the individuals to whom leisure was a term of reproach. The old man, genuinely bewildered by ceaseless activity that terminated only with complete exhaustion, marveled at the force that sought expression solely in physical labor. The dominating spirit of the household, Grace, preached that idleness was sloth and sin. She constantly scored her father-in-law because he produced nothing. The same reasoning accounted for her hostility to pets: dogs and cats and the like ate their heads off, she said significantly. They made no return for their food. She demanded visible interest on her investments, whether of money or time. Her shrewd calculations discounted intangible benefits with the result that, as she boasted, for every penny or every moment expended she had something to show.

Barkley Cooper, unable to forget the dog, ate his well-cooked dinner silently, as had become his habit. He frowned a little over his plate. They all did, for the glare of the electric bulbs tried their eyes. Grace demanded plenty of light, as she insisted on plenty of substantial food. She did most of her housework and all of her baking at night. Her father-in-law, avoiding her restless, boring gaze, told himself that she even ate as if the devil were after her. She made a business of stoking her flat, compact body. Her sandy hair, clipped short, stood up in spikes. She neglected her thin dry skin, so that it usually burned brick red. The old man, who had a theory that women should look pretty, hoped she wouldn't succeed in spoiling Dariel's looks.

Not, he admitted, surreptitiously studying his grandson's wife, that Dariel was exactly pretty. She was too little, too colorless, too scrawny, for that. He suspected she could be lovely when she developed, if she ever did develop, for her tiny features were perfectly formed. She had soft, thick, rather coarse dark hair that fluffed out as a frame for her pointed face, ivory-skinned, very smooth and fine. Her eyes were dark, her mouth delicately modeled. She was rather curiously proud of the fact that she wore a size eleven dress and her reedy

voice suggested the tones of a child. There was something of the child, too, in her attitude toward her
mother-in-law. Dariel, apparently submissive, able to
work in harmony with the older woman, chattered like
a magpie to her young husband when they were alone.
The steady murmur of her quickened voice in their
bedroom over the living-room sometimes wakened the
grandfather long after midnight.

It was from Dariel that he begged a plate of scraps,
when the two women cleared the table. He had known
the dog would be waiting, and he fed it with guilty
haste, weighing in his mind the chances of enlisting
Richard's sympathy. A bed in the warm, dry cellar,
near the work bench would be ideal for a stray. He did
induce his son to come out and inspect the animal, but
Richard vetoed the plan.

"No use, Dad." Richard's beautiful, rich voice
matched his handsome dark face. "If we keep him one
night, he'll think he lives here. Grace would raise the
devil. She says dogs shed hairs in the house and dig
up the garden. None of us could look after a dog during the day. You know that."

"I could." His father thought what it would mean
to have something alive to love and care for through
the empty day.

Grace had overheard. She stood behind them, her
apron fluttering in the wind. "Don't forget you won't

be here more than two or three months," she said to her
father-in-law.

It was funny, the little things you remembered when
you were upset. Barkley Cooper, who opened the front
door the next morning to find the stiff body of the little
spaniel dog at the bottom of the steps, recalled the bit
of steak he had not dared carry out to him. It seemed
to the old man as he examined the pathetic, blood-
stained mass of soft hair, that it would not have been so
tragic if only for his last supper the dog had had meat.
Dogs liked meat. He was still fumbling with the body
when Dariel discovered him.

"Grandpa! What happened?" She knelt on the
pavement, not offering to touch the dog, but staring at
the old man.

He smoothed one forepaw gently. "An automobile
musta hit him. He was trying to crawl up our steps
when he died. He thought he lived here, I guess." To
his surprise she began to cry. "Don't cry, Dariel. A
little dog is better off out of harm's way. He didn't
have any friends, this fellow didn't."

"Don't. Don't." Her tears rained on the matted
hair. "Oh, Grandpa, he only wanted to love us! We
drove him away and *he looked back*. I can't stop remembering how he looked back, hoping we'd call
him." But she sobbed as if for an older, deeper grief.

The old man helped her to her feet, patting her

shoulder, murmuring, "It's all right, it's all right." He
watched her enter the house, then he sat down on the
steps, resting his hand on the spaniel's rigid head. It's
tough for even a dog to have to die alone, he thought.

Grace had only one passion, her house. She had
lived in rented homes for the first fifteen years of her
marriage, and no real-estate dealer ever quoted the advantages of home ownership more fervently than did
she. Her husband, a drifter by nature, acquiesced without cooperating, a tendency that hampered the accumulation of the down payment cash. However, despising
renters, her father-in-law and mother-in-law included,
Grace had doggedly saved. She had engineered the
purchase of a new house in an uninspired development
and the financing must cripple their combined income
for years to come. Buying in good times she had paid
too much for a not particularly well-constructed house,
but in her mind it represented all her dreams come
true. She felt that she and Richard had provided for
their old age. Real estate she believed represented the
only solid investment; no misfortune could overwhelm
those who had their home free and clear. When John
married, so closely had she calculated every penny, the
loss of his board presented an acute problem. She
settled it by suggesting that he and his bride live with
her, until they had saved enough for a separate home.
"Don't waste your money on rent," Grace advised her

son. She herself had worked almost without interrup-
tion since her marriage, and it did not occur to her that
Dariel could have any other plans than to continue to
earn. An able-bodied woman who didn't bring in a
salary was an anomaly to Grace. No matter how much
a husband earned, any sensible wife must agree that
two salaries were better than one. Grace honestly regretted the time she had lost in bearing John. She actually computed the amount in terms of her weekly wage.
Not that she didn't love her only child, she explained,
but in one way and another he had kept her from business almost a year.

She worked indefatigably and assumed that every
member of her household expected to do the same.
The phrases she used to describe herself, "never idle,"
or "not one to fold my hands," she regarded as praise.
She employed no help and work she accomplished evenings allowed her no time for relaxation or amuse-
ment. Her husband and son usually sought their workshop in the cellar where they had a radio. Dariel, if
she didn't do housework, sewed.

The problem of her father-in-law vexed Grace. She
complained that he drove her wild, with his dawdling
ways. There was nothing she could trust him to do in
her absence, for he refused to follow her instructions
unless she stood over him. Often during the day she
worried lest he upset her neat house. At night she
found him more in the way than ever, since he began

to yawn at an early hour. He would have gone peacefully to bed in the living-room at half-past nine, if she had not restrained him. Callers were few, but Grace declined to have her living-room torn apart in a general upheaval before ten o'clock. On the infrequent occasions when they had guests, the old man exasperated her by wandering in and out of the room, eying the davenport significantly.

Grace considered a telephone an extravagance— "We're home so little"—and its absence afforded her a ready excuse for not communicating with her husband's relatives. As she never visited any of them, they paid her no calls. Nellie, she suspected, would bring her mother to see the old father, if asked, but Grace intended to discourage any such plan. Old people, she argued to her silent husband, were peculiar; if the couple were reunited, say for only an afternoon, they might cling to each other, and look at the trouble that would mean! "If George and Anita can't take them both, it's certainly out of the question for us. We've got to get our home paid for."

The factory laid off Richard the first of May. Stunned, he sat in the kitchen till midnight, staring at the opposite wall. He had never been articulate, and his only skill for expression lay in his finely formed hands. He found a medium of escape in his tool-bench. But he couldn't work at home in the daytime, because it humiliated him to remember that his wife earned

and he did not. He left each morning to make the
rounds of the various shops and persistently stayed out
till his usual quitting time. Evenings he worked steadfastly on a cabinet with fitted drawers, a difficult and
absorbing design.

A week later John announced that he had been cut
to two days a week. The usual references to overpro-
duction meant nothing to either man. John, barely
twenty-one, gentle-mannered, boyish, had gone to work
at sixteen. His narrow chest and pinched features suggested a tendency to tubercular complaints. Indeed he
had endured several long and serious illnesses. He and
his tiny wife, bewildered by the demands of living, had
felt a real gratitude to the dominating personality of
Grace, who upon their marriage had taken them in
charge. John had never wished to break away, but
Dariel occasionally rebelled. She continued to pay their
board after John's cut, and Grace announced that by
practising extra economies, she could keep up the pay-
ments on the house.

The old man on the fringe of these lives listened, always hoping that a confidence might be addressed to
him. He sympathized, he offered advice, he dipped
into his memories, but his only audience was himself.
Especially did he long to comfort Richard, who was
never otherwise than kind; Richard, who had been
such a gay, talkative lad and who had grown into such
a silent man. The old father, watching Richard plane

a board with swift, even strokes, longed to be necessary to such a son. Yet Richard's son apparently didn't confide in *him*. The younger generation, it must be, disliked to consult with the old. Richard thinks I'd meddle, reflected Richard's father, and John probably thinks the same of *his* father. Reluctantly the old man admitted that between the generations, as between all men, the possession or the lack of money influenced relationships. The young listened more patiently to the old, if Experience had gold behind it. He wished ardently that he had money to give Richard so that he might feel at ease with Grace.

"He's lucky to have a good wife who makes the most of every penny," Grace liked to proclaim. "I'm sure our meals are as good as when I had more money to spend on them. I'm meeting the building and loan, too. You don't hear me reminding Richard that my salary, and the little Dariel brings in, keeps us going, either."

Nevertheless, her father-in-law knew that she subtly nagged Richard about his jobless state. Her catechism, sharp and searching, exhausted him each night.

When Dariel's married sister died suddenly, Grace insisted that Richard accompany the young couple to the services. "Under the circumstances, I won't ask for a day off," said Grace, an intimation that she, the main support of the family, dared not jeopardize her employment.

The sister had died in childbirth. The evening after
the funeral, Dariel astonished her grandfather by demanding permission of John to adopt the baby. The
old man, reading the paper in the kitchen, could see
from his chair the dining-room table where John and
Dariel had spread a jigsaw puzzle. Dariel, wraith-like
in her black gown, said out of a long silence, "John,
why don't we adopt Edith's darling little girl?"

"Why, it's only a couple of days old!" John, startled,
expostulated.

Dariel smiled wanly as she declared that made no
difference. "She will be just like our own. You always say we can't afford babies, so maybe this one is
meant for us."

In the kitchen the old man rustled his paper, but
they paid no heed to him. If he had sat in the same
room, they would have treated him like a table or
chair. John argued that there was more to raising children than paying doctors' fees. Kids required milk and
cod-liver oil, and cotton, and boric acid. He glibly
rattled off a list of necessaries without, however, im-
pressing his wife.

"Even with you working only two days a week, we
could manage," insisted Dariel, exactly as if she had
not heard him. "Of course, we couldn't stay here and
pay your mother board. We'd have to have our own
place. Or maybe my mother would have us stay with

her. She'd take care of the baby in the daytime for me."

John, fretfully turning the puzzle pieces, asserted she was crazy. She couldn't keep her job and bring up a baby, too. Besides, he added resentfully, it was no time to pull out now and leave *his* mother in the lurch. "You seem to forget how good she was to us when we married. She needs a little help now herself."

"What about the baby?" Dariel's thin voice rose passionately. "My own sister's baby, who has to go through life without any mother? I'm sick and tired of doing for old folks! I want a baby because it's alive and young."

Her husband said, "When we get a little better fixed, maybe we'll have our own." He lit a cigarette, though he had been warned smoking aggravated his chest condition.

He made her laugh, Dariel countered bitterly. What chance had they to get better fixed? As things were now, they made, between them, enough to pay their board and buy their share of gas. "I can't see why we have to help your father and mother pay for this house. They can manage their own affairs. Edith's baby needs us."

"It's got a father." Frowning, John tapped a piece into place. "Sure it has and he'll marry—well, I mean someone will look after the baby all right. But if Mother and Dad lose their home, who's going to look after them? You know the trouble Dad is having to find another job. The older he gets, the harder it will be. I couldn't walk out on them now, Dariel, could I?"

She began to cry, and broken phrases, mixed with her sobbing, betrayed repressions that even in her anger and grief she tried frantically to conceal. Her stifled tones carried intermittently to the old man in the kitchen, who paced the creaking floor, bewildered, uneasy, knowing himself forgotten and unwilling to direct attention to his presence.

She wanted some life of her own, Dariel cried fiercely. John's father and mother and grandfather— what were they to her? Her own home, her own children, were what every woman married for; and she had nothing, nothing, the young voice stormed. Only a husband who wasn't willing for her to mother her dead sister's child. "When we've been married fifty years, like your grandfather, we won't have as much as he has, at the rate we're going now." Dariel's swimming eyes in her white, desolate face stared into the kitchen but saw nothing. "Your grandfather gets taken care of because he had children. Your mother has you. I suppose I can go to the poorhouse in my old age." Not, she added in a final whirlwind of anger, that she would let her children, if she had any, support her. She *hated* grasping parents. Then, using both hands, she swept John's almost completed picture into a hopeless jumble and ran out of the room.

Her husband patiently packed the puzzle in its box and wandered to the kitchen, where his grandfather, uncertain what to say, said nothing. John listened to the sound of his father's saw in the cellar workshop. "After forty it's not so easy to pick up a job," he asserted with a peculiar firmness, as if he upheld an argument. He glanced at his grandfather, then away again. "I guess the funeral got on Dariel's nerves." Another pause. "She's always been mad for kids." As he opened the door leading to the cellar, the murmur of his parents' voices mingled with the filing noise of the saw. "They're both good sports," said John.

Dariel might linger mornings, if she chose. She did not have to reach her office till nine o'clock. When she wanted to press a frock or finish a bit of sewing, she let the others go without her in the car. The grandfather discovered her in the kitchen the next morning, ironing the wrinkled pleats in the black skirt she had worn to her sister's funeral. Her lighted cigarette rested on the edge of a thick china saucer beside the board.

"You tell John tonight," she directed the old man, her sullen small mouth taking a bitter twist, "that I won't be home for dinner. I'm going to Mom's to see Edith's baby. He needn't bother to call for me, either. I can get home. Not that he'd worry about me—a man who doesn't care what happens to a motherless child."

The brown old face mildly admonished her. "Now,

now. John hopes you'll have little ones of your own, some day."

She whirled, leaving the skirt a narrow black funnel on the board. "Do you think I'm going to have children? Never!"

Her husband's grandfather had often said to himself that her narrow body was not of child-bearing build. She was too small, too frail to have children with the easy graciousness that wide-hipped women seemed to him to bring to the task. His own wife, for instance. Lucy had carried herself splendidly in five pregnancies. He sniffed the odor of new black dye, and because he disliked the smell, he decided that he also disliked this discussion. A young woman had no business talking about her children before they were born. Dariel's notions were all twisted, anyway—as tipsy as her high heels. He scowled at the patent leather pumps encasing her slim feet. "All normal couples want children of their own. For your sake, Dariel, I hope you don't come to a childless old age."

Dariel puffed at her cigarette, dipping her pressing cloth in the basin of water as she smoked. "My childless old age will save my kids the trouble of taking care of me. I'd rather go to the poorhouse, than be a drag on my children's lives."

A low painted chest stood against one wall. The old man sat down on this, hoping to conceal the weariness that assailed him lately if he tried to stand. "I'm sure

I don't feel that I'm a drag on any one's life. Nor that my wife is. We had five children, remember. It's only fair for children to pay back some of the care their parents give them. There's such a thing as decent gratitude. My children have it for me. John feels it for his ma and pa."

The vivid scarlet lips of the girl at the ironing-board released one word. "Yeah?"

"You're young, Dariel, and some of your terrible heartlessness is just for effect, I know." He wanted to be lenient, but righteousness mounting within him stirred him to preach. "Any man and woman who have had a child, cared for it, worked and slaved for it, have an everlasting claim on that child. When the parents are helpless and old, it should be that child's pleasure to do for them. Let him remember that but for them he would have died, since a baby is a very helpless thing."

Dariel, bearing down on her iron as vapor sifted through the cloth, eyed him defiantly. "A baby can't help its dependent state. It's born like that. If parents are helpless in their old age, it's their own fault."

"Now you're impertinent." He found it natural to reprove her, for she looked like such a little girl, in spite of her cigarette and lip-stick. "As a matter of fact, Dariel, you don't know what you're talking about. If parents reach their old age penniless, it's because they have sacrificed for their children till they had nothing

left." It seemed to him now that that must be the explanation of his own life. A vagueness, confusing as a
fog, hampered his thoughts when he tried to remember
why he had not saved; he must, he convinced himself
at such uneasy intervals, have spent it all on the children.

His granddaughter lit a fresh cigarette and tossed the
flaming match into the sink. "That's nothing to crow
about. If you did that, you made a big mistake. Do
you know what I think's the most important duty in all
the world? For each one to have enough to keep him
decently in his old age. If a couple can't have children
without being supported by those children later in life,
they haven't any right to have kids. Let them save
their money instead." She breathed as if she had been
running.

The old man stared at her, a growing horror in his
gaze. What kind of a creature was she, this thin, pale
girl who was without religion and without awe? "You
don't think you know more than God Almighty, do
you, Dariel?" He moistened his dry lips with his
tongue. "It's the plan of God for married couples to
increase and multiply. The young folks have a duty to
the old, to care for and provide for them. That's what
keeps the world going. You can't fight the universal
laws, my dear."

She thought of her father-in-law, patient, subdued,
tortured in his weeks of idleness by shame. Not by

word or action did Richard hint that the burden of his old father's support added to the load he carried. Dariel thought of her own husband, of herself, bound by ties of pity and so-called duty to the same wheel. Suddenly she wanted to scream. The iron crashed on its metal stand. "You make me sick!" She clenched her hands. "It's no use arguing with you about what children owe their parents. That's bunk, but you believe in it. What about me?" She flamed, tense and vivid against the cold gray-and-white of the kitchen walls. "What about me? If John's father and mother owe you so much, and John and I owe his parents, too, where do I come in? I'm only John's wife. I can't have my own home, I can't have my own babies, I can't look forward to seeing John get ahead. We're young, and we've got to nurse the older generation. That's what people have children *for*, isn't it? The golden chain of life, I heard some damn fool minister call it. Well, if you ask me, it's a hell of a way to strangle us to death."

He hated her cigarettes and her profanity, but still more he was aghast at the deplorable state of mind her words revealed. "I took care of my father and mother," he said stubbornly. "Was glad to do it, too."

Dariel tossed her butt into the saucer with one hand and disconnected the iron with the other. She deftly slid off the skirt and folded the board, which closed on its legs like a dog on his haunches. Her glittering dark

eyes scorned the old man as she turned in the doorway.
"Maybe you did take care of your father and mother,
but why don't you tell the whole truth? Fifty years
ago, when you married, things were different. Your
mother knitted and made quilts and helped with the
sewing and cooking and preserving. Yes, and you had
a horse and a cow, and your father helped you take
care of them and worked the garden. John's father
told me. They *earned* their keep. You can't compare
today with then." She was like a person in a blind
frenzy, unable to stop dealing blows. In her normal
state she shrank from brutality, but now she delighted
in every cruel word. "Besides, you didn't have to take
care of your father so long, at that," she thrust. "I read
only the other day that people a couple of generations
ago died younger than they do now. The span of life,
the article said, has been prolonged. That means dependent old people may be a burden on their children
for twenty or thirty years." Her laugh had an ugly
sound. "No kid gets a break like that. I was on my
own at sixteen."

After she had clicked down the front steps on her
stilts, the old man remembered that he had not had the
two glasses of water he considered essential for his
health. But when he reached the sink he forgot
to fill his glass. Why, he pondered, nipping a dead
leaf off the sickly geranium Dariel cherished on the
window-sill above the sink, why were the young girls

of today so *hard?* Dariel, who was so little and delicately made, and who ought to be lovable and sweet,
Dariel was like a piece of flint-rock. He could have
understood a girl who cried, or drooped forlornly, but
not a termagent who blew smoke in his face and swore
at him. It must be, he decided, his mind sore and sluggish and heavy with some undefined pain, that business
debased them. Grace was cold and calculating, Dariel
without tenderness. An army of women like them
labored in office, factory and shop, women tense, cynical, hard-eyed. Yes, business robbed women of their
refinement, their gentle qualities.

"My wife," said Barkley Cooper to Mr. Rabonwitz
that afternoon, "was always a sheltered woman. My
mother, too. I don't hold with women working downtown."

Chapter Nine

G RACE began to set Richard tasks each morning, fussily detailed, endless jobs. To polish and repolish, dust and scrub, paint, varnish and wax surfaces already immaculate and seldom used, filled his days. "It makes me sick to see a man sit around doing nothing," his wife said. An unemployed husband marred her record for efficiency, and she pressed him into her service with an eagerness to utilize waste power that was characteristic of her lack of tact.

Her father-in-law perceived that this passionately industrious woman regarded him, not as an idle machine, but as an obsolete pattern, rusted out. She couldn't order him taken up and set aside, but his presence constantly irritated her, hampered her drive. The old man, watching her tireless energy, recalled Dariel's reference to his own parents; fifty years ago there *had* been a place for the elderly in the homes of their young. "People don't live right any more," he complained to his son. "Look at you and Grace. You've got a five-room house on a forty-foot lot. There's no more housework than one woman could do, if she stayed home to do it. With Dariel to help, there ain't anything to do but refine your old dust, as my Aunt Dilly used to say."

He elaborated his theme for the benefit of Mr. Rabonwitz in the increasingly lengthened periods he spent
in the paper store. There ought to be family jobs for
men past seventy, he asserted, such a job as Mr. Rabonwitz enjoyed. "I could tend store, if any of my boys
kept a place." To himself Barkley Cooper added that
he'd clean up this mess, if he were in charge. Neatness
was not a Rabonwitz trait.

"When my sons marry, I have no job." Papa Rabonwitz smiled. "But there is still the Sons of Israel Home.
And I have my violin." He hesitated a moment, natural courtesy struggling with his desire to speak freely.
"Your boys never go in business by themselves? Jews
like their own stores." It was beyond his ability to explain that his music, as a resource within himself, filled
in many lonely hours, so he merely added, "The music
is good, too, for the old."

"There's some good things on the radio." Barkley
Cooper intimated, however, that one couldn't listen to
music, nor read all the time. "I got to keep busy with
my *hands*. I want to earn money so's I can pay my
own carfare at least."

Richard and John no longer had small coins to give
him for tobacco money or for stamps. Dariel, if she
happened to shed her armor of resentment, sometimes
remembered to hand him a quarter. He liked her so
much when compassion softened her that it did not
hurt him to be the recipient of her alms. Her unhap-

piness and his, though widely divergent, formed a kind
of bond between them.

Now that John had work only two days a week, he
tried to sell on commission in his spare time. His efforts at least kept him out of the house, for, as his
mother remarked, three men at home all day would be
"just too much." John used the car in his salesmanship
campaigns, and Dariel, who furnished money to buy
the gas, argued constantly against the plan. She complained, with justice, that there was nothing to can-
vassing, that the money needed for gas and lunches
could at least be saved. John made no sales, but he
doggedly tried one scheme after another and was able
to be optimistic about each for a day or two.

Late one afternoon he drove up to the curb to find
his grandfather sitting in an attitude of dejection on the
front steps. John, whose day had been a total failure,
slumped wearily beside the old man. The thin young
face was set in lines of utter weariness. "Going's tough,
Grandpop."

"Wait till you get to be my age." The old man stared
resentfully, envy edging his voice. "There's no call to
be discouraged when you're young."

John flung out his hands. "For God's sake, where's
the advantage in being young? I'm not getting anywhere. Dariel and I are no better off than when we
married, two years ago. Being young doesn't get you a

thing." But he straightened as he spoke, moved by a thankfulness for his flexible body as he contrasted it with the shriveled, stooped figure beside him. My God, it's hideous to be old, he thought, and the thought renewed his hope. Nothing was permanently lost, neither success nor hope, till Time sucked one into the last trap, old age.

"You've got your life before you." His grandfather's hazel eyes, bright still under the drooping lids, studied him. "Why, after a while when you have your own house and the babies begin to come, you'll be sitting on top of the world. A man always works better when he has a family to do for."

John said, "Forget it." He stood up, his cheap suit wrinkled, though he had carefully pressed it the night before. "We're not going to have kids. I aim to keep out of the poorhouse, and my wife's of a similar mind."

"Children keep you out of the poorhouse." His grandfather puckered bushy gray eyebrows reprovingly.

The young man repressed his desire to shout, "You poor damn fool!" He bit his lip, reflecting scornfully on the capacity of the aged for dodging the truth. I loathe, I despise, the dependency you accept, he wanted to say. I'll be damned if I'm ever the burden on my children that you are on my parents. The whole rotten system is wrong. The old have no right to drag on the young. Seeing the old man wished to rise, John helped him carefully to his feet. "Your dope's all bunk,

Grandpop. If we have kids, we can't save for our old age. If we save for our old age, we can't have kids. The arithmetic books left that one out, but it's easy to figure."

His grandfather followed him into the kitchen. Through the window they could see Richard kneeling, weeding the lettuce planted in a double row. He looked large and dark and vastly patient in the small plot. As they watched, a spray of the rambler, trained on the picket fence, caught his sleeve; he detached it gently, as if the leaves had been human fingers. The old man remembered how Richard as a small boy had helped his mother in the garden. She had boasted that he never bruised nor destroyed a single growing thing. A vivid picture of the old garden, the old house, and his family, as he had seen them one hot summer afternoon rose in Barkley Cooper's mind. His wife had worn a blue dress . . . Then he heard John shuffling toward the stairway, and the urge to admonish the young and foolish, which is one of the most distressing manifestations of old age, crowded to his lips. "It isn't a marriage without children," he said inanely.

John, his coat over his arm, his shirt open at the neck, preparatory to washing up, paused. "Oh, yeah?" Derisive laughter grated in his throat.

Barkley Cooper experienced the thrill of the explorer when he first discovered the farmers' market for himself. He had entered the main market building on a

warm June day to escape the glare of the sun. Inside
he found cool aisles of iced fish, avenues of vegetables,
fresh and green. He lingered at the delicatessen coun-
ters to sniff the odors of sliced meats, cheese and horse-
radish, freshly ground. Strange fruits amazed him.
He paused to appraise the chops and steaks mounted
behind glass like jewelers' wares. The wide, bluff faces
of the market men pleased him. People who dealt in
food-stuff, he decided, usually looked well-fed themselves. They testified to the worth of their products.

The old man, wandering slowly through the long,
narrow building, regretted that Grace did her marketing in the cash-and-carry stores. She occasionally
visited the city market on Saturday and filled the car
with her purchases, but she considered the neighborhood shops cheaper for her daily wants. Her father-in-
law, eying a slab of beef—you couldn't get a roast like
that in a chain store!—would have enjoyed buying
something to take home to her. He had only a nickel,
however, and he had already walked so far he knew he
must ride back. He said to the scarlet-faced butcher
who peered at him over the high counter, "A fine cut
of beef, that!" and passed from the contemplation of
beef to the fragrance of the oyster bars.

Blissfully smeared with butter, the faces of the pa-
trons enjoying the seasonable steamed clams or chowder, grinned amiably at him as he marched resolutely
past. Mountains of salty crackers, battalions of chili

sauce bottles, tempted the hungry to pause. Basins of vivid pink shrimp, scarlet lobsters on beds of cracked ice, promised delicious fare. He had had nothing to eat since breakfast. It was now half-past two. The habit of going without lunch, fostered by what he considered excellent reasons, had lately grown on him. For one thing, he disliked to eat alone. Or, if Richard were home, his silence was worse than the solitude of unbroken thought. Then, too, the old man had recently developed a finicky appetite, much to his disgust. He must pick and choose, he scolded himself, when the bowl of cold boiled rice or the dish of fried potatoes Grace left for him failed to tempt. Partly as a matter of discipline, he had begun to omit the noon meal. It also saved the trouble of returning to the house when, as now, he found himself downtown.

Yet the buttery, steamy clouds of sea-food incense that hovered over these homely bars penetrated to the hollow of his empty stomach. He longed to hoist himself up on one of the painted stools, tuck a checked napkin under his chin, and nibble crackers while he waited for his order to be filled. The thought of his solitary nickel steadied him, and he pushed open a swinging door to find himself unexpectedly on an open square.

The farmers' market spread before him, a gay border, beginning to wilt in the heat. Most of the trading was over for the day, and some of the trucks had already

pulled out, leaving gaps at the curb. At other stands
family groups fanned themselves with folded newspapers and drank iced beer. A few women shoppers
with deep netted bags on their arms moved slowly
from truck to truck. Rotting fruits and vegetables
filled the refuse cans. A farmer chopping ice for his
butter crocks, nodded to the old man and pointed out
an upturned basket. "Sit a spell, Brother. You're
purple from the sun. Summer's early this year."

A slight feeling of giddiness vanished as Barkley
Cooper took the offered seat. The truck cast a narrow
shade. From under its awning a voice said, "Would
you care for a glass of cold buttermilk?" A woman,
gowned in black, her hair as white as her apron, smiled
down at him. She was as serene as if she stood in her
kitchen doorway.

"Well—" He hesitated. If he spent his nickel
now——

"I'm not selling it. One of my customers cancelled
her order and left two quarts on my hands." She
smoothed her apron with a gesture he remembered as
like his wife's.

The man, whose resemblance to her identified him
as her son, said, "Sure he'll have a glass, Ma. So'll I.
Ice-cold buttermilk needn't go begging a day like this."

Barkley Cooper had never been fond of buttermilk,
but he gratefully accepted the tall, thick glass. Perhaps if he drank something the trembling in his knees

would cease. Across the square he saw an old man,
surely as old as himself, presiding over a vegetable
stand. The crimson of tomatoes made a splash of
color against the dark and light greens. The old
farmer, bareheaded in the blazing sun, sat on a high
stool shelling something, most likely peas.

A wandering, friendly conversation, in which the
mother asked many questions, and her son managed
to include himself though busily sorting a barrel of
early cabbages, did more than the buttermilk to revive
their tired old guest. Contact with small-town minds
and interests, from which he had been long shut off,
roused him to feel the importance of an individual
again. These people spoke his language. He wanted
to hear what they did for a living, how they managed,
something of their family relationships, as they questioned his. The old woman proudly announced that
she kept house for her son. She had three married
children, but no one could hire her to live with them.
"I pray every night that Dave won't marry till I die,"
she confided in a moment when her son had gone to
fetch a second barrel. Her home, she added, was just
as her husband had left it. "Dave's a good son, but no
wife of his would want to use my old things." She
quoted the old saw, "A daughter's a daughter all the
days of her life; a son's a son till he gets him a wife,"
but added that she couldn't be persuaded to live under
the roof of a son-in-law. "An old person like me's

entitled to her own home. We can't be moved around like trunks. I guess you know that, trying to live as you do."

Her son, rolling an empty barrel over the curb, heard the end of her speech. "Folks can't be always choosers, Ma." He hoisted the barrel to the truck, and his mother rolled it inside.

"There don't seem to be a place for old folks any more." Barkley Cooper crushed a cabbage leaf under his foot. He had removed his hat, and his front peak of hair straggled limply wet on his forehead.

The farmer's light blue shirt showed large dark wet patches across his back and under his arms. He was about fifty-five, muscular, lean. His shrewd, kindly face puckered when he meditated. "Well, now, it's worse in the city, ain't it? Most everything is. Out with us there's always room for the old folks and plenty to keep 'em busy. I never saw a farm with too much help, yet."

"Maybe on a farm," said the old man. He meant that perhaps on a farm the situation was more hopeful, but unexpectedly the effort to talk wearied him.

"You have to hand it to the Eyetalians and the Jews," pursued the farmer. "Them families makes a place for the old fathers and mothers. Know why? It's because there's always a store to tend or a vegetable stand, something light, where the old folks can sit down. They don't even have to be able to speak English. We got a store at the crossroad, kept by Eyetalians. The mother's nearly eighty and can't speak an American word. She sits in a chair all day—she must weigh two hundred—and shines up the fruit. Doesn't do another damn thing but polish stuff and wrap it up in tissue-paper."

His listener recalled Mr. Rabonwitz' theory that working for an employer was bad. A man who was his own boss could provide jobs for his kith and kin. "I don't suppose you know of anything I could do?" He held his head down, for if Richard and John could find no work, what chance had an old man?

The brisk mother of the farmer peered out from the canvas side curtains that hid her mysterious activities in the interior of the truck. "Could he fill in for Cousin James, Dave?"

"It's washing dishes at the oyster bar," the farmer explained. "My mother's cousin had to fire his man 'cause he was drunk. It pays only twenty-five cents an hour, but you get your lunch."

Well, no one knows me, no one knows I once earned my sixty a week, reflected the old man, suddenly tremendously concerned to suppress details which might invoke the pity of these stranger folk. It seemed to him that he might preserve his pride only if no one pitied him. After all, washing dishes in a market's not much different from washing dishes in a kitchen, he stoutly reminded himself. "If your cousin will hire me, I'll take the job," he said.

The farmer lost no time in leading him to Cousin James. That opportunist welcomed the applicant on condition that he set to work at once. The rush, Cousin James declared, was over, but a stack of dishes had accumulated. "It's three o'clock now. You work till five and I'll give you fifty cents and all the chowder you can eat." He had a fairly clean apron and a pan of water heated.

Delicious hot chowder and crackers renewed strength in the old body that did not always now respond to the stimulation of food. Barkley Cooper attacked the leaning towers of soiled crockery with an energy that surprised himself. He washed and dried the thick white china for the next two hours with no intermission, except when he stopped to clean out the sink or to heat more water. The inadequate supply of dish towels annoyed him and the tiny space in which he must work hampered his movements. He feared to slip on the wet floor, slimy with garbage that had escaped the cans. Toward the end of the second hour the overpowering odor of fish from the surrounding stands sickened him, the noise of voices shouting against the loud-speaker in a near-by stall set up a ringing in his head. His feet, of which he had never been particularly conscious, throbbed and burned with a pain that dug into his arches and tunneled through the bone up

into his legs as high as his knees. The intensity of the
agony roused a dull wonder in his mind. He had never
regarded his feet as furnished with sensitive nerves.

At five o'clock new noises marked closing time.
Fire doors rattled into place with tremendous crash
after crash. Boys, pushing wide brushes, swept debris
down the aisle. Here and there an electric sign winked
out.

"Guess you'd like to be paid by the day?" Cousin
James regarded his employee with obvious approval.
"You've cleaned things up fine. Come around eleven
tomorrow, will you? I don't need nobody till near
noon, and you can get away a little after two. I got
snowed under today, 'count of that skunk getting
drunk on me."

The farmers' market lay as deserted as if the border
of trucks, the canopied stands and the friendly folk
who had lined the curb had all been dreams. Barkley
Cooper assured himself that he would see his friends
next Thursday to thank them. They came in twice
a week, they had told him.

He paid his nickel for carfare and presented the fifty-
cent piece to Dariel. "Go to the movies." He always
thought of the little oval face, colorless except for two
vivid patches of rouge, as that of a child. "Get some
candy, too," he added. To earn money, to bestow it,
was the prerogative of the male. He forgot his aching
feet.

In the morning, after a tortured, sleepless night, he discovered that he could barely stand. His extremities, puffed and discolored, were for the present quite useless. He managed to get his socks on, but not even his soft felt slippers would cover the monstrous shapeless mass of his feet. His hands, too, were swollen to twice their normal size.

"What in heaven's name were you doing?" Grace had no patience with illness or incapacity, weaknesses she frequently stated to be avoidable.

In response to her father-in-law's reluctant confession, she made no comment other than to assure him the pay was too small. Richard covertly mumbled to his father that he had no call to overtax his strength. "They're talking of putting on more help next week, and I'll be among the first to go back. You don't have to worry, Dad."

To himself Richard said that he had to lie or be a brute. He regarded the burden of his father's support as unjust; he had moments of fierce resentment against the complacency of the old man who assumed that his children owed him a home. Yet who could balance justice against pity? Only Grace succeeded in being consistently objective, and Grace was damnably hard. She loved only her house.

Four days later when Barkley Cooper returned to the market, it was to find his place filled. Cousin James explained regretfully that he had had to have help at once. "I got a coon. He can take it. I never saw a nigger yet whose feet gave out on him."

Hot nights exhausted the air in the small front room. The atmosphere thickened so that the old man fancied his breath pressed back against his lips like a suffocating cloth. He lay awake for hours, staring at the outlines of the furniture as revealed by the street light. Sometimes the fragrant smell of wet, cut grass seeped through the screens, but more often the odor of street dust, stirred by a passing car. When his back ached from lying on the seams of the davenport upholstery, he rose and sat by the window. After midnight practically all traffic ceased on the dead-end street. At long intervals a pedestrian, furtive because solitary, might hurry past. The sound of his footsteps echoed the length of the block. The old man, peering, listening, had no interest in sight or sound, except as it immediately engaged his senses. He never pondered the destination of a passer-by, nor speculated on his errand. The prolonged ringing of a 'phone bell, sharp, insistent, agonizing in its import at two o'clock in the morning, he classified merely as a definite sound. If a window in some black square of a house suddenly flared into orange light, the possibilities of illness, of birth or death, never smote him. Motionless, panting, his nightshirt clammy with perspiration, he huddled in his chair, grateful for suspended thought. Toward daybreak a cooling breeze usually freshened the stale air. Then he returned to the davenport bed, to sink into a heavy sleep. He rose groggily when Grace called him, fatigued, dazed.

The long empty days dragged hour by hour. Richard went back to the factory at reduced wages, John secured temporary employment in the suburbs that eked out a full week for him once more. The old man, again alone in the house, sat by the open windows, idle, motionless, except when the sun forced him to seek a shadier spot. The small, poorly constructed house absorbed the heat and retained it. Cheap paint blistered on the clapboards, the vines in the window-boxes bleached yellow in spite of Grace's devoted attention. She said they couldn't afford a hose, and the front lawn lacked water, even in June. Acting under her instructions, her father-in-law closed the windows at the first hint of a thunderstorm. Often he nearly suffocated in the oppressive interior, but he dared not run the risk of letting the rain spot the varnished window-sills. He had no thin suits, and he insisted on wearing his coat because his wife had never liked him to go coatless in the house. They wrote each other less and less frequently; indeed, concentrated thought on his part had become laborious. He followed no topic through in his solitary meditations, arrived at no conclusions. Recurring worries harassed him, but he diffused his anxieties among his several problems.

Intermittently the subject of cemetery lots visited his mind, when he read of the death of men of his age, or when the papers mentioned a burial in Potter's Field. He remembered the small country cemetery where his parents lay. Once he would have been sure that his children would give him what he called a decent burial, but now, he sometimes muttered to himself, he had his doubts.

Another day the whole dreary business of death and interment might awaken only a contemplative wonder, in which he reflected that there had not been a funeral in the family for thirty years. He had never purchased a cemetery plot, and, as far as he knew, his children owned none. If he might know where he and his wife would finally rest, he fancied it might be a comfort to him; yet he remained uncritical of those who refused to make final plans. He still regarded death as one of the emergencies of life.

A breathless, humid morning in the last week in June so weighted his limbs that he found it impossible to rise. His entire body felt sticky and gummy, but his eyes burned dry in their sockets, and it hurt him to turn them. When Grace rapped on the living-room door, he called to her.

"You have some fever." She felt of his forehead and hands. "Well, I suppose you'd better lie quiet a little while." Her gaze roved over the room, betraying regret at the disorder.

She brought a basin a few moments later and sponged his face and hands. Her touch was capable, not unpleasant, but as impersonal as it was thorough. She called Richard to help her sponge and dry his body and to change his soaked nightshirt. Sickness, she told her husband as they worked over the thin old body, upset everyone's schedule. "Some one will have to stay with him."

He caught at her hand as she turned to follow Richard, who carried the wash-basin out. "Grace! Why don't you send for Lucy—for Richard's mother? She'll stay with me." Raising up on his elbow he peered at her, his hazel eyes oddly faded.

Grace refused to meet his gaze. "I must get these windows washed, soon as you're well," she said.

When Dariel came softly in with a breakfast tray, her compassion touched him. She sat on the edge of the couch and coaxed him to eat. "That's what made you sick, Grandpa. You don't eat enough."

He drank half the coffee. "I can't eat, Dariel. 'Tain't just being sick." His voice dropped to a husky whisper. "It's unhappiness wears me down, Dariel. I couldn't eat a banquet, the way I feel now." A desire to move her, to capture her sympathy urged him. He would have indignantly denied that he dramatized his suffering, but to secure her pity was distinctly a part of his deliberate plan.

Tenderness softened the girl's dark eyes. She laid

a thin little hand on the dry, withered one. "Oh, Grandpa, you know I'll do anything I can to make you happy. What is it, dear?"

"Will you telephone your grandmother? She's at your Aunt Nellie's house, you know. I want your grandmother to sit with me while I'm sick." He wriggled on the thin slab of the divan so that he nearly upset the tray. His wife, he thought fretfully, would pin the bedclothes in place, if she ever got her hands on them. "You will, won't you, Dariel?" he pleaded.

She couldn't reproach him with unfairness, but she instinctively resented the trick. The next time she would be a little less responsive to the pathos of his appeal, a little quicker to suspect an ambush. "You know Grace wouldn't like that," Dariel said.

A crafty, furtive expression narrowed the old face, yellow against the white of the pillow-case. "Dariel, nobody need know. You could 'phone on your way to the office. Don't give your name. After your Grandmother gets here, Grace can suppose she just dropped in. You don't have to worry a mite." He watched her hopefully, eager for signs of capitulation.

"Grandpa, we *can't*. Grace would guess in a minute." A nervous fear of her mother-in-law's displeasure betrayed itself in the girl's manner. Dariel glanced over her shoulder as she spoke and started when the old man clattered a spoon against his cup. At the sound of a brisk step in the hall, she seized the tray, released by the entrance of Grace from further debate.

Grace fought against her irritation each time she saw the davenport as a bed. She yearned to fold the sheets, twitch the rug straight, remove the heap of clothing from the club chair. "I'll pull the shades, and maybe you'll sleep, Father," she said with a fair imitation of kindness. "This noon I'll come home and heat some soup for you. That way Richard won't have to lose any time. John's already gone."

"I want my wife." He spoke to her back as she twitched at the curtains. "Lucy's a splendid nurse."

"What on earth do you want to worry Mother for?" Grace signed to Dariel to carry the tray away. "I should think you'd try to save her in weather like this."

The old man's hands, brown and shriveled, wandered aimlessly over the tangle of sheets. "She'd sit with me. If I'm going to be sick, she'll want to nurse me." He looked from Grace's sharp, intense face to Dariel's puzzled one, for the girl still lingered in the doorway. "I can't get out to telephone. One of you'll have to do it for me."

Grace darted at him and spread the twisted top sheet smoothly in place. "Don't talk nonsense! You won't need any nursing. This is just a let-down from the heat. You'll be as fine as silk by tomorrow." She stooped to pick a crumb from the rug, then tiptoed out of the room as a concession to the invalid.

"Send for the doctor?" Her father-in-law heard the

rising inflection of her voice ten minutes later. She
was arguing with Richard. "Your father's old, and
the heat's played him out. That's all." Richard said
something in a low voice, and Grace retorted with
shrill vehemence, "Well, if it turns out to be anything
serious, he'll have to go to the hospital, and stay there.
Better people than he have been sent to hospitals."
Again the murmur of Richard's guarded tone and the
loud resistance of his wife's. "All right, suppose you
do have the doctor for him? Who'll pay for it? You
know you can't get a cent out of your sisters or George."

The clumsy kindness of Richard, who, torn between
two loyalties, found speech more difficult than ever,
expressed itself in rather pathetic attentions, when he
hurriedly looked in to say good-by to his father. The
son carefully arranged a morning paper, matches, tobacco and a pipe, ready at hand. "You'll be feeling
better soon, Dad, and ready for a smoke." Surreptitiously he slipped a bit of change into the old man's
palm.

"Richard, will *you* 'phone your mother? I'd like to
see her. Grace don't understand, but it's been nearly
three months since your mother and me's had a talk.
You could telephone her and not mention it." His
son towered above him with a strength that comforted
the old man. Richard was neither old nor ill. His
must be a strong spirit, too.

A confusion of uncertainty harassed Richard. He

would have denied that he feared his wife, but like most men he refused to analyze his dread of her ill will. He accepted her own estimation of her virtues, which subtly belittled his. Her terrific industry blinded him. Without her, he felt, he must always fail. She practically told him so. He often temporized with his self-respect to avoid her anger, but without Grace, he had once said, he would be a bum. He tried to smile at his father. "You get well quick, Dad, and I'll take you to see Mother. That's better than having her come here."

Grace, hurrying off, repeated that she's be home at noon to heat soup for him. She intimated that he was fortunate to have nothing to do but rest quietly in bed. Even Dariel, her pallor intensified by her rouge, said wistfully that she wished she could stay in bed a whole day.

The sun filled the living-room with a humidity that, fused with the accumulated heat of the previous day, was stored in the stuffy walls. The glare penetrated every corner, burning yet damp. The old man, panting, felt his head wet on the pillow, but did not shift his position. He noted that the curtains at the windows hung limp. Not a breath of air stirred. He was expected to lie there, simmering in the cauldron, till noon. Out of the shimmering haze a memory of the palm-leaf fan his wife kept behind the clock in their dining-room formed a picture photographically clear.

It amazed him that he could trace the veiny ribs in that
familiar, ragged fan. When he closed his eyes he could
see his wife in the chair beside his present couch. She
wore a spotted blue-and-white dress. He even fancied
he felt her hand on his forehead; he would have sworn
that he caught a faint breeze wielded by the palm-leaf
fan she held. The delusion slipped from him, and his
loss renewed his resentment against Grace. He remembered that he had coins—Richard had seen to that. "I
can do my own telephoning!" His defiant voice
sounded reedy in that hot, still room.

To dress in his weakened state taxed his patience almost to the point of tears. His hands trembled, his
garments weighted him, vertigo forced him to grasp at
a chair; if it had not been for his horror of womanish
behavior, he might easily have wept. Yet, when he
finally gained the street, he told himself that he was
well. The outdoor atmosphere was less oppressive.
Some of the walks had been sprinkled and were still
damp and cool. The old man drew a deep breath. He
tried to step briskly, though after the first few efforts
he unconsciously slackened his pace. The paper store
represented his goal. Once there, he knew Mr. Rabonwitz could be relied on to look up the right number;
he would even press a stray customer into service to
operate the dial. Yes, Mr. Rabonwitz would supply a
man the assistance his own kin denied him.

A trash box on the curb tempted Barkley Cooper to

rest. No reason for killing himself, best to be careful on a day like this. A woman hugging a bag of vegetables passed, and eyed him sharply. Her competent, searching glance reminded him of his daughter-in-law, who appeared to tabulate people as she talked to them. Grace, the old man mused, would be mad when she discovered what he had done. She had a nasty tongue when she lost her temper, had Grace. Most likely she would take her fury out on Richard, because any one with half an eye could see that Richard was deathly afraid of her. Well, I'm not, maintained Richard's father firmly. My good Godie, there ain't any female living going to tell me I can't 'phone my own wife. A piercing pain, keen enough to interrupt his continuity of thought, shot between his eyes, then centered in a dull ache that throbbed. He wondered in instant alarm if it meant anything. Like a warning the reference Grace had made to the hospital repeated itself in his brain. His imagination painted for him the charity ward of a great city hospital, lined with rows of narrow beds. Out of the mass of hearsay he had accumulated over a period of time, he recollected most vividly that the nurses put a screen around the bed when they expected a patient to die. He wondered how it felt to die behind a screen with half a hundred strangers speculating on one's passing. The sweat ran down his face. He pulled himself up, standing woodenly for a moment, because he discovered that he had to think specifically of his feet before he could move them.

Very stiffly he walked on. Caution accompanied him now. If he made himself worse, he had no doubt that Grace would keep her word. She'd never let him be seriously ill in her living-room. He anticipated the arguments she would marshal to prove that the hospital was the best place for him. A sickening wave of heat from the asphalt of the street staggered him. He clutched the iron pickets of a fence and pretended to be admiring the crimson rambler that half covered it.

As he clung to the fence, a new worry attacked him. Suppose Nellie, siding with Grace, refused to give the message to her mother? He dared not hope that his wife would answer the 'phone; if Nellie were the intermediary, could he count on her loyalty? Even if she were sympathetic, she would probably compare notes with Grace. The old man frowned. Let her. My good Godie, I don't have to take any lip from Grace, he heartened himself sternly. She's got Richard where she wants him, but I'm some one else again.

"Hello, Grandpop! Out of bounds, aren't you?" The grinning young postman had swung across the street to greet him. Concern replaced the banter in the blue eyes, as he recognized the signs of illness in the tired old face. "Why, Grandpop, you're white around the gills. Don't you feel right?"

"Maybe I walked a little too far. I was sick last night." The task of getting himself home began to present insupportable difficulties. Yet one couldn't, Barkley Cooper admonished himself, voluntarily give up.

The postman, born to be an executive, hailed a lad driving a light delivery car. "Say, Buddy, give an old gent a lift? I can't leave my route to help him, and he's all in. He lives a block or two down the street—No. 34. That's not much out of your way."

Their matter-of-fact kindness impressed the old man only vaguely. He tumbled, rather than climbed, to the worn leather seat. All he had to do was to tell the youthful driver to take him to the paper store. The opportunity to 'phone his wife was in his grasp. He turned, putting his hand on the boy's bare freckled arm. Then he saw the discolored face of a clock on the dashboard. It lacked ten minutes of twelve.

Grace had said she'd be home at noon to warm the soup! The disorder of the room he had left must instantly reveal his absence, if she reached the house before he did. The idea of facing her after discovery dismayed him. He had meant to be safely in bed again before she arrived. Why, it would be a catastrophe to have Grace walk into that empty house! No one could predict what she might do, foretell what she might say. The old man's heart pounded in his side, the lining of his mouth dried. The agony of his apprehension mounted to torture, as the car slowed at an intersecting street. "Can't you *hurry*, Bub?" he urged.

Chapter Ten

" A young man has no respect for a girl who lets him talk loosely." Grandma Cooper's upper teeth took a firm pleat in her lower lip. The corners of her mouth showed tiny sprouts of black hair.

Rhoda twitched her shoulder. "Tracy's all right."

"You'll find that men don't ask such girls to marry them. It's for you to put that young fellow in his place. Then he'll respect you."

"He's already asked me to marry him." Rhoda in the porch swing stretched her slim length. She reached for her cigarette-case on a near-by chair.

Her grandmother was amazed, delighted, fluttered. She leaned forward to pat Rhoda's knee, then removed her spectacles and wiped her eyes. "Why, darling! So he's proposed! Why didn't you say something about it? Does your mother know?"

"My God, don't try to make me out a romantic fool," said Rhoda in sincere alarm. "There's nothing to tell. I'm merely proving to you that Tracy respects me. I believe he even considers me worthy to be the mother of his children."

She wasted sarcasm. Her grandmother, with the peculiar, secret smile old ladies reserve for all topics connected with love and marriage, rocked while she selected a suitable platitude from her store. "The engagement is the happiest period of a young girl's life, dearie." She wished privately that Rhoda would put her legs down and not expose her pink silk underwear. Three months ago the grandmother would have remonstrated and also suggested that nice girls didn't smoke. Now she knew that nothing she said would influence Rhoda to acquiesce and that a single word might be sufficient to drive her to exaggerate her posture.

"I think that's a lot of rot." Rhoda's voice always thickened when she smoked. "No one's happy, except when he's asleep."

The old lady in the rocker took a neat darning stitch, then laid down her work. "When will you be married, dearie?" she coaxed.

Rhoda flared impatiently. She had no idea. Probably never. She wasn't engaged to Tracy Bennett and didn't intend to be. She lit another cigarette and puffed nervously, her mocking dark eyes challenging her grandmother.

"You mean this Mr. Bennett asked you to marry him, and you said 'No'?"

Rhoda protested. "I don't see why you're surprised. You've been running Tracy down ever since he's been coming here. Just because he's asked me to marry him doesn't make him any more valuable, does it?"

It did, but how explain that to this cynical young person? Grandma Cooper had been bred to respect eligible suitors. In her girlhood a proposal of marriage was not to be lightly tossed away. The dread and danger of spinsterhood menaced every maiden and prompted her to show a becoming gratitude for the offer of a "good man's love." Grandma wasn't even certain that Tracy Bennett was good, but he had proved his intentions honorable at least. "I don't see why you won't marry him," she said.

Rhoda lay still. Her beautiful ivory skin set off by her crimson lips glowed flawless under the rays of the reading lamp. She wore a thin white silk dress with a scarf as red as blood, tied under her chin; red buttons, like drops of blood, fastened the front pleat of her frock from throat to hem. A wild impulse to confide in some one, any one, even this old, old woman, stirred unexpectedly in Rhoda's soul. She longed to explain, to let go. Why won't I marry Tracy? she fancied herself saying and a torrent of words tore at her locked lips. What is Tracy to me, when every word he says, every thing he does, only makes me hungrier for Lee. For Lee, *who passed me by!* She tried to imagine her grandmother's shocked expression if she should be told that her granddaughter loved the bridegroom of a girl chum. Granny's so old, thought Rhoda desperately, she's forgotten desire. Her idea of happiness is peace. She thinks she's good because she has no more wants.

A car slid to the curb, and the lights dimmed. "There's Tracy." Rhoda did not turn her head.

Tracy Bennett's eager, furtive face quickened whenever he looked at Rhoda. He possessed a veneer of good manners, because his occupation of society photographer for a number of newspapers gave him the entree to smart homes. Debs and their older sisters made a tremendous fuss over him. He gossiped shamelessly and had been divorced. Fifteen or twenty years older than Rhoda, he fancied that he dazzled her by his interpretation of his success, his exaggeration of his income. This evening he had brought a portfolio of his most recent photographs to show her. "We'll be all right in the swing, Mrs. Cooper. Don't let us disturb you." His creased smile, professionally friendly, concealed his irritation at the old lady established under the bridge lamp.

The murmur of his voice reached the grandmother intermittently. ". . . Julia Nagle. She's drunk from after breakfast, till some one puts her to bed. Been around the world twice . . . delirium tremens on the highseas . . . That's Cassie Twills. Scads of money. They say the colored butler . . . Stunning, isn't she? Bernice is a nice girl, but she can be had . . ."

"You can't stay too late," Rhoda hurriedly informed him when her grandmother withdrew so ostentatiously that the girl nearly giggled aloud.

"Why not?"

She pushed away his hands. "Because Gram sleeps out here on the porch now. She has a cot. Her asthma bothers her, and she likes the air."

"Then we'll go for a spin. Get a coat. It takes more than a grandmother to spoil Tracy's evening."

Rhoda noticed that his hair was already thinning across the top of his head. Lee had thick, butter-colored hair. Tracy will talk to me, thought Rhoda, help me to forget. Yet at that moment Lee stood between her and Tracy, silent and tall. She knew that all Tracy said or did, contrasted with Lee's voice and hands, must miserably fail to satisfy the longing in her. "I don't think we ought to leave Gram alone," she said.

"For Pete's sake!" He had a great deal of respect for old people, Tracy added, but when it came to letting them clutter up every one's plans— "Where's the family?" he demanded.

At the movies, Rhoda informed him, thinking that the balls of his eyes looked hot and swollen under the heavy, wrinkled drooping lids. She suddenly questioned him about his mother—was she alive? Was she very old? Did he think parents should live with their married children?

"Why the catechism?" The lines of his face shifted slyly when he talked. "My mother's got her own home —a little brick house in a little dead town. My father left it to her, free and clear. I pay a housekeeper to stay with her. The old lady's got her way of living, and it wouldn't match with mine. Besides, I don't hold with uprooting old folks. They're set in a mold by the time they're sixty or seventy, and it's like lopping off their arms and legs to try and change 'em."

Rhoda told herself that she liked him a little better now. She was uneasily aware that her grandmother would like to be abed. It upset the household terribly to have her ensconced on her cot on the screened front porch by half-past nine each evening, and sometimes she snored. It meant that no one could use the porch and that the living-room was practically a loss, because the lights interfered with Grandma's sleep. Yet the old lady's choking asthma was a dreadful thing to listen to, and no one could be responsible for letting her suffer an attack. Old people should live in little houses of their own, decided Rhoda, with a housekeeper in a white apron to do the work for them.

Tracy, out of a silence, yawned. "You'd think my mother would be contented, but she isn't. She thinks I ought to live with her. Or she'd come live with me, she says. That's because, being a woman, she figures out one or the other of us ought to be a living sacrifice. Mothers are strong for sacrifice. Get your coat, kid, so when your folks turn up, we can go for a little ride."

Diane, at fifteen, couldn't get a license to drive a car, but her chum, Marian Holt, had her own coupe. This friendship distressed the Tuck family, because Marian,

four years Diane's senior, so obviously preferred
younger girls. Diane was her confidante. Marian's
dish-shaped face, her flat, nasal voice and eccentric hats
and frocks labeled her a nut in Diane's circle, but the
younger girl hotly defended her friend. Marian was
wonderful, Marian was intellectual, Marian would
some day show the world, always too ready to laugh at
genius.

"That Holt woman's a genius, all right," Tracy Bennett commented to Rhoda. "A genius for making your
sister the cat's paw. All this night driving the two of
them do is to clear Marian's brain for her reading, isn't
it? Well, they drive downtown and pick fellows up.
I've seen them. Diane gets the boys; Holt couldn't attract a one armed blind man."

"Why aren't you content to spend an evening with
your family?" Grandma Cooper frequently demanded
of Diane, who never had a satisfactory answer.

None of the replies to her questions were satisfactory,
if it came to that. It sometimes seemed to the old lady
that the family, as a unit, dissolved and flowed away
from her at the sound of her first word.

She began gradually to realize she had been prepared
to fill the rôle of grandmother in a household which
apparently had neither time nor inclination to appreciate the part. The traditional grandmotherly attentions
missed fire. No one praised fine darning in a day when
cheap silk stockings were discarded at the sign of a

hole. Colin and Patty preferred the movies to any fairy
story or cooky bribes. The talk of vitamins and calories
and marketing budgets stripped Grandma of authority
in the kitchen. Nothing she had learned, she perceived,
was needed here. Instead of holding her in esteem as
became her years, the entire family accorded her a careless pity she was powerless to combat. This pity, which
she now comprehended had colored George and
Anita's attitude toward her, had its edge sharpened,
like a knife, by daily use. No one had ever pitied her
when she had her own home. She wondered if her
husband understood that they were now detached fragments with no place in any scheme of living.

It would, however, have surprised the old woman to
learn that Diane honestly regarded grandmothers as
superfluous gadgets in a world already sufficiently clut-
tered up. "My God, you have to explain everything
twice to her," Diane confided to Marian, who had no
close relatives to trouble her. "She's worse than a child.
Some one has to stay in the house with her nights.
She's supposed to be wise, because she's old, but she
can't talk about anything I want to know. What do
you suppose she told Rhoda? That she didn't know
what marriage meant till her wedding-night, and then
her husband explained to her. All nice girls are like
that, she says."

But, by accident or design, Diane discovered, much
to Rhoda's scorn, a use for grandmothers. She and

Marian, Diane announced, would take Grandma for a drive. Daylight saving lengthened the evening and not even the most stuffy parents could pick flaws in a plan that included a grandmother and two girls.

"Where'd you like to go?" inquired Marian civilly, when they had tucked the large old lady into the small new car.

The hesitation, growth of insecurity, which recently impeded Grandma Cooper's simplest response, colored her reply. "Could we go to Richard's—to my son's house?"

"Oh, Grandma!" Diane's sharp, impatient young face was a rebuke. "That's too far. Aunt Grace wouldn't like it, either. Let's see, where shall we go? Don't you want to visit that old friend of yours in the Home, the old lady you knew when you were first married?"

A little bewildered, because she thought the girls must be bored by Virgie Wheeler, Grandma Cooper assented. She insisted on explaining to Marian that she and Virgie had gone to school together. They had lived next door to each other for the first year of their married lives, then had lost track of each other, till Virgie, a penniless widow and childless, had been placed by a niece in this Home. "My daughter-in-law has a maid who has a sister working in the Home," babbled Grandma Cooper breathlessly. "Virgie happened to mention my name to Bebe once, and she told

Mitzi and so I heard. I've been to see Virgie twice now."

Marian glanced at her wrist watch. "Yeah? It's a small world, isn't it?"

Grandma continued to believe the girls meant to call on Virgie Wheeler with her, until she found that Diane who had helped her out of the car and up the white stone steps of the Ashby Memorial Home, was making a hurried farewell.

"Marian and I'll be back for you, Granny. About ten or eleven. Have a good time." Diane spoke rapidly, as if rehearsing a speech. She was halfway down the steps when her grandmother called after her that the Home closed its doors at ten o'clock. "All right, we'll be here at ten." Diane skipped to the curb and scrambled into her seat as Marian started the car.

The matron, black-haired, black-eyed, gowned in black, but healthily red and white as to complexion answered the doorbell. She relieved the maids of this duty after six. "Why, Mrs. Cooper!" The matron was friendly, with the merest trace of condescension because she had been humoring old people for twenty years, and it is impossible to patronize dependents for that length of time and not betray a taint. "Surely you didn't come out at night alone!" Expertly the matron guided the visitor across a glassy expanse of floor to the oasis of a small sofa on a square of rug. "I want to speak to you about Granny Wheeler, before I take you up."

Granny Wheeler, the matron revealed, was causing the Board of Managers a great deal of worry. "We're afraid her mind is going. She's been eccentric for several months, but the condition is worse. Of course, if actual insanity develops, she'll be sent to the state asylum."

"I thought you were supposed to take care of them when they're ill." Grandma Cooper recalled the spotless infirmary on the second floor.

"Not a mental case. We haven't the facilities, and we have to consider the other ladies." The matron repeated, like a parrot, the glib assertion that the state hospital was a beautiful place. "The patients love it there. They're perfectly happy, and they have the most marvelous care."

She suggested that the daytime would be better for a visit, but Grandma Cooper, concealing her involuntary shrinking, stood firm for her original plan. The matron took her in the automatic lift to the fourth floor and left her, after rapping at Mrs. Wheeler's door.

"Is that the matron?" High and sweet, Virgie's old voice drifted through the panels.

"It's Lucy—Lucy Cooper." She tried to answer naturally, but her heart fluttered. A horror of diseased minds haunted her. What she expected to face she hardly knew. Yet when Virgie, shrunken, bent, her

knitted shawl in a huddle about her shoulders, finally
opened her door, the other at first perceived no change.
The shadowy room looked instantly familiar, like a
place she had known in her youth when details were
easily memorized. Even the pink glass vase which had
been filled with flowers on her two previous visits, still
stood on the window-sill. "I didn't bring you anything,
dear, because I didn't know in time that I was coming
to see you." She had forgotten that it made her feel
younger to be with Virgie, who was so feeble and so
old.

They drew their chairs close together, after Virgie
had closed the door. She fumbled a long time with the
lock, but there was no key. "That dratted matron tries
to listen." Virgie peered shrewdly at her guest. "She
thinks I'm crazy." Her hands twisted in her lap, and
a spasm of pain slanted across her face. "It's only that
I can't remember. What was it you told me about
your husband?"

"Do not try to remember; let us both forget," implored Grandma Cooper, who had forgotten, too. She
did not stir as Virgie put out a little dead-white hand
ridged with dark veins and touched her knee.

"You have children. Now I know you." Virgie
smiled, pleased to have set her poor wits in order without aid. "Children who are good to you. No one in
this place has living children. That's why we're all
here."

The street light's reflected glow dimly outlined the large woman and the small, but the room itself retreated into uneven precipices of black and gray. Noises from the street ebbed and flowed in almost rhythmic waves of sound. A clock somewhere ticked tinnily, and the odor of old age, which is compounded of dust and mildew, hung heavy in the hot gloom. Beyond the door in the body of the house, no life stirred; no voice called, no footsteps clattered on the polished, shining stairs. The piano and radio in the wide double parlors on the first floor remained mute. Outside, on the lawn, fireflies winked gaily, but no cars waited at the curb. The neighborhood houses twinkled with lights, but the Home displayed only hall and stair bulbs and here and there the subdued glow of a reading lamp.

"They've buried us before our time," said Virgie Wheeler's quavering voice, with its strange undercurrent of faint music like a fragrance that has dried.

Grandma Cooper began to speak of Nellie, her lovely daughter, who had four beautiful children. The laughter and noise and bickering of Rhoda and Diane, Patty and Colin stimulated the speaker as she recalled the vital family atmosphere. That, she told herself, was what kept her alive. Shut away from all living, like Virgie, condemned to pass her days in the company of those facing in one direction, toward death, she too must, she believed, inevitably lose her mind. Perhaps the aged had logically no future for which to plan, but one shared vicariously in one's children's plans. That was the cruelty that hid beneath the surface of existence in these comfortable, scientifically managed Homes. Settled in their rooms, old women no longer contrived or dreamed or hoped. Their lives finished except for the incident of dying they lived in no other lives. Even when they died, no young life paid them the tribute of a moment's grief. I must get out of this room, thought Grandma Cooper, shrinking from the thoughts that crept out to her from the shadows. She reminded herself feverishly that she had children, that no woman with children entered a Home. "Is it ten o'clock yet?" she asked aloud. "My granddaughter promised to call for me at ten o'clock."

Virgie, who had been dozing, switched on a small lamp and held a cheap alarm clock under the paper shade. It lacked ten minutes of the hour, she reported. As they moved toward the door suddenly Virgie whispered, "Would you like to see my baby boy? I keep him in the bed where the matron can't find him."

Grandma Cooper read nothing in the gentle old face to alarm her. "What do you mean, dear?" After all, suppose Virgie did imagine her baby lay beside her in the empty bed? A hundred times she, Lucy Cooper, had put out her hand to touch her husband in the dark silences of the long nights. I suppose the matron would call me crazy, too, she reflected indignantly.

"Did I say anything out of the way?" Virgie
Wheeler, alarmed, clutched her visitor's wrist. "Of
course you know all my trouble's in my head," she
added quietly. But she denied any pain. "It's just my
head. I can't describe it. I forget, and sometimes I say
foolish things. The things that happened fifty years
ago seem like yesterday, and before I know it I talk to
myself about them. My baby lived two days."

Downstairs Grandma Cooper had to wait for Diane
a quarter of an hour. The curious matron probed. She
had found Mrs. Wheeler much changed, of course?
Had she wandered in her speech? Said anything out
of the way? "The maid has to make her bed while
she's at breakfast now. She flies into a terrible rage if
any of us go near the bed when she is in the room.
She has some queer delusion about it. The doctor has
her under observation, but he says she isn't dangerous
yet. That's why I let you go up."

Diane and Marian, voluble, apologetic, arrived.
Their ability to view the matron with detachment, as
if she had been a tree on the landscape, soothed
Grandma Cooper, though she had often found fault
with this attitude of the young toward herself. Seated
in the car between the two girls, she persuaded herself
she had waked from a bad dream. Her relief occupied
her to the exclusion of other thoughts until she found
herself on the lighted porch and heard Nellie asking
the perfunctory question of perfunctory motherhood.

"You kept Grandma up pretty late. Where did you go, dear?"

"Oh, we just drove around," said Diane.

The next morning Grandma Cooper followed Nellie into the kitchen and then stood in the center of the room, looking about her in a vague, helpless fashion as if she could not find what she had come to see. In the small kitchen the old woman took up such an awkward amount of space that Nellie, who must pass her each time she carried food to the refrigerator, wished fervently she would at least sit down.

"Why don't you go out on the porch, Mama, where it's cooler?" Nellie remembered then that the cot bed had not been put out of the way. Her daughters bitterly complained that the front porch was ruined for social use, but Grandma insisted on airing her bed till after breakfast. The reminder of this constant controversy together with the pressure of Saturday's duties crowding her worried Nellie. She began to feel that she had altogether too much to do, and she assured herself it was much too early in the day to indulge in that feeling.

Her mother apparently had not heard the suggestion about the porch. "Nellie, will you promise me one thing?" She came quite close to the younger woman and put a dry, hot hand on Nellie's smooth round arm. "Promise me, Nellie, that you'll never let me be put in

a Home. There isn't any *life* in such places. I couldn't
be happy one moment, walled in like that."

"I should think it would be kind of nice." Perversity
dictated Nellie's response. She had never thought seriously about the matter. "You'd be with people your
own age, and they'd have similar interests. Rhoda's
always telling me that you can't mix two generations."

Tears welled into Grandma's eyes. She had slept
badly, and she was dismayed by the weight of her
spiritual and bodily fatigue. The burden of another
day to be endured frightened her. She had always felt
the heat, but this sensation of utter exhaustion she believed to be new. "Nellie, I'd die in a Home. Promise
me you'll never let me be put in one."

Nellie's emotional affection, maternal, protective,
rose easily to the surface of her nature like cream on
good milk. "Darling, don't be foolish. No one's going to send you to a Home. I'll take care of you." She
kissed her mother and patted the barrel-shaped shoulders. "That is, we'll all take care of you," she added,
apparently as an afterthought.

Virgie Wheeler's image, which had set eerily beside
her cot half the night, lingered in Grandma Cooper's
mind. Grateful for Nellie's reassurance, the old
woman perhaps unconsciously laid it aside for confirmation. In her insecurity she dreaded nothing more
than the promise of a security that might prove false.
She had never admitted even to herself that Nellie's

character, flowering into softness and charm, had no
roots in bedrock. Nellie was too pliable, too adaptable,
ever to fight very fiercely for her pledges. This was
perhaps the reason why she so readily made vows.

Her mother heard her arguing with Rhoda later that
morning. The girl's clear young voice, that discounted
modulation as an affectation, rang harsh with bitterness and scorn. Rhoda, wandering into her grandmother's room an hour or so afterward, still retained a
belligerent air. A necessity to review her grievances
impelled her to confide in the old woman, to whom
ordinarily Rhoda was only too transparently indifferent.

"I had a run-in with Mother." The girl began to
pinch the waves of her hair into place. Whenever she
had a moment to spare like this, Rhoda automatically
did something to her hair or her nails, as if talk in itself wasted her time. "I intend to get a job right away,
and Mother hates the idea. She wants me to stay home
and do nothing."

The grandmother, contentedly busy with her Saturday task of regulating her bureau drawers, ducked her
white head in a pleased nod. "Of course, my dear, a
daughter at home can have a lovely life. You're just
the age to be companionable to your mother now."

"I wanted to go to college, but we're too damned
poor." Rhoda scowled at her image in the glass.

College was well enough in its way, her grandmother
conceded. Still, it took four years out of a girl's life.

"And you have little enough time to spend with your mother, before you'll be married, Rhoda. Perhaps it's all for the best."

Rhoda muttered that she didn't know what some people called all for the best. "I don't intend to be a housekeeper, or a trained nurse. That's what this house will need soon. Before that day rolls round, I intend to be earning my own living on the outside."

"Why, dearie, what are you talking about? What do you mean?" The veined hand patting a starched frill trembled.

"I suppose you know Mother's going to have another baby?"

The announcement, against which she had supposed herself braced, dealt the grandmother a heavy blow. The words seemed to tear a hole in her body, and all her reserves of strength, endurance, and composure drained out of her through the wound. She put up a hand to feel of her stricken face because the muscles locked. "If she is happy, then of course I am glad for her," she said valiantly.

Rhoda paid no heed. "What a hell of a nerve she has, to bring another child into the world." Her cold bitterness was more shocking than her choice of words. "But then I don't suppose she's learned anything from the mess you've made of *your* life. She probably thinks it's sweet to have five children for the same reasons you did."

"None of my five children ever spoke to me as you do, Rhoda." Indignation afforded a measure of relief. "There's something horrible and unnatural about a young girl who doesn't love children. I do hope you're not going to be one of these disgusting mannish women."

Rhoda said with deceptive mildness, "What do you think women have children for, Gram?"

The old woman's answer, confident, assured, had an exultant ring. It was the natural, the right thing, for a woman to desire children, she declared. The highest, holiest joy a woman might ever know she found in her motherhood. There could be no greater gift than to bestow life, and this supreme privilege compensated women for all maternity cost them. The rush of words invoked their own memories and quite simply it seemed to the grandmother that her arms again ached to hold a tiny form close to her heart. "Why, Rhoda, when I think of holding another baby, a little, new baby——"

"Oh, yeah?" Rhoda cut in. "Now you're stating facts. The rest is bunk. Women have children because they like to fool with them. Mother gets a kick out of working over a baby, tending to it, presumably sacrificing herself for it. It's the one form of selfishness that gets a big hand. But what about the kids themselves? Mother already has four, too old to be her dolls, you know."

Nothing I can say will move her, thought the grandmother, but she resolved to administer reproof faithfully. "I hope you're not going to be jealous of a poor, helpless, little brother or sister, Rhoda."

"Listen, Gram, I'm so sorry for that kid I could cry, but when I think of the rest of us, I could scream. Here, Mother's almost forty-three, and Dad is forty-seven. They've no guarantee that they can afford to put the children they've already got through high school, and college is, of course, out of the picture. Don't they owe us a fair start? Don't they even think about their own old age? When are they going to begin to start saving, so they won't have to be millstones around the necks of their children? They'll be old by the time this kid is grown up, and they won't have saved a cent. Uncle George is the only one in this damn family who has an ounce of brains in his head."

The old woman folded and unfolded a white lawn collar. An inward, tremulous anger sickened her. To think that a girl would dare talk as Rhoda did! Nellie had spoiled her children, boasted that she never spanked them. As a result of her laxity, she had a selfish, impudent hussy, instead of a sweet, companionable eldest daughter. Of course, Nellie had no judgment, her mother admitted, or she would not have confided in Rhoda so far in advance. The grandmother had abandoned her opposition to another baby and now

allied herself with Nellie, who surely did not have to
ask her headstrong daughter's permission to have another child. "Your father and mother have done and
will always do, the best they can for all their children."
Grandma struggled bravely to conceal her flounderings.
She had no armor against an adversary bound by no
reticences or restraints.

"How do they expect to take care of themselves when
they're old like you?" Rhoda probed.

Grandma murmured resentfully. She guessed they'd
manage.

"How? They can't pay into an annuity—not with
five children. Dad's earning-power will decrease, not
advance. I'd like to know just how they plan to lay
anything aside for their own future."

"That's your father's and mother's business."

Rhoda asserted doggedly that it was the business of
their children, too. She intimated that modern children did not expect to support their parents in the
latter's old age, but believed it to be the duty of parents to make deliberate provision for their own care
when their ability to earn should cease. "Children
are no longer regarded as an excuse for dependency,
nor insurance against it, even if my parents do cling
to that quaint idea."

"Why, Rhoda, I never heard any one talk as you do!"
Genuine horror colored Grandma's expostulation. "You
sound like a monster, or some kind of inhuman ma-

chine. I'm sure I don't know to whom you've been talking, to get such terrible notions. If every one felt as you do, there wouldn't be any children born."

There would be no more born than could be adequately cared for and guaranteed a fair chance, declared Rhoda's hard young voice. "And a fair chance means they shall be free to live their own lives, not bound down by financial obligations to improvident old parents."

"You don't know what you're talking about!" Rage lent its temporary strength to the emotionally exhausted flesh. "There is no sin more terrible than the ingratitude of a child toward its parents. The more children in a family, the greater their debt to the parents who gave them life. A father and mother are sacred responsibilities; their care is a duty on each child."

Rhoda, out of her own pain, made a vicious thrust. "Suppose responsibilities conflict? Suppose a woman has so many kids she can't afford to take care of her own mother—what then?" She knew nothing definite, but cruelty is based on logic.

What then? Her grandmother paused, her automatic utterances checked. She rubbed one hand over the other, swallowed hard. Her first impulse had been to say that a child had a right, under any circumstances, to be born. Nellie's baby must claim its place in the world. Only, if his coming should cost his mother's

mother too dear; if she must leave Nellie in whose
gentle affection she had been happier than at any time
since the collapse of her own home; if there could be
no chance to persuade Harvey to let her remain permanently under his roof; if she must adjust herself in
turn to Richard's wife, to Cora's undemonstrative ways
—what then? "There can be no *real* conflict." The
old woman clicked her teeth as if she bit off each word.
"The first duty of every son or daughter is to their
parents—to their mother. You can have but one
mother, Rhoda. I can't think of a more horrible fate
than for a mother to be abandoned by her children,
for any cause." She began to praise Nellie's devotion,
asserting that a woman like that could be trusted to
know where her duty lay. "And you, Rhoda, you owe
your mother far more than you can ever repay. As
long as you live, you'll be in debt to her."

Derisively Rhoda suggested, "Side-stepping, aren't
you, Gram?"

"Nothing of the kind. You're too young, dear, to
understand." Dignity, like a lace collar, dressed the
grandmother's manner. She put away her fears. "You
may discover that this lovely new baby who is coming
to your mother proves to be the biggest blessing our
family has ever experienced. When you're married,
Rhoda, you'll feel differently about these things."

The grating harshness of Rhoda's laugh set up a

smothered pounding in the tired old heart. She waited dumbly, swiftly prescient, suddenly deeply afraid.

But when Rhoda did speak, after a little pause, all the fire had gone out of her tone. "It happens that I *am* married, Grandma," she said.

CHAPTER ELEVEN

DIANE, who drove into the city nearly every afternoon with Marian Holt, reported she had seen a crazy woman carried out of the Old Ladies' Home. "Marian and I noticed the crowd, and stopped to watch. She was a little bit of a thing, but it took four men to get her down the steps into the car. We asked some of the people standing round what was the matter, and they said she had gone raving mad. She was screaming when we saw her."

Grandma Cooper, the only one at home to hear this recital, shuddered as she listened. "Do you know who it was?"

"No. We didn't stick around. Her shoes came off. I suppose they took her to the asylum. Where's Rhoda, Gram?"

The grandmother sighed. So Virgie Wheeler had been sent away! Her tiny, obdurate figure, battling every step, had been carried down from the room on the fourth floor, hustled over the white stone steps, thrust into the waiting car and whirled to a strange and dreadful prison more cruel than the grave. Surely no kind God devised such harrowing substitutes for death.

"Where's Rhoda, Gram?"

"Rhoda? She went to look at apartments with her husband, I believe." Grandma Cooper turned on the porch reading light. A feeling of desolation oppressed her; she regretted that she had not accompanied the others to the block party on the other side of town. The thin, restless Diane would be released to join them as soon as an obliging neighbor who had promised to sit with Grandma arrived.

The radio shrieked. "Sorry, Gram." Diane reversed the dial. "Do you know, Gram, I wasn't a bit surprised to hear Rhoda was married. She was wild for Lee Wood, but life's too short to give in to a broken heart. Of course, she'll divorce Tracy in less than a year. That's why she's got herself a job."

Grandma Cooper blinked doubtfully at her voluble grandchild. "Do girls go to work in offices because they're married? It used to be that they gave up their positions to keep house."

"They don't now." Diane had no doubts. "In the first place, most husbands expect their wives to work, say five or six years. In the second place, Rhoda says statistics show that over seventy per cent of American women are widowed or divorced by the time they're forty-five. Any girl with sense hangs on to her job. When Rhoda's divorced, she'll go into one of those smart shops where everybody goes after they're divorced. She can model or sell. Rhoda has style."

Outraged seventy-two frowned at philosophical fif-

teen, who smiled sweetly back. Grandma recalled a
distracted comment of Nellie's, following the revelation of her older daughter's marriage. "The young
girls of today are so brutal!" Rhoda's retort had dealt
another blow. "Honesty is brutal. Your generation
and Grandma's, swimming in sentimental slush, were
rotten *soft.*"

"Diane—" Grandma lowered her voice. "Do Patty
and Colin know about your mother—about her condition, I mean?"

"Lord, yes." Diane did not lower her voice. "So
will all Freeland school by the time the term starts in
the fall. Patty lost no time spreading the scandal that
the Tucks are going to have a baby in February."

"Why, how dreadful! What will your mother say?"
Grandma thought helplessly there must be something
in the *air*. What didn't children talk about!

"She told them, didn't she? Last year one of the
families in town expected a baby, and all the kids in
primary school were anxious it should be a boy. There
were already four girls, and even the youngsters understood that another female wasn't needed. They were
really concerned about it, and when the baby was born
and they heard it was a boy, they behaved as if a load
had been taken off their minds."

A week later Grandma Cooper read in the paper of
Virgie Wheeler's death. The brief notice set the funeral

hour for that afternoon at the Home. Nellie, who was
more demonstrative than ever, because she had not
been honest with her mother about her pregnancy,
ordered a taxi and apologized for staying home. "You
know I simply go to pieces at funerals, Mama. I'd only
disgrace you. I'll get some flowers for you to send,
and you must be sure to take a taxi home. I'll worry
about you in this heat."

The double parlors of the Home, cool and shaded,
seemed almost dark after the sunny glare of the streets.
Grandma Cooper staggered slightly as she groped her
way to a chair. The heavy scent of cut flowers drifted
out from the adjoining room where the casket rested.
Presently she must go in and gaze on Virgie Wheeler.
A truck rattling past shook the building, and an inside
shutter swung open, letting in a flood of light. The
undertaker's young man, blond, plump and smelling of
soap, brushed by Grandma Cooper to close the slatted
blind.

"My dear Mrs. Cooper! So glad you could come!"
The matron leaned down to her. "It's terribly sad,
isn't it? But of course the troubles of Mrs. Wheeler
are over now. Have you been—" she nodded her dark
head toward the inner room.

Grandma Cooper smoothed her black silk gloves.
"In a moment. I wanted to ask you, first, where she'll
be buried. Has she a family plot, or any relatives to
attend to putting up a stone?"

The matron whispered hoarsely, glancing about her
as she talked and nodding to people who recognized
her in the dim light. Burial, she explained, was "all
taken care of" when one paid the entrance fee. The
Home had a beautiful section in Hollowbrooke Cemetery; each grave was marked with a simple stone.
"You'll see for yourself today, Mrs. Cooper, if you
come to the cemetery with us. Some of the members
of the Board have offered their cars, and there'll be
room for you."

Well, it didn't matter to the incredibly shrunken
figure in the satin-lined depths of the coffin, Grandma
Cooper consoled herself, when she quietly studied the
alien features of what had been Virgie Wheeler. The
vital, fighting spirit that would have bitterly opposed
burial in a plot labeled the property of the Home had
abandoned the flesh, and the deposition of the frail
shell suddenly lost all significance.

But as she listened to the service, surrounded by rows
of silent, hatless, black-gowned old women, their arms
folded across their breasts, their eyes gazing steadfastly
into the abyss of the years, Grandma Cooper began
to wish she had not come. The bitter draught poured
for these ranks of waiting women was loneliness, old
age, and death. No words of the gentle, superanuated
preacher, intent on quoting comforting texts, could
make easier their halting march, since each saw clearly
the end of the road. In this funeral each knew that

she witnessed her own, complete in detail except for
the change in seasons and the identity of the corpse.
The agreement signed when one entered the Home, the
matron had disclosed, stipulated the exact amount to
be spent. Grandma Cooper scarcely heard the closing
prayer, so anxious was she to escape. The desire to get
back to her daughter's house made it difficult for her
to sit still. To have Nellie or one of the children glance
up and smile at her as she came in; to take off her
black dress; to lie down on her own bed and listen
drowsily to the distant, cheerful sounds of activity in
the other rooms; perhaps to drop asleep, then wake to
smell food cooking, or to find Nellie standing beside
her asking if her head ached— Oh, as long as she
lived with some one of her children, surely the horror
that surrounded her in this Home could not fasten
upon her.

She settled in the taxi with a sigh of relief. The matron had reluctantly agreed with her that the trip to
the cemetery might be too much of a strain. Several
of the old ladies had wistfully pressed her to visit them.
"If I am near here, or some one will bring me, I'll
come," promised Grandma Cooper, a little tremulous
herself, for she remembered that she had been with
Nellie nearly three months. The ordeal of another
change, another adjustment, worried her. She discovered that she had no faith in her ability to persuade
Harvey to let her remain indefinitely in his home. Her

husband, she hoped, did not dread this shifting as acutely as she did, but in her heart she knew it worked a greater hardship on him.

As the taxi grated against the curb where Colin's bicycle sprawled on the thin grass, Red, the dog, raised his head and wriggled without leaving the front steps. Harvey Tuck, looking cool and freshly tubbed without coat or vest, hurried down the walk. His mother-in-law decided he must have reached home in time for a shower, since no shirt could be as immaculate as his at the end of an office day. Harvey paid the fare and helped her out, a process she always made as difficult as possible by twisting and backing in a series of astonishing bends.

"You're home early, aren't you?" She glanced at him a little timidly, because she distrusted his sense of humor.

"A little."

She suspected nothing, until she stood in the hall. Then Nellie, who had probably been watching from one of the front windows, stepped through the doorway of the living-room and cried hysterically, "Oh, Mama, Mama!"

Harvey said, "Let her sit down."

They eased her into one of the slip-covered chairs in the living-room and Nellie, whose face was swollen and blotched as if her tears had bruised the skin, sat on the broad arm.

"It's Papa," Nellie sobbed. "The telegram came half an hour ago."

Her mother, struggling to rise, mutely questioned Harvey, who shook his head. No need to go to him, that negation told her.

She sat quietly for a moment, looking straight before her. It surprised her that Nellie could so easily cry. The weight that pressed upon her own chest hampered even her speech. It seemed to her that she had to drag her dry, hoarse voice out of her aching throat. "At least he didn't die among strangers," she said.

They were, overnight, quite simply her children again, who expected her to tell them what to do. She demanded to be taken to her husband and George obediently drove her to Richard's house. There, in the small oven-like front room where Barkley Cooper had died, his widow, encircled by her children, made his funeral plans. She realized vaguely that beneath the subdued manner, the new, respectful attitude of her daughters and her sons, lay a childish fear of this strange, close contact with death. They avoided viewing the body of their father, shunning the room where he lay. They protested that their mother need not consult with the undertaker, but she perceived they secretly welcomed her presence at the conferences. She remembered that they had had no experience with the stark details that hedge round the disposal of the dead. It seemed unnatural to them, perhaps shocking, that she liked to sit beside her husband, gaze tearlessly upon his face. They were, of course, almost as much afraid of her, of her calmness, her superior experience, her lack of terror, as they were of the peaceful, waxy features of the father they had never feared in life.

Whatever she suggested or asked for they hastened to obtain or supply. Dariel and John volunteered to stay with the former's mother till after the funeral, so that the widow might be under the same roof with her husband till the end. George agreed without demur to purchase a cemetery lot large enough for two in the country cemetery not far from Cora's house. It startled George to hear his mother discuss her own passing, as she phrased it, and it distressed him that she insisted on personally inspecting the plot. The willow tree that grew at one side pleased her. She said quietly that his father would be glad to be buried near a tree. George, who saw nothing but the raw, damp earth of another grave freshly dug, privately resolved to make sure that his own body was cremated. He knew his mother to be violently opposed to the practice, but she, poor soul, fought any change. He failed completely to understand the eager interest she displayed in the endless details of the arrangements for the services; or the comfort, amounting at times, to almost a pleasure, afforded her by the messages, the flowers and the calls from distant relatives and friends. Addie Moss, the

California daughter, telegraphed an expensive wreath, which her mother proudly placed on the coffin herself. Anita's suggestion that no one wore veils any more pained the old woman, who construed the remark as a slight to the dead. George and Richard purchased a new suit of clothes for their father, and it was Grace who urged that they also buy shoes.

"He wanted a new pair of shoes before he was taken sick," she reminded them.

Grace watched the narrow margin of her careful savings disappear, without murmur or complaint. Like the others she had discovered the crushing, if temporary, power of remorse that had in a few short hours brushed aside their strictures of reason and justice and left them only the sharp regret that they had not been kind.

The funeral would be held in Cora's house. She lived near the cemetery, and the pastor of the local church would be available to conduct the services. Again George wondered ironically what kind of sermon a man could preach for a non-churchman. Neither of his parents had been religious folk, although his mother as a young woman had attended church to mingle with her friends. In old age neither of the Coopers had been interested in church services, except as they might be dialed on the radio. Yet George noted that his mother talked earnestly to the serious, freckled-faced young pastor for half an hour in Cora's dining-room. It half-baffled, half-amused George; his father had been inclined to doubt the sincerity of all ministers of the gospel. Still, as a man of strong conventions, he would doubtless prefer one of the clergy to handle his last rites. Funny, we're all trying to figure out what Father would like and do it for him, mused George, depressed by the insistent silence of the house, an appalling, enveloping stillness that he fancied to be constantly prowling about him like some great dumb beast.

The evening before the funeral day, Nellie announced to Cora and Richard and George, assembled in the dining-room—the living-room with its drawn curtains through which a single light burned dimly, was across the hall—that their mother thought it would be nice to have a quartet sing. "She says Papa was fond of the hymn, 'Just As I Am.' I hadn't thought about any music, but I suppose if she wants it——"

Richard glanced at George, who nodded assent. Each would have considered it heartless to have mentioned the expense, but the indisputable fact that these demands were final influenced them. Their inner, secret calculations, the bedrock communications of their souls which no human being can bear to reveal to another or read himself except in snatches, urged them to be liberal; their responsibilities had been halved; there would be nothing more asked of them on their father's account.

Cora 'phoned the leader of the choir, who promised to arrange for the quartet. Nellie murmured something about "going up to Mama," but Cora, hanging the receiver in place, said as if she continued a conversation, "I want to know what we're to do about Mother."

They stiffened as if braced against attack.

Nellie reproachfully murmured, "Oh, Cora! And Papa isn't buried yet!"

"Well, tomorrow there will be precious little chance to talk." Cora's thin, dark face, chiseled with lines of fatigue, challenged them. "I want a few things settled now. The important question is, 'Where is Mother going to live?'"

Richard spoke with unusual swiftness, his beautiful rich voice roughened by haste. "She ought to stay with one of you girls, it seems to me. I don't believe she'll fit in so well with a daughter-in-law, now she's upset over losing Dad."

"I'd love to have her, I really would." Nellie fluttering, explored her blouse for her handkerchief. She just *couldn't* take Mama through all the hot weather, she anxiously explained. Rhoda was threatening to separate from her new husband and return home to live. Harvey feared a pay cut. "And of course I have to consider my own health at this time," said Nellie solemnly.

It was Cora who suggested that a trip to California,

to visit Addie, might be marvelous for their mother.
Addie, they unanimously agreed, ought to do something. She had successfully evaded all her obligations,
but it would be strange indeed if her conscience didn't
trouble her now. It gave them intense satisfaction to
excoriate Addie, as if in listing her shortcomings they
in a measure justified their own. Let Addie supply
the money for the fare, let Addie offer her mother a
home for the next six months or a year. "Mother needs
a change," Cora urged. "California is a Paradise for
old people. I'll send Addie a night letter and put it
squarely up to her. There's no reason why she
shouldn't do her part after all we've been through. The
trouble is, she knows she's protected by law." Cora,
after studying the legislation enacted to compel the support of dependents, had become bitterly opposed to
states' rights. She agreed now to care for her mother
until they could receive Addie's reply.

The stone-cutter, all of a granite grayness like the
materials in which he worked, called a few days after
the funeral. Cora, who still kept the shades in the
front room drawn in deference to her mother's mood,
helped choose the headstone. The paper patterns,
pinned to the portières, represented the cutter's best designs, he assured them with an artist's pride. A plain,
simple marker for the foot, something solid and handsome for the head of a grave was what *he* liked to see.

"Just be sure to leave a line for my name and the date of my death," the widow stipulated, when they deferred to her. She had previously queried Cora about the expense, to learn that her children were paying for the stone in equal shares. None of them would discuss details with her, none except Cora saw the design. They insisted on branding her references to her own death as morbid, if not actually lacking in good taste. Cora protested it wasn't natural to be interested in one's own gravestone.

"Land knows, there's plenty of other things to be settled that can't wait," Cora informed her mother that afternoon.

The yellowed Miss Besmer, working on a piece of needle-point, nodded. Miss Besmer had stayed with Cora through the funeral and was apparently prepared to make one of her indefinite visits that often lasted a month or six weeks. She had explained to Cora's mother that Cora really needed companionship, because May, in a girl's camp, would be absent till September. "No woman should be alone too much," Miss Besmer stated.

The old woman, rocking listlessly on the screened side porch that formed a pleasant summer living-room, rested in silence. Normally loquacious, the shock of recent grief and excitement had left her limp, dry like a piece of driftwood exposed by an ebbing tide. As she recovered, she might recapture some of her lost resiliency, but it would always be a surface quality, requiring a conscious effort on her part. At present her thoughts noticeably lacked continuity, a phase that led Cora to suspect that she was childish, or might be. "I thought it was real nice of that woman at the Library to send a wreath," she murmured now.

"I've got more on my mind than wreaths." Cora raised her voice as if she spoke to the deaf. "This California trip of yours means a lot of work, just to plan. Bill said last night he'd feel better if we knew some one else who was going; but no one tours California in the summer. Not from here."

"No, that's so," concurred Miss Besmer.

Cora's mother glanced from one to the other in instant alarm. These references to California as her future home had assumed a finality that set a ball of cold fear rolling sickeningly under her ribs. To her it seemed that she was being propelled toward a shining, treacherous quicksand that waited to swallow her. The glories of a great state, as recounted to her, only intensified her dread of an alien land. Distance appalled her, strangeness intimidated her. Addie, her daughter, she had not seen for eighteen years; better, far better to remain in her own country, as she identified the East, to stay with those of her children whose ways were at least familiar to her. "I don't know as I feel up to the trip, Cora." She sat forward in the rocker, her body tense. "It's a long trip. And then I get to thinking, suppose

I died out there? There'd be all the extra expense of
bringing me back for burial beside your father."

"What difference does it make to any one where
they're buried? I can't see." Cora twitched her crochet
thread.

Her mother rubbed one hand over the other, as if in
pain. "Why, I must lie beside your father. I couldn't
be buried in California. There's the lot, the stone with
room for my name——"

"Here's the minister!" Cora's kite-shaped face assumed a conventional smile. "Unhook the screen,
Fanny," she directed Miss Besmer.

The widow understood that the Reverend Theodore
Bailey had called to see *her*. He had preached her husband's funeral sermon and had made beautiful references to her in the course of his remarks. She was sure
that as a young man, married only a month or two, he
must be interested in the experiences of a couple who
had lived together for more than fifty years. He would
doubtless be willing to listen while she talked of Bark.
Ministers of the gospel, she assured herself, could have
no reluctance to speak of the dead. She smiled as he sat
down beside her, and she remembered to be glad that
she had put on her new black dress.

Yet, at the end of a half-hour, she and the minister
had exchanged barely a dozen words. Cora and Miss
Besmer, interested in parish activities of a social flavor,

firmly engaged the attention of the young man. The
mother must perforce listen, but as an outsider, grateful
to be included in a smile or a hurried, explanatory
phrase. Her uneasiness lest the pastor's visit be spoiled
revealed itself in her worried glances, her spasmodic
attempts to bring the conversation around to her own
affairs. Had she but known it, the nervous divine
thanked the stars that had saved him a tête-à-tête with
her; the grief-stricken old women who sobbed as they
talked embarrassed him, even when he recognized the
duty imposed on him to comfort them.

"Well, I don't care if it is summer, Mama can't start
on a journey like that without a coat." Nellie eyed her
mother as if she had been a dressmaker's dummy. "I
think a three-quarter length would be right."

Her mother said hesitantly, "Well—I'm not sure I'm
going, yet——"

"Fanny and I were looking at travel prints yesterday." Cora rummaged in her basket for samples.
"Only, Mother has this silly idea that she must wear
mourning."

"Your father hasn't been dead two weeks—" The
old woman drew the folds of her black gown over her
knees, as if for protection. Her daughters, she thought
resentfully, need never expect her to wear colors again.
If they had little respect for their father's memory, at

least his wife intended to be faithful in her grief.
"You'd better not buy me things ahead of time, in case
I don't go to California," she cautioned.

Not that they listened to her. The clothes for her
California trip interested Cora and Nellie—and Miss
Besmer—precisely as if they were conducting a shop-
ping service for an incompetent client. Materials and
styles, quantity and cost, they discussed freely among
themselves, but they brushed aside the preferences and
opinions of an old woman as so much chaff. In only
one point did the mother have her way: she refused to
wear anything save black.

This morning an old friend had called to see her, a
woman she and her husband had known years before
in the friendly town where they had lived when their
children had been born. Lucy Cooper, whose widow-
hood was so recent that the greeting of a mutual ac-
quaintance roused poignant longings for her husband
who could not share it, longed to talk of her bereave-
ment. She had been touched when Mrs. Ames, whose
husband had been dead for years, had attended the
funeral; they must look at life, Lucy Cooper felt confidently, from similar viewpoints. It would be good
to talk privately with a woman of her own age.

"Be sure you tell Mother *all* about your California
trip, Mrs. Ames." It was Cora's morning for dusting
the dining-room, which opened on the porch. "Explain to her about berths and meals in the diner, and

everything. You know Mother expects to make Addie a long visit."

Mrs. Ames had obeyed. Cora cross-questioned as she worked. It seemed to her mother that, if one died and the spirit returned to earth, it might be to find existence something like that she now endured. She inhabited a body, but was denied a will and mind. Sometimes I think my children believe I *am* dead, the old woman mused, letting the voices flow on past her.

At other times she listened intently, eager to be included in the futures for which her children planned, Cora in her interminable dialogues with Fanny Besmer; George and Richard in their spasmodically mentioned hopes to Bill Payne; Nellie, as immersed in hand sewing as if she tucked batiste for a first child. None of these in anticipation drew up to their tables an extra chair. It finally occurred to the mother that they regarded her as already provided for, removed from their horizons, settled as Addie's permanent charge.

The continued silence of Addie fretted the old woman whom the years had failed to reconcile to uncertainty. She refused to consider the plan confirmed, yet in the absence of a definite negative from the West, she dared not hope. The mounting intensity of her desire to remain with Cora, where she might visit the cemetery daily, added to her uneasiness. Occasionally she assumed an air of importance, when some one in the town envied her such a marvelous trip. Then she might display her little fitted overnight bag and the few new dresses that hung on her closet hooks. Even as she glibly recited the benefits of a year-round sunshiny climate, her heart protested at the thought of being uprooted.

When Cora and Bill conferred over railroad maps and folders, chartering her journey day by day, as if, she flared once with a momentary display of her old imperiousness, she had been a checker on a board—she sat tense. Her fumbling perceptions, not naturally keen and further hampered by her poor mental habits, had delayed the realization of her true position; but she was beginning to see herself as pitied by her children, relegated by them to their past. The need for preserving her individuality, if only in her own eyes, urged her to dwell constantly and proudly on the days when she had been active and young. She studied old photographs, tried to recall her glad memories, to recapture old dreams. Not even to herself could she bear to acknowledge there were days and hours in which none of her experiences as a wife and mother seemed real. The impressions of her early childhood, however, often startled her in their clearness, and she discovered how tenderly she felt toward the child she had been.

"My father always thought I was just about right," she would say proudly to Cora, who didn't pretend to listen. "My mother thought he didn't appreciate her boys, but it was just that he loved me dearly as his only daughter."

Cora, mixing a cake, might let her lips move as she read the cook-book propped open before her.

"—He couldn't bear me out of his sight, not even to be educated. Once I went away to school and he came after me in the middle of the term."

"If you'll move your chair, Mother, so I can get into the dish closet——"

The old woman would petulantly hitch her chair out of range of the cabinet's swinging doors. I do believe my mother was jealous of me, she said to herself, my father made such a fuss over me. She saw nothing to shrink from in the desire to be loved as a cherished daughter, protected, comforted and indulged, after a lapse of sixty years.

Chapter Twelve

THE willow tree that grew at one side of Barkley Cooper's grave had a scarred, twisted trunk, from which a gracious curtain of green swayed like drapery above the slight mound. His widow, exhausted from trudging the dusty road, glaring under the midsummer sun, sighed deeply as she gained the circle of shade. She bent her stiff knees, and let herself drop on the grass. Fatigue, exquisitely keen, amounting almost to torture, cramped the bones beneath her flesh. The agony of being so tired she wanted to stop breathing possessed her, dulling all other thought. She forgot even the grave.

When she had rested a moment, she stretched out her hand mechanically to pull a dandelion from behind the headstone. Weeds forever flourished, she thought in vexation, noting that the grass on the grave showed bare patches. She must bring more grass seed. Or perhaps it would be better to have it sodded. The peace that suffused her if she sat long enough in silence beside this plain, gray stone, gradually soothed her aching body as well as her soul. She told herself contentedly that she meant to live within walking distance of the cemetery, and with her daily care Bark's grave would soon be neat and trim.

"How's the grass comin'?" Harry Hand, the general caretaker, edging a bed of geraniums, called to her. A cheerful, strong young fellow to whom caskets and graves meant no more than the bulbs he buried in the same earth. "Maybe I can mow over there next week," he suggested.

"If you'll cut around my plants," she assented. "I mean to set out some begonia slips. He—liked begonias."

The caretaker agreed that he liked to see a grave look nice. It paid, he instructed her, to take pains the first year. After that, with occasional extra attention and the perpetual care furnished by the Cemetery Association, there'd be no need to worry about the plot. He brandished a bright steel sickle, tested it on the glistening red hairs of his forearm and departed whistling to attack the weeds at the entrance gate.

Lucy Cooper folded her hands in her lap. The tree-trunk supported her back; her legs, extended primly straight, had ceased to tremble. She had walked too fast, she admitted now. A woman her age should be careful not to overdo. I'm not so young as I once was, but my feet are pretty good yet, she thought. She slipped a hand under the top of her black cotton stocking to feel a swollen vein. Her feet didn't bother her, but her legs gave out.

A scurrying chipmunk startled her, and she pulled her skirts down over her ankles. With the movement control of her thoughts slipped; like the chipmunk, her mind scurried back to the house she had quitted, to the group in conference she had left there. It surprised her to discover that she was feverishly wondering what the children were saying to each other. She had not meant to allow herself to speculate on the topic of their discussion, and here she sat overtaken by the turmoil from which she had tried to escape.

The letter from Addie must have brought them together, she told herself. No one had divulged its contents to her, but she chose to accept that as a hopeful sign. Addie had certainly refused to have her mother visit her—otherwise Cora would not be so extremely cross! The old woman thought she cared little what became of her, if only she need no longer face the prospect of California and exile.

Her lips trembled as she pictured the group gathered in Cora's living-room, her two daughters, her two sons. They had deliberately excluded her; they meant to talk about her; they would read and re-read this mysterious letter from Addie, but their mother they persistently regarded as a child. For a moment she longed to put her head down on the grass that covered her husband's grave and let her tears pour into the cool dampness of the ground. Before she could alter the position of her

stiff limbs, her thoughts had flowed into another chan-
nel.

Now that Addie had failed to agree with their plans,
perhaps the children might ask her where she would
prefer to live. I couldn't go back to Nellie, the mother
mused, watching the sunlight darken on the graves,
then flare into light as a cloud passed. Nellie wants to
talk about the baby, but not to me. Rhoda and the
other children don't want a grandmother around. They
don't *need* me—I'd rather stay where I'm needed.

She recalled her room in George and Anita's apartment, the orchid-and-silver room she had not remembered for weeks. Mitzi had been compassionate and
kind, but must she rely on the sympathy of a maid?
The clear, relentless sharpness of Anita's driving schedule, the swift march of George's days, stirred vividly in
the mother's mind. They worked hard, they played
hard. Their lives rushed past her and she shrank from
the knowledge that they must force themselves to remember her, if they looked back at all. It would be
better, she decided, brushing an ant from her skirt,
not to live again with George.

There remained her other son. Richard. His kind,
dark silence often rested her. She had never been sure
of what he thought, but then had she ever known a
single passageway in her children's minds? Her husband had died in Richard's house, died in his sleep,
they said. She hoped this might be the truth, but the

fear nagged her that alone in the blackness of that last night he might have called in vain for aid.

"I couldn't live there—not with Grace." The old woman started at the sound of her own voice, cracked and hoarse as if corroded with pain. She rubbed one hand agitatedly over the other and her heart quickened its beat. "Mustn't get worked up," she reproved herself in a whisper. "Only I can't forget that Grace wasn't good to him. It would always come between us." It wasn't likely, either, she admitted, that Grace looked forward with pleasure to any arrangement that brought her mother-in-law into her home.

Hidden in the vegetation, a regiment of locusts began to drum. The hot, sweet odor of sundried grass swept toward her in a little puff of fragrance. Perspiration beaded her heavy eyebrows and ran down in the hollows of her neck, and her eyelids felt weighted. She fought off this drowsiness because it seemed to her that she had some decision to make. What had she been turning over in her mind? Oh—where she might best make her home. The place for her, of course, was with Cora, who lived within walking distance of Bark's grave. Lucy Cooper recollected confusedly that Cora had lately made mysterious references about giving up housekeeping. As if a woman who had a husband and child could give up housekeeping. Maybe I ought to go back to the house and talk things over, Cora's mother worried. I've never told them what it

means to me to be near the cemetery—it's all that matters to me since Bark's death. She saw again the dusty
white road, and the length to be traversed before one
reached the haven of Cora's house dismayed her. It
seemed to her she could feel the heat of the sun on
her unprotected head. Clumsily she struggled to her
feet and tottered on swollen ankles to the iron pipe
and faucet set in the center of a flaming petunia bed.
A rusty tin cup was chained to the length of pipe. She
drank the warm, brackish water in little, sucking gulps.
Her hands busied themselves with hanging up the cup
to drain, but her gaze rested on the tilled fields lying
breathless in the sun, beyond the cemetery walls. A
placid world, flat and burned the color of straw, spread
for miles till it fused with a molten sky. Lucy Cooper
saw no sign of life, heard no sound. The locusts were
still. She stared fixedly for a moment at a handful of
wilted flowers in a glass jar on a nearby grave, then
turning, she slowly retraced her steps to the willow tree.
As she settled herself with her back to the trunk again,
a hot, dry wind fanned her puckered face. I ought to
go back to the house and talk to the children, she
thought irresolutely, but her chin dropped forward and,
breathing heavily, she slept.

She woke with a jerk. Her heart pounded in her
side, a slight dizziness confused her. "Why, George!"

It did not, somehow, surprise her to see him standing there. "Have you been here long, dear?"

He had been watching her so intently that he wondered if the concentration of his gaze had drawn her up from the depths of sleep. In the somberness of his dark eyes, his lined face and the white hair at his temples, the last trace of boyishness had vanished, leaving only an impression of soul fatigue that impressed even the mother who could not analyze it. She only asked if he were tired, to which he answered that the heat had played him out. But when she tried ponderously to rise, he delayed her, a hand on her shoulder.

"Didn't you come for me, George? I thought that was your car there in the drive."

"It is. I want to tell you something before we go." He continued to stand looking down at her with the same curious intentness that had pierced her dreams.

Her hands strayed restlessly; she squinted as a ray of sunlight shot through the screen of leaves. "Where are the others? Is anything the matter?" Silence provoked in her an instinctive dread. "Can't you speak out?" she had always admonished her children when they were small.

George let himself drop on the ground beside her. He picked a twig from the grass and began to strip it of leaves as if the task absorbed him. "I want to tell you something, Mother," he said again, but he did not glance toward her.

Startled, the old woman raised her head. It was a gesture of listening, but she scarcely heard the mournful whistle of a distant train. She felt as if an invisible yet heavy curtain had dropped between herself and George, and that, if he mumbled a word, she must lose its import. Her body strained forward, anxiety burned in her feverish eyes. "You mean about where I'm to live?" It seemed to her that she whispered like a person in a nightmare who vainly strives to shout.

"Yes." George, dissecting the midrib of a leaf, nodded.

"Not with—Addie?" She cleared her throat before she could utter the name. Unconsciously her gaze shifted to the inscription on the headstone. She could not read it from where she sat, but she made out the space left vacant for her own name and the date of her death.

George said, "Addie writes us she isn't in shape to have you." He stripped a fresh leaf and rolled it flat on his knee. It grieved him to find that he resented his mother's inability to make his story easier to tell. *The poor soul doesn't guess what I'm driving at, and I sit here waiting for her to give me an opening,* he reflected. The picture of his mother, as he had found her asleep, urged him to be gentle. It had been months since he had seen his mother plainly, he admitted, recalling the white weariness of the unconscious face, the pathetic emptiness of the relaxed hands. For the first time he had noted disintegrating imprints of old age—the large body had definitely begun to shrink, the white hair to thin so that the scalp showed pink in spots. One or two discolored patches, liver spots his mother called them, reddened her cheek-bones. Feebleness, poverty, old age—the last of life for which the first is made, eh? George had held himself rigid as his mother's gray eyes, opening suddenly, had stared into his.

"Mother, it's like this." He tossed aside the twig and fumbled for his pipe. No matter, he had left it at the house. "We talked things over, and every one was willing to do the fair thing, only we're all pretty hard up, just now." He mentioned the struggle of Richard and Grace to pay for their house. Grace, he explained, meant to let nothing interfere with getting the mortgages cleared off. "It's her way of saving, and you can't blame her. She and Richard want something to fall back on when they're old." George forebore to add that John and Dariel had refused to contribute further board money if a dependent were added to the household.

The old woman shrewdly filled in the gaps. That little Dariel, she told herself, had enough to do to get along peaceably with Grace. "Anyway, unless there's no other place for me, I'd rather not go to Grace's house," she said aloud. "She wasn't good to your father."

George sighed, impatient for the sound of her voice to cease. Then he methodically continued his report. "Nellie, of course, is concerned with her health. She strikes me as being a little hysterical, but Harvey and her doctor don't want her upset. Nellie assured me twenty times that if it wasn't for the baby's coming, she'd be glad to have you with her, Mother."

The longing to be settled in Nellie's house again revived in the troubled old heart. Suppose she went to Nellie, to Harvey, and pleaded frantically, passionately, if necessary on her knees, could she persuade them to change their minds? Nellie's easy affection, the careless, comfortable atmosphere of her home, the vivid, rich presence of her children who, if they ignored their grandmother, at least connected her with life, must all this, the old woman brooded, be lost to her? She realized vaguely that Nellie's attitude toward life, unquestioning, tranquil, conveniently blind to all that might be painful to see, more closely duplicated her own acceptance and compromise than the philosophy of any of her other children. Nellie, her mother reflected complacently, lead a normal existence; she was as God intended women to be. Perhaps, thought Nellie's mother hopefully, Harvey will change when the baby comes. He may be more—more generous.

"Do you know about Cora?" George seized upon severity with relief as a weapon to which he was entitled. "The damn fool's kept her plans pretty dark, but she had to lay her cards on the table today. She and Fanny Besmer are going to share an apartment. Bill keeps May."

Dark secrets, shameful intrigues, cloaked the image of Cora that flitted like a shadow across the mother's mind. "What do you mean?" The cherished hope that she might stay with Cora, be near the cemetery, perished in the murky flood of fear that chilled her. Cora, Cora, what have you done?

"I can't make Bill out." Puzzled distaste thickened George's voice. Cora, he said, had decided to form a partnership with Miss Besmer. Their technical explanation was that they meant to study Art. They had rented an apartment in New York together, taking a year's lease. Cora had planned to have May with her, but Bill refused to let his daughter go. "I believe he and May will live with his married sister, until he can sue for divorce." George, frowning, shook himself as if he struggled out of mire.

What would Bark say, if he knew a divorce had been discussed in his family? Married folks got along in his day and mine and they could now, if they had a mind to, the mother argued to herself. She hastily reckoned Cora's age. At forty-six, perhaps— "If Cora would let me talk to her, George——"

"Well, she won't. No telling how many years back it goes. No, Mother, there's nothing to be done. Bill will put the house up for sale. Now about us—Anita

and me—" his detour finished, he had returned to his
main theme. He and Anita, he informed his mother,
were more than ever convinced that their foremost duty
in life was to make their old age secure. Independence
must be bought and paid for like anything else of value.
"I'm late in starting, too, and we've got a long pull
ahead of us. Then Anita's mother, worse luck, expects
to have a major operation soon. She expects Anita to
help with the bills. It will come out of our joint account, of course. Anita earns almost as much as I do."

All the doors had closed. It seemed to Lucy Cooper
that the echoes still rang hollowly in her ears. Where
do I go, what is to become of me, she wondered in
despair. The reasons, the explanations, the grotesquely
fantastic affairs of her children as just recited to her
whirled, a chaotic jumble, in her dizzied brain. She
couldn't remember why she mustn't go to Nellie's
house; she strove in vain to recall what Cora's excuse
for not having her might be. I'm sure I never heard
tell of a woman who had four children that *one* of
them wasn't good to her, she fumbled, calling the silent
roll. Five! She had overlooked Addie. What had
George said about Addie, whose mysterious letter she
had yet to read? Once or twice in her lifetime she
had known a premonition of approaching grief. Such
a moment of prescience nudged her now. Do not ask,
do not ask, the warning flicked her consciousness, a
whisper spun from nothing more tangible than the

sunshine, or the white butterfly that circled above her whiter hair. Do not ask, do not ask, the words beat dully in her brain and a fragment of a fairy-tale from her childhood wove itself into the tangle of impressions that bewildered her: "into that closet you must not go." Do not ask, do not ask. "George, *what* did Addie say in her letter?" Out of the distance an airplane's motors hummed, and the deafening noise rushed at her, intensifying the roaring that filled the spaces in her aching head.

George tilted his face mechanically to observe the plane's flight. Its shadow, like that of a giant bird, swiftly shaded the grassy graves and as swiftly cleared them. The pilot flew so low that the noise rendered speech impossible, a respite for which the listening man thanked his fates. Yet, as the staccato clamor faded to a drone, George spoke hastily, like one who shunned or feared an answer delayed. His voice was level. He studied his mother with the peculiar intentness she believed to be new in him. "You might as well know." He remembered afterward that she was holding in her hands the twig stripped of leaves that he had tossed away. "Addie writes that she is willing to pay your entrance fee into an Old Ladies' Home— that and nothing more."

She was still a strong old woman, and she did not faint. Her mind, however, stunned by shock, refused to function. She mechanically rubbed one hand over the other, her piteous dazed eyes staring blankly into space. It seemed to her that a gray fog enveloped her, and faintly, as from a distance, she heard George's voice. "I don't know what you're talking about," she said almost irritably.

"Don't take it so hard, Mother. Try to understand." He forced himself to speak calmly, a little more slowly than his wont, in the effort to focus her attention. The pathos in a situation like this, he reminded himself, did not alter the fundamental truth. Once his mother accepted the idea, she would be infinitely more comfortable in a Home. "We talked it over, Mother, and we came to the conclusion that Addie is right. She wrote that you'll be more independent in a permanent place. This moving from one of our homes to another has been hard on you. We all know that." He painstakingly listed the advantages of a residence in a wellmanaged Home. His mother would be free to come and go as she liked, yet her room would always be waiting her return. She would have the convenience of an elevator, excellent meals, the companionship of women of her own age. No matter what financial losses her children might sustain, she could be sure of shelter, of medical care and all the necessaries of life. It would be like living in an up-to-date hotel. "You can come visit us, Mother, you know, and we'll come visit you." He hurried a little over that. It had a hollow sound. His mother, he suspected, would be quickly forgotten, once she had been provided for; he hoped to spare her this knowledge, but the quick intake of her breath at his mention of the visiting arrangements was significant. At rare intervals she surprised him with such a flash of keen insight.

He quoted a few more disjointed fragments from Addie's letter, neatly censored to satisfy his sense of fitness. Addie had stated it as her belief that no old person could be happy in any home of which he or she was not the head. "They make trouble if they live with married children, and they raise ructions if you place them in a boarding-house," Addie wrote. She disapproved, too, of permitting her mother to keep house alone, even if the expense could be met. Old people, Addie observed, were not physically able to do their own housework; they might set themselves afire, fall down stairs, forget to turn off the gas. "Since we're responsible, financially and otherwise, we should do what is best for her, regardless of her personal wishes," Addie's firm, back-hand script urged. A Home, she reminded her brothers and sisters, eliminated extras by the payment of a flat fee. If the entrant lived twenty days or twenty years, she would receive comprehensive care. "No matter what happens to us, we'll know our mother is in good hands." Addie had thrice underscored her convictions on the subject of make-shifts, temporary solutions, sentimental cliches.

Her letter had agreeably surprised George, who had not expected to concur with her views.

The cessation of sound, when George's voice died away, relieved the mother because the silence allowed her to listen to the words repeating themselves in her brain. These words, she fancied, might be attached to an endless belt that turned smoothly on a wheel. "You are Lucy Cooper," ground the wheel regularly, monotonously, "this is your husband's grave, your children want to put you in a Home. You are Lucy Cooper, this is your husband's grave, your children want to put you in a Home." She thought she had tasted supreme bitterness on the day when she and her husband had learned that because they were penniless they must live apart. The pain of that revelation was transcended by the agony of this hour. "You are Lucy Cooper, this is your husband's grave, your children want to put you in a Home." The wheel, she thought wildly, had already worn a groove, and still it turned. I cannot live in an institution, she protested to herself frantically, but the terror that possessed her blocked the outlet of speech. She remembered her visits to Virgie Wheeler, she recalled the starched matron, the dead calm of the ordered rooms through which only old women ever passed. Must she become an inmate, an object of the solicitation of the Board of Managers, wealthy women who talked volubly of their pet charities? It can't happen to *me,* she writhed in an inferno of humiliation and shame.

"I'm glad your father will never know," she said aloud, her lips stiff, her eyes watering and stinging as they filled. But she hoped passionately that Bark *did* know. She yearned for his pity, for his indignation and resentment, to supplement her own. As the first numbness passed, anguish gripped her, squeezed her heart till she wanted to tear her hair and scream aloud. The outward control she could not abandon unless she lost her mind, intensified the inward frenzy that maddened her. An instinct to escape suffering drove her to construct flimsy harbors of hope, in none of which, however, could she rest. The raging torrent of sickening despair wrenched her from each frail mooring as fast as she contrived it. She told herself that George only teased her; or that the children had been unable to agree among themselves, and one or two had advocated a Home; or that God would surely take her before this final disgrace crushed her.

Death, anticipated, momentarily soothed her. It would mean that she might lie down beside Bark, here in this sunny place, beneath a protecting tree. She would be no longer a supplicant, no longer alone. Death, under such circumstances as she endured, could come in no guise save that of friend. Suicide she had always dismissed briefly as a sin, but she wondered about it now. Perhaps her reflections were not alto-

gether free of a childish wish to impose remorse upon
her children, to "pay them back." If she killed herself,
they must feel that they had forced their mother to such
a dreadful alternative. Regret must henceforth shadow
all their lives.

Lucy Cooper's body ached from long sitting on the
ground. The discomfort of her wincing muscles
nagged her vindictively, and anger forced the hitherto
sluggish blood to race hotly through her swollen veins.
Only cowards would take advantage of her like this!
If Bark had lived, she told herself fiercely, if Bark had
lived! She forgot that at the end of his life he had
been unable to protect her. The incontestable fact that
his negligence was responsible for her present helplessness, she either failed to recollect or chose to ignore.
Instead she assured herself that, because she was a
widow and penniless, she had special claims. The Bible
preached compassion for widows. She longed to stand
up and denounce George and the rest of her children,
who had no mercy in them! Their mother, old as she
was, could teach them their duty—yes, she would!
You have got to take care of me, you shall not leave me
to strangers, she would tell them, tell them so sternly,
so furiously, that they must heed. She thought she
tried to rise to her feet, but in reality she did not stir.

A weariness more devastating than pain or anger,
weighted her body and soul. She shrank in dismay from
the physical effort involved in standing up, doubted if

she could turn an ankle or a wrist. The thought crossed
her mind that she might be a thousand years old. Her
skin and the membranes of her mouth and throat felt
puckered and dry, as if the blood had drained out of
her along with the last flare of emotion. She knew she
must ask George to help her rise, and she cautiously
turned her head toward him as if she feared the stiff
muscles might snap.

Two little piles of grass-blades lay beside his hand.
He had pulled each spear separately, laid it crisscross
on another, while God only knew what went on in his
logical mind. He was grateful to his mother for not
making a scene, a little surprised at her self-control.
To allow her time to adjust herself to the shock had
been part of his plan, so he had not attempted to hurry
her. Even now, though his stomach demanded lunch,
though he had promised to return to his office that
afternoon, he did not suggest to his mother that they
might set out for Cora's house. He had himself in
hand; he no longer feared that his pity might swamp
his reason, and he dared to let himself be patient and
kind.

"I guess we might as well go." The old woman
looked around her vaguely, identifying the familiar
scene. It would not have amazed her to find herself
sitting in dusk, instead of the undimmed power of a
noonday sun. How could one's whole life be wrecked
and the unimportant background remain unchanged?

She heard the rattle of a chain and perceived the caretaker had come for a cup of water to wash down his
lunch.

George put his arm around her, and she leaned
heavily on him, honestly terrified at the failure of her
limbs to respond to her directions. The thought that
she might one day be bedfast menaced her. As long as
I can get around, I won't complain, she hastily promised whatever Providence might be listening ready to
check up on complainants. I don't want to be bedrid-
den in a Home, with only strangers to wait on me.
Besides, I've always been able to get down to my meals.
She stood, a silent figure in her wrinkled black dress,
until returning circulation supplied her a measure of
confidence and she leaned down to pull a piece of
crab-grass from the grave.

As she straightened up she laid her hand on her son's
arm. Her eyes searched his face, but he bore the scru-
tiny unflinchingly and she knew he would not yield.
They began to walk slowly down the cinder path between the graves, to the car.

She's really taking it very well, thought George,
carefully guiding her around a stone urn filled with
myrtle and striped grass.

THE END